Salt Is Leaving

Salt Is Leaving
J. B. Priestley

Carroll & Graf Publishers, inc.
New York

First Carroll & Graf edition 1986

Carroll & Graf Publishers, Inc.
260 Fifth Avenue
New York, NY 10001

ISBN: 0-88184-227-3

Manufactured in the United States of America

Salt Is Leaving

ONE

1

A few years ago, W. H. Smith had no branch in the High Street, Hemton. *(County town of Hemtonshire; population 13,600; early closing Thursday; Market Day Friday; see medieval Guild Hall and almshouses, University of Hemtonshire—2 miles N.E. on Hemton–Birkden Rd.)* Where Smiths are so bright and imposing now, then there was a smaller and far less imposing shop: *E. Culworth, Bookseller and Stationer.* And it was at the back of this shop, towards closing time on a Monday in early October, that Maggie, only daughter of E. Culworth, might be said to have first set foot in the maze that finally turned into a high road.

She had spent all the afternoon doing accounts in the little office at the back. Now she came out to ask her father to sign some checks. In the near room, with children's books on one side and paperbacks on the other, Sheila Holt was pulling her mouth down to give it more lipstick.

"Where's Mr. Culworth?" Maggie asked her.

Sheila stopped lipsticking. "I don't know, I'm sure." This was not surprising. At work she wasn't sure of anything except that she didn't know.

Maggie looked through the archway into the larger room, which led to the street door. Mrs. Chapman was attending to a customer, the only one in sight, at the stationery, fountain pens and gifts counter. The old reliable gave Maggie one of her slow fat smiles. Not seeing either her father or the boy, Reg Morgan, Maggie thought they might be rearranging some of the secondhand books down in the basement. The lights were on down there. Beginning to feel impatient, Maggie rushed below, risking a fall at the turn of the stairs.

"Don't overdo it, Reg." Still holding a duster in one hand, he was deep in a book. He was smallish, even for sixteen, and had a curiously wizened face, so that at times he looked like a professor on the edge of retirement. He wasn't stupid like Sheila, who, Maggie guessed, never really thought about anything except young men, making love, bedroom suites and where she would spend her honeymoon. Reg, poor lad, failed all examinations and yet carried about with him a kind of bookworm atmosphere; her father believed he might be turned into a first-rate assistant. But where was her father?

"I don't know, Miss Culworth. He told me this morning to come down here and tidy up and make more room in the top shelves. Sounded as if he might be going off to some auction sale —y'know, to buy some more secondhands."

"Yes, I suppose that's it, Reg. But he almost always tells me. Well, you can pack up now. And don't forget to turn the lights off." She hurried upstairs.

Mrs. Chapman's customer had gone, and she was clearing away, ready to close the shop. Once a teacher, married and then widowed in her forties, now well into her fifties, fat and comfortable but very conscientious, Bertha Chapman had been her father's chief assistant for years when Maggie came back from London and agreed to work in the shop, taking charge of accounts and correspondence.

2

"What's the matter, Maggie?"

"It's my father, Bertha. Where is he? There are checks and things for him to sign."

"He's not been in all afternoon. Didn't he tell you at lunchtime where he was going?"

"I don't go home for lunch on Mondays, Bertha. Mother gets up early on Mondays and does some washing, then she meets her friend Mrs. Holroyd somewhere for coffee and cakes, and then they go out to the Cottage Hospital and spend the rest of the day there, doing mysterious good works. So at half past twelve I nip round to the Primrose for some coffee and two poached eggs or one of their rather revolting little messes—"

"And your father goes to the Red Lion for a glass of bitter and a couple of sandwiches," said Mrs. Chapman, smiling. "Usually about one o'clock. Well, I can tell you this, Maggie. He went earlier today—about quarter to one. He took a telephone call in the office and then went straight off, without a word. And he looked worried—really worried. He often looks anxious—he's an anxious kind of man, your father is, Maggie, as you must know as well as I do. But this time he looked so worried and in such a hurry to get away, I didn't like to stop him and ask him where he was going." She was serious now.

Maggie knew that Bertha Chapman was no fusspot. She felt disturbed, but pretended not to be. "Probably somebody rang him up to remind him about some sale he's forgotten, so he rushed off to it." She looked hopefully at Bertha, who was now crumpling a paper on which somebody had been trying a fountain pen. "Don't you think so, Bertha?"

After disposing of the crumpled paper, Bertha gave her a long, hard look. "I'm afraid I don't, Maggie. Your father isn't going to try rare books again, and he doesn't want to carry much more secondhand stock. But that's not it. I know his anxious business face—I ought to after all this time—but the way he looked when he went out today was quite different. He wasn't thinking about this shop. He was worried about something else.

3

But that doesn't mean *you* have to worry about it, Maggie. Better not, I say."

"And you're sure you don't know what it might be?" It was Maggie's turn now to stare hard.

"I couldn't even start guessing, Maggie. We'd better close up, hadn't we?"

Maggie liked to walk briskly, and as a rule she was home in ten minutes. But this time it took her nearly a quarter of an hour. Not being afraid of taking an interior look at herself, she realized as she approached the house that she had been deliberately loitering a little in the hope she would find her father already there. He might have decided, she told herself, that it was not worthwhile to return to the shop at closing time. He might. It was just possible. But she was not surprised when she had to unlock the front door. Her mother would still be at the Cottage Hospital; her brother Alan at the university, where he lectured on physics; and wherever her father was, he certainly wasn't back home.

It was a tallish but narrow house, one of a row of twelve built about 1900. Everything except the stairs was to the right of something that began as a hall and ended as a passage to the kitchen. In front was the sitting room and behind it was the dining room, close to the kitchen. Her parents had the large front bedroom and she had the back bedroom, too poky even after the bed-sitter she had had in London. Alan claimed both attic rooms, sleeping in one and filling the other with books, his moths and other nonsense. Maggie had often complained that the house was now too small for them—she couldn't begin to turn her miserable room into a bed-sitter—and that anyhow it had far too many useless things in it. But this evening, for once, it seemed quite large—and disturbingly empty. Halting for a moment at the half landing, where the bathroom was, she decided to stop wondering about her father and to have a very hot bath.

Strictly speaking, the Culworths never had dinner. Their midday meal was lunch, and their evening meal, usually taken at about seven o'clock, was supper. And it was apt to be rather sketchy. Mrs. Culworth was an indifferent caterer; Alan and his father would eat anything in an absent-minded way; and though Maggie knew better and liked good food—and Hugh Shire had taken her to some splendid West End restaurants during the three years she had been his mistress—the attitude of the other three made any effort look ridiculous. Supper that Monday evening consisted of macaroni and cheese, peas, fruit salad and custard, and like her mother and her brother she mechanically consumed it. But unlike them, she kept worrying about her father's absence. She had not expected Alan to share her anxiety. It wasn't rational, she knew, whereas Alan was nothing else but, and anyhow never really *saw* people as persons, only caring about figures and subatomic particles and moths and things.

Her mother, however, was a fretful woman, full of odd grievances and regrets for a past she had never really had; very much a molehill-into-mountain type. She was capable of nattering away or sulking throughout a meal just because her husband had been five minutes late for it. But now, when they didn't know where he was, probably out of sheer contrariness she refused even to appear vaguely worried.

"I don't know why you're going on and on about it, Maggie," she had said. "I expect it's some silly business that won't do him or any of us one bit of good. Alan's not bothering. He knows what your father is."

Maggie felt like telling her that Alan didn't know what anybody was, but restrained herself. She might lose her temper; not being able to share her worry and talk it out, she could feel it might be explosive. And if a row started, Alan would go striding off to his books-moths-and-mess room, giving her no chance to explain why she was the worrier for once—though she couldn't really understand it herself—and depriving her of his calm science-don act, which she might need soon. Alan was thirty-three, and four years older than she was, a secretly rather desperate twenty-nine. But because he had taken his degree at Birmingham, and then had only gone to Newcastle for a few years before coming back here, whereas she had spent five years in London and had this tremendous if messy love affair, taking her to all kinds of exciting places he had never seen, she always felt she was much older than he was. In some ways he was just a giant schoolboy. He dressed appallingly and never tried to improve his appearance, which was a pity, because really he was quite handsome in a tall, somberly dark, Abraham Lincoln kind of way. His mother adored him—she was dark too, though not tall—and talked about him in company as if he might be another Einstein, much to his annoyance, for Alan was a modest fellow. There was no such boosting of her husband's and daughter's abilities. But then they were just Culworths, a kind of mistake she had made when she might have done so much better, and they looked rather alike, being shortish and rather squarely built and having the same blunt noses and gray eyes. There were times when Maggie felt she was quite attractive, but there were other times, and now more and more of them, when she was almost sure she was just a thick, dull lump.

As they finished their fruit salad, and after several minutes' silence, Maggie could bear it no longer. "The trouble with this family," she found herself saying, "is that we're all too dry."

"There's some sherry in the cupboard." This was one of Alan's more maddening tricks, pretending he had just heard a literal statement.

"Don't be idiotic. You know what I mean."

"Well, I don't." Her mother looked and sounded cross. "And I doubt if you do."

"We're all too dry. There isn't enough juice in us. That's why nothing happens."

Alan caught her eye and then raised his right eyebrow and lowered his left one, a feat that Maggie had wasted too many years of her childhood trying to copy. "I'm not with you, Mag girl. First you try to spread alarm about our pa popping off somewhere. Then you complain that nothing happens. Is too much happening or too little?"

"Both," she replied promptly, an old hand now in dealing with Alan's logic-chopping questions. "If anything *is* happening, then it's the wrong kind of thing. Like me being left with a lot of unsigned checks and things because Daddy's suddenly vanished. But nothing that we want to happen. And perhaps that's because we're all dry."

"It suits me. Most of the types I try to instruct are much too wet."

"I think you're both being rather silly," their mother told them. "Now about your father . . ." She hesitated.

Maggie couldn't resist it. "I believe Alan should go to the police."

"The police? You're out of your mind, Mag. They'd rock round the station laughing at me. Come off it. What's the matter with you tonight?" His tone was still mocking, but the inquiring look he gave her wasn't.

She shook her head. "Sorry. I don't know why I suggested it. Not sensible, I agree. Forget it."

Their mother was now leaving the table. "I'm going upstairs to look round. You two clear and start washing up." And she left them to it.

As they took the supper things out, they agreed that there should be some coffee but disagreed about who should make it. Alan always said hers was too weak; she thought his too strong. As they prepared to wash up, they went through the coffee argument for about the hundredth time, but there was no passion in the debate. They were like actors waiting for an important scene that had been delayed.

Then their mother appeared in the doorway. She looked triumphant rather than dismayed. "I know what this is all about —your father going off like that. One of you must ring up your Aunt May." Mrs. Culworth never trusted herself to make long-distance calls. "I'm sure it's that wretched husband of hers again, in some sort of trouble and expecting your father to get him out of it."

"How do you know all this?" Alan demanded.

Maggie pointed to something her mother was holding. "Is that a note he left for you?"

"If it is, then it's mine, isn't it? And you started fussing before you even looked round."

"I don't search other people's bedrooms, if that's what you mean," Maggie began angrily.

"Quiet, Mag. Now, Mother?" And Alan gave her an inviting smile.

"Thank you, Alan dear. Well, as soon as I got upstairs, I realized he'd taken the smaller case and some things for the night. So that was that. Then I saw this note hanging out of the little box where we keep some money for sudden emergencies. And this is what it says: 'Have taken ten pounds. Suddenly called away. Explain later.'" She looked at Maggie. "Did anybody telephone him at the shop?"

"I was out. But Mrs. Chapman said he took a call."

"Then I know exactly what happened. That wretched brother-in-law of his, May's husband, is in trouble again, and she asked him to go at once to Luton. He didn't explain what it was because he didn't like to. He knows I think he's done enough for them, and he promised me he'd say no next time. But of course he's just *weak* where those two are concerned. Always was. And I've told him over and over again that she's nearly as shiftless as her husband is. She says he *drinks,* but if you ask me, so does she. Alan, ring them up—the number's in the little book

8

by the telephone—and if your father's still there, say I want to speak to him." She came in to take the towel that Alan had picked up. "Go on, hurry up! Goodness knows what those two might be persuading him to do!"

The telephone was in the sitting room and Alan, being knowledgeable, was no shouter on long distance, so he was completely out of hearing. Having restrained their curiosity, Maggie and her mother proceeded to wash up in a rather detached and dignified manner, as if they were demonstrators of washing up at an exhibition of detergents. Mrs. Culworth, who had detested her sister-in-law for nearly thirty-five years, added a few acid comments on the double-whisky life in Luton, while Maggie used unnecessary force on the little mop thing and said, "Yes, I know," at intervals. She was feeling curiously let down and depressed.

"Well," Alan began quite cheerfully, "he isn't there. And Aunt May never called him at the shop. And they're very well, thank you, and Albert is doing quite nicely in the used-car business." And as if to prove that none of this worried him, he began lighting his pipe.

"I knew it," said Maggie.

"What—all of it?" said Alan.

"No, of course not. But I knew somehow he wasn't there."

"All right, then," her mother began angrily. "If you know so much, then just tell me *where* he is, if he isn't there." She turned to Alan. "Who answered? May, I suppose?"

"Yes, he was out. Probably knocking them back somewhere. Why, Mother?"

"She could have been lying. Perhaps your father asked her to say he wasn't there."

"No, lady, I can't buy that," Alan told her, doing his American act. "She's not that good a performer. She was gen-u-winely surprised, ma'am."

"Besides, Daddy would never ask her to tell a lie for him." Maggie was indignant. "He isn't that kind of man."

9

"He certainly isn't, sister."

"Oh, do be quiet, both of you. I'm trying to think where he could have gone, intending to spend the night. What about some silly book sale, a long way off?" She looked at Maggie.

"It's just possible," said Maggie carefully. "But I doubt it. I suggested that to Bertha Chapman and she said he wasn't keen on sales now and that anyhow he looked different—really worried."

"I don't want to know what Mrs. Chapman thinks," her mother told her sharply. "She's always seemed to me a stupid woman. Now be quiet and just let *me* think."

During the next hour she thought aloud of various relatives and some dubious old acquaintances, but Alan flatly refused to try to trace them on the telephone and told the women they were making a fuss about nothing. His mother finally pretended to believe him. Maggie didn't, and she took her deepening anxiety to bed.

3

Next morning, Tuesday, was fine, with that curious mixture of a mellow sunlight and a smoky atmosphere peculiar to early autumn. Maggie felt less anxious than she had the night before, the sunlight and stir of the morning making everything seem more reasonable and reliable. Nevertheless, on her way to the shop she decided to inquire about her father at the bus station. There was no longer a railway connection between Hemton and Birkden, the nearest large town, apparently in order to make the road between them even more congested with buses and cars, to Maggie's disgust because she liked trains, hated buses and could not afford a car of her own. (The only Culworth car was Alan's, an old sports model, really too small for him and almost too small for anybody else. Moreover, it was very noisy, given to sinister explosions.) Even though it rules Hemtonshire, Hemton itself is a small town, not a tenth the size of Birkden, but it is the center of a considerable network of bus services.

So Maggie wandered about the bus station, feeling an idiot. The drivers and conductors she tried couldn't care less about a man in his late fifties wearing a gray suit and carrying a small brown suitcase. She was just telling herself to give it up when, as often happens, a bit of luck came her way. An older man, some kind of inspector, asked her if she wasn't Miss Culworth of the bookshop. And when she explained why she was there, he said, "I know your father, of course, and I had a word with him when he was here yesterday. Yes, he had a bag with him. And he caught the one thirty-five bus to Birkden Central. Oh, yes, I'm positive, Miss Culworth."

Well, now she knew something, but not much. He might have gone to Birkden on the way to somewhere else. Then she seemed to spend half her day dodging in and out of the main shop, to and from the little back office, to see if her father had come back. She said nothing to Sheila and young Reg, but whenever Bertha Chapman was free she asked her useless questions or gave her useless answers. There were not many telephone calls—there never were—but the people who did ring up were answered abruptly by Miss Culworth, just because they weren't her father. There was no news at home at lunchtime, and now her mother was really worried. Maggie rang her up in the middle of the afternoon, only to be told that no telegram, no letter, no anything had arrived.

"But so what?" This was Alan, cutting short their vague feminine speculations over the supper table. "You're going on like a pair of witches. It's ridiculous. You might be talking about Aunt May's Albert. So far Dad's been away one night. All right, we don't know where he is. But does it matter? He's just about the most respectable careful man in Hemtonshire. Cautious, considerate of himself and everybody else—"

"But that's the point," cried Maggie. "Just because he *is* like that, then why hasn't he let us know where he is? It simply isn't like him. Apart from Mother naturally wanting to know, I have to know because of the shop. There are things waiting for him to sign, and he knows that. Unless . . . something's happened to him."

"Just what I've been wondering," said Mrs. Culworth rather miserably.

"But for Pete's sake—what *could* have happened to him?" Alan still sounded exasperated.

"How do I know, you idiot?" Maggie began sharply, but then trailed off. "Something . . . anything."

"Look—if you're thinking about accidents, then don't. If he'd been involved in any serious accident, we'd have been told by this time. He's got various things in his wallet that would identify him. Business cards and private cards with addresses and telephone numbers on them. You suddenly become important when you've been in an accident. No, that's out."

"But what if he'd had his wallet stolen?"

"What? And *then* had an accident? That's too much."

"What if he's lost his memory?" Which seemed silly to Maggie as soon as she'd said it.

"I can do better than that," said Alan. "What if he's barmy and is now addressing a street-corner meeting in Birkden or Birmingham, telling 'em he's John the Baptist?"

Maggie giggled. Their mother told them both that that was quite enough of that. "Now listen, Alan. If we haven't heard anything by, well, say ten o'clock, then you must go to the police—"

"Honestly, Mother. They'll tell me I'm wasting their time. It'll make me look a fool."

"Well, I don't care if policemen think I'm a fool," Maggie announced with more heat than truth. "If you won't go, I will."

"They'll take much more notice of Alan, dear."

"Why should they? Just because *you* do . . ."

"Maggie, I won't have you speaking to me in that tone."

"Drop it. You're both on edge," Alan told them. "I'll go, but Maggie can come with me. That'll make us look twice as silly or half as silly—I haven't worked it out. Which reminds me—I have some work to do. But I'll be down just before ten."

He wasn't, but it was only about a quarter past ten when they arrived at the police station. It was so near that even Alan, who hated walking, agreed that they needn't take his car. That was one reason why Maggie didn't feel fussed about marching into a police station: this one was so near home. The other reason was that she had seen so many police stations on television.

This one didn't look any different, and the sergeant across the counter was first so polite and then so much like a kind uncle that Maggie began to feel they were all characters on television. He listened quite carefully and made a few notes on his pad. But his meaty face, his uniform, the telephones that kept ringing, the general atmosphere of the place, did combine to make their appeal to him look very small and silly. Alan did almost all the talking. Maggie felt that while the sergeant might be ready to lend her a handkerchief, give her a cup of tea, pat her hand, he wouldn't want to listen to her very long. And Alan, of course, was really on the sergeant's side; they formed immediately, on sight, one of those irritating masculine alliances.

"Well, let's see now," the sergeant said finally, still their dear old uncle, no doubt, but not having any more time to spare for them. "Mr. Edward Culworth packs a bag and takes the bus to Birkden yesterday early afternoon. All you know is that he was urgently called away—might be business, might be a private and personal matter. It's inconvenient and a bit worrying that you don't know where he is and when he'll be coming back. Eh? Quite so. Well, I think you can take it for granted that he's not met with a serious accident. All I can do is to put through a call to the Birkden police asking them to let us know about Mr. Culworth if anything should come to their notice. And I must say I'd rather do that tomorrow night about this time—that is, if you've still heard nothing—than do it now."

"In other words," said Alan, "you really think we're making a fuss about nothing."

"In these particular circumstances, sir—Mr. Culworth being the sort of man you say he is—I don't think we come into the picture yet."

"But why is he not *telling* us anything?" This was Maggie, who felt she had to make one last protest.

Then she wished she'd kept quiet, for now the sergeant gave her a bleak look. "He's not a child, miss. He's a responsible middle-aged man, and if he doesn't choose to tell you everything he does, that's not a police matter. Unless, of course, you haven't told me *all* you know about him."

"What do you mean?" Maggie began furiously, but Alan, loud and clear, said, "But we have, sergeant. Good night," and swept her out.

"I'm sorry, Alan, but you saw how quite suddenly he stopped pretending to be so kind and fatherly. And that's how they really are, I suppose."

"It's how they have to be, Mag. But let's stop all this fussing around. You heard what he said. Father's all right. He's minding his own business. We'll mind ours."

"That's all right for you. But I'm not just indulging in Mother's kind of fuss. You forget that it's *his* shop I've got on my hands, and unless he comes back soon, I shan't know what the hell to do next." And then, to her disgust, she found herself noisily bursting into tears. And three youths, monsters from other planets, stopped and cried, "Hoy—hoy!" or something, and she grabbed Alan's arm and broke almost into a trot— hurrying forward, we might say, into the maze.

TWO

1

That same Tuesday, but during the morning, not in the evening, Dr. Salt was also calling on the police. Their headquarters occupied one end of Birkden Town Hall, a very large building that looked as if an Italian palace was trying to get out of a warehouse. Dr. Salt ran his car into a parking space labeled *For Official Use Only.* It was an old gray-green Citroën, not unlike an enormous battered frog. While Dr. Salt was examining a crack across one of the headlights, a policeman arrived and told him he couldn't park there.

"I'm Dr. Salt," he replied. "And I have an appointment with your chief constable. Now where do I go in—um?"

Respectful now, the policeman showed him. Dr. Salt had no appointment with the chief constable, had never even exchanged a word with the chief constable, but when a quick lie was called for, he believed in lying firmly and well. Moreover, he did want to talk to some police officer.

The sergeant who seemed to be on desk duty was a man he knew called Broadbent. Mrs. Broadbent had been a patient of his.

"I didn't expect to see you here, doctor," said Broadbent, a smiling man. "And I heard you'd left us."

"Not yet—though I'll be leaving quite soon. I've already handed over my practice—to Dr. Baldwin, pleasant young fellow. Your wife will like him. Now I want to talk to somebody about a former patient of mine—young girl—who's missing."

"Do you think it's important, Dr. Salt?"

"Yes, I do. If I didn't, I wouldn't be here, Sergeant Broadbent. And I don't want one of your ordinary CID chaps. I want to go as high as possible—please."

"I'll see what I can do, Dr. Salt. Take a seat, won't you?" Dr. Salt did, realizing that the tactful Broadbent was putting him out of earshot of the telephone. But having very good ears, he was able to make out that Broadbent was telling somebody he was a clever and reliable doctor, who had been kind to Mrs. Broadbent, and there wouldn't be any harm in listening to what he had to say even if it turned out to be something and nothing, sir.

"You're going as high as possible, Dr. Salt," said Broadbent, pleased with himself. "Superintendent Hurst will see you. Straight along the corridor—last door but one on the left." He leaned forward and became a conspirator. "And you'll be doing me a favor, doctor, if you make it sound important—even if it means piling it on a bit, you know."

"I don't need to pile it on," said Dr. Salt, not using the same whispering tone. "I suspect that everything's been piled on already."

Superintendent Hurst was a large man in his fifties who made his desk, the two chairs, his whole room, look too small. "Dr. Salt? Think I've seen you in court once or twice, haven't I? Giving evidence, I mean, not in the dock—eh?" He followed this with one of those mechanical laughs that the other man is supposed to echo.

Dr. Salt didn't even produce a smile. He stared steadily at a point somewhere between the superintendent's eyes and his mustache.

"Well, let's sit down." The superintendent's manner was not quite so hearty now. "Then you can tell me what we can do for you—that is, if it's any business of ours."

"If it isn't yours, it's somebody's," Dr. Salt told him firmly. "I've disposed of my practice here and I'll be leaving Birkden shortly. I want to leave everything nice and tidy."

"I'd feel the same. In fact, I will in a couple of years—when I retire. But what's wrong?"

"A patient of mine—a young girl called Noreen Wilks—is missing."

"Noreen Wilks." Hurst made a note of it, or at least pretended he did. "Can't say I know that name. Give me a few particulars."

"Age nineteen, perhaps twenty now. Mother died about a year ago—sarcoma. Never mentioned her father. Probably cleared out and left them years ago. After her mother died she lodged with a Mrs. Pearson—I have the address." Dr. Salt pulled out a rather fat and untidy notebook. "Yes, Mrs. Pearson, 45 Olton Street—"

"Now just a minute, doctor. I think that rings a bell. Hold on." He spoke on his intercom to an Inspector Frith and asked him about Mrs. Pearson of Olton Street. And it was soon obvious that neither of them cared for her. "That's it," he continued to Dr. Salt. "Nothing much wrong with my memory. Yes, we've had her here twice, screaming her head off—half pissed each time, I gather. And about this same Noreen Wilks, who's gone off somewhere, not telling anybody. What sort of girl would you say she was, Dr. Salt?"

"What you'd expect from a bad background and the kind of muck the papers and magazines feed these girls now. Not vicious, as she might have been with that background, no real harm in her, but empty-headed, sloppy, silly."

"Just another of these little fly-by-nights," cried Hurst triumphantly. "And Birkden's full of 'em these days. I'm sorry, Dr. Salt, but if you're looking for her, then you're just wasting your time."

"I don't think so, Superintendent."

"Now look—we've no evidence she's really missing. Girls of this sort—and we know she was on the loose—go rattling off anywhere with anybody. They don't tell their mothers, sisters, brothers, landladies—*or* their doctors—when and where they're going. It's all gin and impulsiveness and sex with them. Go anywhere, do anything—except steady work. We've had scores and scores of 'em through here. So don't waste your time asking about this Noreen Wilks. She might have gone to Birmingham—London—anywhere. So just you forget about her." He stood up and held out a hand.

Ignoring the hand, Dr. Salt didn't even get up. "I haven't finished yet, Superintendent."

"Now look—unless they're involved in a criminal offense, we can't begin tracing these little fly-by-nights." He was annoyed now and didn't sit down again. "I agreed to see you because of something that Sergeant Broadbent said—but I'm a busy man."

"*Sit down*, Superintendent." This came out with such astonishing ferocity that Hurst found himself back in his chair without meaning to move. He was about to protest when Dr. Salt broke in sharply: "Now let me explain why I'm here. And don't give me any more about little fly-by-nights going to Birmingham. I know what goes on in Birkden. I ought to, after seven years of it. So just listen, please. It's more urgent than anything else you'll hear today."

"Want to bet on it?" And Hurst stared back at him.

"Certainly—five pounds," the doctor replied promptly. "Though I don't know who'd hold the stakes and decide upon the winner. Now then—Noreen Wilks. She seems to have been missing for about three weeks. And she's suffering from a very unusual form of chronic nephritis—a kidney disease. If you want the medical details, you can have them. It's rather a specialty of mine—so far as an overworked GP can have a specialty."

"I'll take your word for all that, Dr. Salt. But where's the urgency?"

"I'd worked out a treatment for her that just kept her going nicely. And I'd impressed it upon her that wherever she went, she must report to a doctor within ten days. I'd made her understand that if she went without treatment for several weeks, she'd soon be very ill indeed and might die. She could be silly and irresponsible about most things, but she knew this was serious, she was frightened, and she gave me a solemn promise. She carried in her bag a note from me to any doctor she might report to, giving details of the treatment and asking him to get in touch with me for her case history. Now she's not been heard of for three weeks. Dr. Baldwin has her case history now, of course, but the point is that no doctor, in or out of a hospital, has been in touch with me about Noreen Wilks."

"But in spite of her solemn promise—and I know what these girls are—she may not have seen a doctor—just not bothered."

"Then she'd be in a hospital now—or dead."

"You can't prove that, Dr. Salt."

"I can't even prove I'm fit to attend anybody, not beyond having a few pieces of paper that say so. But I'm willing to show that girl's case history to any specialist, or body of specialists, you like to name."

"I'm not querying your medical opinion, Dr. Salt, just trying to follow your line of argument."

"Good morning, Superintendent!" The man who had walked in was tall and thin, elderly and authoritative.

"Yes, Sir Arnold?" Hurst was on his feet, eager and smiling.

"I've just been having a word or two with your chief, Colonel Ringwood."

Dr. Salt, not on his feet, produced an explosive cough.

"Oh. This is Dr. Salt—Sir Arnold Donnington. Dr. Salt's worried about a patient of his—a girl called Noreen Wilks—who seems to have disappeared. But I'm sure he won't mind—"

"Dr. Salt?" Sir Arnold, who had the face for it, gave him a glance full of distaste. "We've met before, I think. In court when I was on the bench. You gave some rather controversial evidence on behalf of that fellow—"

"Yes." Dr. Salt looked up at him, rather like a sleepy little bear, but he had cut in very sharply. "He was a sick man."

Sir Arnold was obviously not a man to avoid battle. "But I seem to remember he was given a stiff sentence at the Assizes afterwards—several years, I think."

"And he's still a sick man; probably worse. Sick in the head."

"Society has to be protected—"

"Some of it's not worth protecting," said Dr. Salt sharply.

"No doubt some of it isn't." But Sir Arnold's tone was equally sharp. "You should try being an industrialist these days, Dr.—er—Salt. We have to employ about fifteen hundred women and girls. They come and go as they please, say and do what they like, swear like troopers or pack up and go if a foreman criticizes their work. No idea of order, responsibility, of trying to earn the wages we have to pay them. Foul-mouthed sluts, half of them. Perhaps the young woman you're inquiring about—er—"

"Noreen Wilks," said Dr. Salt carefully.

"Perhaps she was one of them."

"She did work at United Fabrics for a time, I believe, Sir Arnold." Dr. Salt now sounded amiable, perhaps even a little respectful. "But talk to the superintendent. I can wait."

"Thank you. I shan't be long and you needn't go. Nothing private about this." He turned to the superintendent. "It's about the old Worsley place. You were keeping an eye on it for us."

"Yes, Sir Arnold. We still are. Why? Nothing's happened up there, has it, sir?"

"Not to my knowledge—no, Superintendent. Though I must admit I haven't been near the place for months." Sir Arnold was

20

easy and fluent. "As you probably know, the old Worsley place adjoins our United Fabrics Club, and we bought it so that we could turn it into an annex to the club. We approved a scheme and accepted an estimate, and for the last three months I've been pressing the contractors to start work there. Maddening people. However, they're now making a start in a few days' time, and as soon as they do they'll put in their own night watchman. Now I'll tell my secretary to notify you when the contractors are in. But just for these last few days I'd like your fellows to keep a particularly sharp eye on the place. Nothing worth stealing inside except possibly a few fittings, but of course there's the lead on the roof."

"And that's what the villains like, Sir Arnold."

"Well, we don't want to lose it now. So tell your fellows to chase anybody out of the grounds. A dog would be useful."

"I'm afraid we couldn't justify that, sir."

"No, we people who keep the town going mustn't ask too much, must we?" He had flared up, but now controlled himself. "Well, keep an eye on the place for the next few days, that's all I ask."

"We'll do that, Sir Arnold."

"Excellent! Dr. Salt, I hope you find your patient—Dora Jilkes."

"Noreen Wilks." Dr. Salt said it very carefully.

"Quite. Well, I hope you find her. Good day to you both." And he didn't give Superintendent Hurst, who was dithering at the edge of his desk, time to show him out. However, Hurst lumbered to the door and went out into the corridor, in the hope that that would somehow show respect. When he came back, Dr. Salt was busy lighting a pipe.

"What Americans—would call"—Dr. Salt was speaking between puffs—"the Mr. Big of Birkden. Chairman—United Anglo-Belgian Fabrics. Chairman—*Birkden Telegraph* Publishing Company. Senior magistrate. Other things too. Mr. *Very* Big of Birkden."

21

Hurst, back behind his desk, regarded his visitor with some disapproval. "Sir Arnold Donnington can be a bit stiff and sharp, but he's a fine man. He needn't have stayed here and identified himself with Birkden, but he has done so. I don't know anybody who's done more to make Birkden what it is today."

"No doubt," said Dr. Salt. "But what's that? No, don't tell me. I've spent too much time at the wrong end of it. By the way, Donnington didn't strike me as being stiff and sharp this morning. In fact, he was extremely nervous."

"I didn't notice it. And I can't imagine why he should be."

"He was, though. Take my word for it."

"He might have been a bit on the fussy side about that old Worsley house. But it's not a month since he lost his only son. And Colonel Ringwood, the chief constable, who's a friend of his, says it's hit him very hard."

"Well, when a man's son commits suicide—"

"Dr. Salt," Hurst came in heavily, "the verdict was 'Accidental Death.' And it's not going to be anything else in this office. Yes, I know. He was cleaning a gun at five in the morning. But it's still accidental death here. Now have you anything more you have to say to me about this Noreen Wilks?"

"Not much." Dr. Salt took the pipe out of his mouth and looked hard at its mouthpiece. "She hasn't reported for treatment anywhere. She isn't in any hospital. Not unless the country's medical service is even worse than I think it is. And if she left Birkden, nobody so far seems to know when or how." He got up and then pointed his pipe at Hurst, who had also risen. "The girl's missing. Where is she? Is she alive or dead? You could begin making a few inquiries."

"We'll do that, of course."

"It's something I'd like to clear up before I leave Birkden."

"We can do that better than you can, Dr. Salt. And we don't encourage amateur investigations."

"Don't worry. I've never fancied myself as a detective."

"Glad to hear that, sir," said Hurst, smiling. "Very relieved. I just had a feeling you might."

Dr. Salt nodded but didn't return the smile. "I've a feeling too. Not based on any real evidence. Kind of gloomy hunch. I can't help believing that Noreen Wilks never left Birkden. And if she didn't, then I think she's dead."

2

Dr. Salt drove to a garage he knew, where he persuaded one Bert to take a little time off from his football pool sheet to attend to a headlight. "I'll be back about three, Bert."

"Why? What's the idea, doc? It's been like that for months. Why the sudden rush?"

"I'm hoping to sell it, that's why."

"Then you're dead right. The least bloody thing, they want to take quids off." Bert gave him a sly look. "How much you asking, doc? I might know somebody."

"Bert, you attend to that headlight first. And before three o'clock, don't forget."

There is always a lot of traffic at midday in the center of Birkden, and even the broadest pavements seem crowded with people busy not working. Dr. Salt tried to saunter to enjoy his pipe and the pleasant October day, but soon realized he had chosen the wrong place and gave it up. He looked in a bookshop but found nothing he wanted. He spent twenty minutes, making rather a nuisance of himself, in the phonograph and record department of Birkden's largest store, which was very warm and seemed to smell of hot pastry and face powder. Every time he asked the girl about another record, she closed her eyes, as if he mightn't be there when she opened them again. Finally it worked—he felt it was the least he could do—and without waiting for her answer he hurried away, sweating it out down to the street level.

A few minutes later he turned into a side street and found his way into the snack bar of the George. The counter was thick with high blood pressures and potential coronaries, shouting either at one another or at the waiter and the barmaid. After a few more minutes he extracted from this tumult a bottle of stout and a slab of veal and ham pie, out of which a profit of about four hundred percent was being made by somebody. There was one small unoccupied table in the far corner, and there he munched and swallowed and read an early edition of the *Birkden Telegraph* that had been left behind. Before trying to find any news—not always easy to find in this early edition —he looked carefully through the advertisements of Birkden's larger cinemas. His eye rested longest on that of the Lyceum.

Just before two o'clock he was climbing the stairs up to the balcony entrance of the Lyceum. The stairs were broadly and deeply carpeted; the walls below and above the photographs of film stars were paneled in wood or plastic of the same light-brown shade; and the general effect suggested a palace made of milk chocolate. The old-gold lighting did nothing to spoil this effect, but a bright-green notice, above a door on the left of the half landing, was out of key: it said *Gents*. The next flight was shorter than the one below; it led him into a great milk-chocolate space that had two or three doors marked *Private* on the right, and on the left, in the center, showed him the curtained entrance to the balcony. A girl was standing there, waiting to look at tickets. She wore a brown uniform coat and short skirt, a pink blouse, black stockings: a neat compromise between the severe and the sexy—the severe to demand the tickets, the sexy a foretaste of the lush pleasures inside. At first Dr. Salt did not recognize her, and it was only when he was a few feet away from her that he saw that she was Peggy Pearson.

"Peggy," he began.

"Oh—it's you, Dr. Salt." She had rather prominent muddy eyes, a wide pout of a mouth glistening with lipstick, not much

24

nose and chin. "Are you coming in? Everybody seems to like it this week."

"No. I want to talk to you, Peggy."

"Well, it's a bit awkward here."

"I know. But it's important."

"I'll bet it's about Noreen, isn't it? Well, if you don't mind me stopping all the time—y'know, people coming in. There's one now."

He waited, standing on one side, until she had looked at a ticket, torn it in two and dropped one piece into the tin receptacle. Then he went close to her and spoke in a low voice. "You were a friend of Noreen's and she stayed in your house after her mother died—um?"

"That's right. But that was my mum's doing. She got two-ten a week out of Noreen just for bed and breakfast. Noreen and me were always together, one time. But then, when she lodged with us, I hardly saw her. I was up when she was still fast asleep, then at night she was still out when I'd be going to bed. She'd stopped working then and was going out to posh parties. But still, some afternoons she'd come to the caffy here and if I could get half an hour off we'd talk. Excuse me."

He waited on one side again while she dealt with a slow-moving elderly pair of patrons. "When was the last time you talked?" he asked as soon as she was free. "Try to remember, Peggy."

She waited a moment, trying hard. "It was sometime in the second week of September—"

"The last time she came to my office was the morning of September the twelfth."

"And if you ask me, that's the day she went out at night and never came back. I'm nearly sure my mum says it was the twelfth. And I'll bet anything," Peggy continued, excited now, "it was the day before that when she came here for the last time. She was in a great state of excitement and had to tell somebody. And if you want to know where she is, I believe I can tell you—if it's important, Dr. Salt."

"It's very important, Peggy, or I wouldn't be bothering you now—oh, I'm sorry!" He disentangled himself from two young men and a girl. One of the young men gave him a curious glance while the other produced their tickets. Even when they had gone through the curtains, Peggy shook her head and waited a few moments.

"They could be a bit nosy, that lot," she explained, speaking now in a rapid whisper. "Well, you see, Noreen told me that one of these posh party boys she'd been playing around with had said he'd take her to the south of France. And after that she thought he'd want to marry her. He was mad about her, she said. Well, of course we've all heard that before, but I believed the south of France part. She wouldn't tell me his name. No, not me. I'm just Peggy Pearson. I don't go to parties at the Fabrics Club. I've just got to wave and cheer, not ask for names—me. But if you want to know where she is, I think she's somewhere in the south of France, drinking martinis in bikinis—"

"No, Peggy, she isn't."

"Just a minute. Here's another one." She was soon rid of her. "Right, doctor. How d'you know she isn't?"

"She hadn't a passport. I signed her application form on the morning of the twelfth."

"She could have gone to London with this chap and got one there, couldn't she?"

"She could, but I don't think she did. Now—this Fabrics Club. Is that where she used to go with her boyfriend?"

"I think so. But they went elsewhere. She was sleeping with him, I know that much. And I'll tell you something else. From what she told me, some of these so-called party boys would never see fifty again—dirty old men—but this one who was mad about her really *was* young, not much older than her. Money there too, she said. But that's Noreen. Not much sense, if you ask me, but lucky—lucky all the way."

"I don't think so, Peggy. Only part of the way—and not very far, at that." He had to stand aside again. He asked the next question hurriedly, as if he had had enough of this dodging about. "Nothing else you can tell me?"

"W-e-l-l." Peggy drew it out as if uncertain what to reply. "I can tell you this much. Noreen had a special secret she shared with me when we were always going out together. And I promised—cross my heart—I'd never say anything about it to anybody. And I never have and I won't break my promise."

"You can tell me this, though." Dr. Salt stared hard at her. "Could this special secret have anything to do with her disappearance—the night of September twelfth?"

"No, it couldn't. And that's something I'm absolutely positive about—I really am, Dr. Salt."

Another two patrons were arriving. "I believe you, Peggy," he said quickly. "And thank you."

He walked away and went down the stairs rather slowly. An observant man for all his abstracted air, he noticed in passing that the door of the gents' was slightly ajar. Halfway down the lower flight, he stopped just as two people passed him, and looked up. He caught a glimpse, the merest flash, of a young man with reddish hair and a leather jacket, who must have come out of the gents', turning at the top of the upper flight. He hesitated, slowly descended three or four more steps, but then, just catching a sound from above, swung round and hurried back upstairs, passing the two people who had passed him. Peggy was not there and neither was the young man with the reddish hair and the leather jacket. The tin receptacle was lying on its side, with tickets spilled around, two or three yards from where it had been standing near Peggy, as if the young man had booted it hard before hurrying down the opposite stairway. Dr. Salt looked at the doors marked *Private*, as if Peggy might now be behind one of them, waited a moment or two, then went on his way downstairs again.

27

Recovering his car from Bert, who swore he was nearly ready to offer a lovely price for it, Dr. Salt drove to Olton Street, which was only about half a mile from his own flat. It was a monotonous and miserable street, filled with very thin women, very fat women, crying babies. He stopped at number 45, and Mrs. Pearson had the front door open before he had reached it. She was looking rather less slatternly than usual. "Come along in, doctor. And what about a nice cup of tea? Be no trouble."

He thanked her but said he hardly ever drank tea, which was a lie because he drank a lot of tea but not the kind that women like Mrs. Pearson made—stewed tannin.

"Well, sit down, then. That's right. No—you go on. I like to see a man smoking his pipe." She was, in fact, sitting very near him—they were facing each other, but it was a very small room —and he was lighting his pipe to defeat that now familiar sour smell of unwashed bodies and clothes, which had been strange to him seven years before, after the brown and yellow people he had been attending.

"You went to the police this morning—about Noreen—didn't you?" said Mrs. Pearson. "Well, I had one of them plainclothes sergeants here this afternoon, asking me all sorts of questions. Taking an interest now—and about time."

"What did you tell him, Mrs. Pearson?"

"Just what I'd told them before, only they weren't interested then. Though I'll admit that both times I'd had a drink or two with my friend, Mrs. Muston, who'd egged me on to go. Well, I told this sergeant—CID chap, though he didn't look a bit clever, I must say—I told him she'd gone out that evening—"

"September twelfth, wasn't it?"

"That's right—the twelfth. I told him she'd gone out just the same as usual—an' looking very smart, I'll say that for her— expecting to come back. All hours, of course—an' I knew what was going on, of course—an' I'd warned her. So I told him she wouldn't have left Birkden without coming back for some of her things. Not even if he was going to buy her some clothes, whoever he was. I don't care who a girl is and what she's up to, she's not going to walk out an' leave everything. This, for instance." Rather like a conjurer now, Mrs. Pearson triumphantly produced from nowhere an object that Dr. Salt stared at blankly. He decided finally, while Mrs. Pearson sat quietly, radiating triumph, that it must be what was left of a rag doll after many years of hard wear.

"Yes, Noreen told me she'd had it ever since she was five. And she'd never stir without it—always took it on her holidays—always there on her bed. I said to that sergeant—an' he's a fool, if you ask me— 'She'd have come back for that if for nothing else.' My Peggy's just the same with her old Baby Bear. God knows what they get up to nowadays, not out of their teens, but they're still babies in some ways." And Mrs. Pearson began to cry softly.

"We're all babies in some ways, Mrs. Pearson," said Dr. Salt, feeling he ought to say something.

"Doctor, what do you think has happened to her? I know Peggy thinks she's gone to France or somewhere with some chap. But I don't. I can't help it, I just don't. She'd have come back for some of her things. It wouldn't have taken her five minutes to get 'em. And it's no use—I feel uneasy in my mind about Noreen and I can't stop wondering about her. Three weeks, an' never a word. What's happened? Where is she, doctor?"

"I don't know, Mrs. Pearson," he said slowly as he stood up. "But I'm going to find out. And I'm not leaving Birkden until I do, even though I've had quite enough of Birkden."

"I used to think it such a nice town," said Mrs. Pearson, through her final sniffles, "when I was a girl and just after I got married. But now—I don't know—it's different. Nothing like so nice and friendly."

"Perhaps there aren't any nice towns anymore, Mrs. Pearson," he told her on his way to the door. "Perhaps instead of making them bigger and bigger, we ought to set fire to them and then start afresh."

"And where would we all be—camping out? Will you be seeing the police again, Dr. Salt?"

He turned at the front door. "I think so. I hope so. We ought to have something to tell each other soon."

4

Dr. Salt had lived well away from his office, which he had shared with his three partners. He had a ground-floor flat in a row of coming-down-in-the-world Victorian houses. It had its own front door to the left as you entered the still imposing hall. This door led directly into an unusually large sitting room with windows at each end of it. Here, an hour after he had left Mrs. Pearson and Olton Street, which he hoped he had visited for the last time, Dr. Salt was finishing a pot of China tea, without any nonsense of milk and sugar, and losing himself in a muddle of books and phonograph records. He was trying to decide which books and records he could sell or give away and which he ought to keep, packing them to be stored until he knew where he was going. And so far he had made very little progress with this rather urgent chore. He would light a pipe and then begin dipping into books instead of deciding which pile should receive them. With the records—and he had several hundred, together with a magnificent stereophonic record player—he wasted even more time, especially where he had two versions of one work. He would play a particular movement, then try the same movement on the alternative record, which might be older and monaural and yet more worthy to be kept. And so far, though he had started on Sunday morning, he had not yet clearly separated the rejected and the accepted: it seemed to be more and more of a muddle. His heart wasn't in it. This was when he needed a woman, or at least the kind of woman who was all will and energy when faced with disorder and indecision.

He was listening to the fifth movement of the Schubert Octet in F Major, played by the Vienna Octet, when the young man with the reddish hair and the leather jacket walked in. He had found the door unlocked and apparently did not care about ringing or knocking. He was wearing dark glasses, which he might have been wearing earlier—Dr. Salt had only seen him from the back—and which were certainly unnecessary late on an October afternoon.

Dr. Salt carefully stopped his machine and lifted the record from the turntable. "This isn't a surgery and, anyhow, I'm not in practice here now."

"And I'm not ill." The young man grinned, pleased with himself.

Even apart from that funny business with poor little Peggy, Dr. Salt would have disliked this young man—everything about him. "Well, don't wear those damn silly dark glasses too often; you'll ruin your eyesight. Good afternoon."

"Not yet. Want to talk to you. You're leaving Birkden, aren't you?"

"Yes, quite soon. Why?"

"I've a friend who wants this flat—and right sharp."

"Go away."

The young man brought out and held up what looked like a number of banknotes. "A hundred quid here. Nice new fivers. All off tax. Lovely money. And my friend says it's all yours if you'll walk out tonight—like that—bingo!"

Dr. Salt was curious now. "It's a bargain. I leave here tonight, and you or your friend book me a suite for a few days at the Queen's Hotel."

"Oh, no. That's out."

"I thought it would be. Put your money away."

"You think you're being clever, Dr. Salt, but you're not.

31

You're just being bloody stupid. Look—if you're leaving Birkden, you can't like it much."

"Not much—no."

"Lovely town. And I'm not one of the locals. Only been here a year. But I go with the right kind of people. You don't—you're bloody stupid."

"You've made your point," said Dr. Salt wearily.

"Oh, no. Just coming to it. Look—if I want you to clear out of Birkden, right sharp, it's only for your own good. You're not popular, y'know, Dr. Salt. You've been careless. You've made enemies. Didn't matter before. Not safe to start monkeying with a doctor who's working hard. He's got too many people on his side. But you've finished here now, haven't you? You're not working anymore. You're not important to anybody. You're *redundant*, man. And it can turn out to be a nasty experience."

"Can it? What are you proposing to do?"

"Me?" cried the young man. "I'm not going to do anything. I'm just giving you a warning, that's all. After that I mind my own business. And you ought to mind yours."

"I am." Dr. Salt went to his desk and picked up a telephone directory.

"Look—I've given you a warning; now I'll make you a nice offer. My last. Clear out now and you can take ten of those fivers with you and I'll see that everything here is properly packed and put into store. There's a good train to the Smoke at half past six. You could catch it. And two or three to Birmingham—if you like Birmingham."

Dr. Salt was now looking through the telephone directory. "I don't," he threw over his shoulder. "And I don't like you. Now go away."

"And you go screw a duck." The young man slammed the door so hard that a color lithograph jumped its nail and crashed on a pile of books.

After blowing out his breath in a long sighing sound, Dr. Salt began dialing. "This is Dr. Salt. Is Mr. Duffield there, please? He knows me." A youthful but surprisingly precise voice, belonging, it said, to one Godfrey, personal assistant to Mr. Duffield, replied that Mr. Duffield was away and would not be back until the following afternoon. "Well," said Dr. Salt, "tell him I'll be coming round to see him about something that might be rather important. About this time perhaps . . . Yes, Dr. Salt. He'll remember me because his brother was one of my patients."

Then he recalled that he had been trying to make up his mind about the Schubert Octet. He started the fifth movement again, listened carefully, decided in the record's favor, but then had some trouble finding the pile of chamber music recordings he was keeping. After listening to several more records, he went into his kitchen, which was larger than most and also served as a dining room, even when he had two or three guests. He examined some tins in the cupboard and chose a French one— *tripes à la mode de Caen.* He brought it out but did not open it, knowing that he had plenty of time, but he peeled a few potatoes and cleaned and shredded half a cabbage. Then he put the potatoes into salted water and started them going over a low flame, poured some whisky into a tumbler, added a couple of ice cubes, and then took the drink into the sitting room. There he sat at his desk, lit a pipe and, after taking one slow sip of the whisky, forgot about it, began thinking hard and making notes in a scribble that was as good as a cipher. Sometimes even he couldn't read it after a few hours; but he just managed to make it out, later that evening, when he began thinking again.

THREE

1

The letter came by the second post on Wednesday morning. It was the only letter, the rest of the mail being bills and receipts. Reg Morgan, looking important as well as scholarly, brought it into the little back office, where Maggie and Mrs. Chapman were sitting over their cups of elevenses.

"Just one real letter, Miss Culworth," said Reg. "I can't imagine what's in it. Looks very peculiar."

"So do you, Reg," said Mrs. Chapman sharply. "Hanging about here, making silly remarks. Go and help Sheila."

"What doing, Mrs. Chapman? She's just standing there—in a dream."

"I'll find something for both of you to do in a minute. Now off you go, Reg."

Maggie was staring at the letter. Printed in red at the top of the envelope was *Lyceum Cinema, Birkden*. But it was addressed in a childish hand to *Mr. Culworth, Bookshop, Hemton*. "I must say Reg was right, though. It *does* look most peculiar. See for yourself."

"Must be one of these silly young girls they have working in some of these offices now. Can't get anybody else. Not even a big cinema like the Lyceum. Are you going to open it, Maggie?"

"I think I ought, don't you? After all, it's addressed to him here at the shop. It might be something we ought to attend to. I think he'd *want* me to open it, don't you?"

"Certainly." Mrs. Chapman brought that out promptly, but then she hesitated. "Besides, if it isn't business—well, it's from Birkden, isn't it? And all you know so far about your father is that he went to Birkden. So if it isn't business, if it's personal, then it might tell you something about where he is and what he's doing. You read it, Maggie." She took a look into the shop. "Damn. Two customers. I'd better go and cope."

The sheet inside was headed *Lyceum Cinema* again. The letter was written in the same childish hand that had addressed the envelope.

Dear Mr. Culworth,

Dr. Salt came here to ask me about Noreen and from what he said I think I was wrong what I told you about her. And now there is trouble so look out but I am in a hurry to write this so can't explain.

> Yours truly,
> Peggy Pearson

Maggie read it three times, her mind racing round and round it. And then, before she settled down to consider the letter carefully, she realized something. She was suddenly more alive than she had been for the last two years, ever since she fled from the ruin and misery of her affair with Hugh. Not joyously alive, of course—she hated this letter—but still, alive. Or at least far less desiccated, instantly more capable of real feeling, than she had been ever since she came back home.

"Was it anything?" Bertha Chapman was back, for once inquisitive.

Maggie had to think quickly. She had already decided that she must show the letter to Alan, but must make him agree that it ought to be kept from their mother. But what about Bertha? Yes, she needed one ally in the shop. "You read it, Bertha, but please don't say anything about it to Sheila and Reg."

Bertha, built for it, gave a snort. "I wouldn't tell those two what I was having for lunch. Now then." When she had read the letter twice, she stared inquiringly at Maggie.

"What do you make of it, Bertha?"

"Well, it's obviously written by a girl, probably quite young, who works at the Lyceum Cinema, and not in the office, though she's used office stationery. She knows your father, but not well, I'd say. What she and your father have in common, so to speak, is this Noreen. And my guess is that she's another young girl. Where this Dr. Salt comes in, I can't imagine. Noreen could be a friend of his—or just one of his patients, which I think is rather more likely. But obviously your father's involved somehow in this Noreen-Peggy-Salt business."

"I know. But how? Can you see him being mixed up with cinema usherettes or whatever they are?"

"That's this Peggy Pearson. He went to ask her about Noreen."

"Yes, but then what? That must have been on Monday. What happened then?"

"You'll have to go and find out, Maggie. At least you know *something* now. And if you don't want to do it, then let me do it."

"No, of course I must go, Bertha. You'll have to manage without me this afternoon."

"Your first duty to the shop, Maggie, my dear, is to find your father and bring him back as soon as you can. I think all these bigger cinemas open just after lunchtime. So you have your lunch—and try to eat a good lunch; you're all excited and using up nervous energy—then take the first bus into Birkden and find this Peggy Pearson."

"That's what I thought, Bertha." She hesitated a moment. "I'll have to tell my brother, Alan, about this letter, of course, as soon as I can—he's at the university all day today, and it's hopeless trying to ring him up there—but I thought I wouldn't worry Mother with it."

"You're quite right, Maggie dear. In your place I shouldn't dream of it." Mrs. Chapman and Mrs. Culworth had no liking, not even any respect, for each other. "Keep her right out of it for the time being, until you know more. You go off to lunch, then to Birkden. Don't go there first; all the lunch places there are always so crowded."

Maggie laughed at her. "Food first for Bertha!"

"You may laugh, but I believe in stoking up—specially at a time like this. And another thing, Maggie dear—be careful."

"Careful about what?"

"I don't know. If I did, I'd tell you. But Birkden isn't Hemton, don't forget. Different sort of place altogether."

"And don't you forget that I'm a big girl who used to live and work in London—the *real* wicked city."

"Well . . ." And Bertha left it at that, but gave her a long look. Maggie could feel the flush that Bertha must be noticing. Annoyed with herself, not with Bertha, she said rather quickly, "All right, I'll be careful."

Just over an hour later, she went at forty miles an hour into the maze and another kind of life.

2

She never did see the manager of the Lyceum, but after talking to two girls and a male attendant in a chocolate uniform, she reached the assistant manager, a pale and melancholy youngish man in a cubbyhole of an office.

"Peggy Pearson. Yes," he told her. "One of our usherettes."

"I'd like to speak to her."

"So would I," he said wearily. "She was supposed to be here, putting on her uniform, at one o'clock. It's now nearly quarter to three and she isn't here. No message, of course. This happens all the time. You'd think these girls would enjoy wearing an attractive uniform in a picture theater. The work's not hard. We do everything we can for them. I'm referring to the company now, which owns eleven picture theaters like this one, all in the Midlands. We're already employing over thirty coloured girls. Why? Simply because these Peggy Pearsons are here today and gone tomorrow. They don't even tell you they're dissatisfied—"

"Could you give me her home address, please?" said Maggie, tired of this long grumble.

"I could, of course. But if it's anything to do with her work here . . ."

"It isn't. Purely a private matter. And rather urgent."

He opened a filing cabinet. "It's 45 Olton Street."

"Thank you. Do you happen to know where Olton Street is?"

"I'm afraid I haven't the faintest idea. I came here from Coventry only a few weeks ago. And between ourselves, I'm hoping to be transferred to our Wolverhampton theater any time now. 45 Olton Street," he repeated as he opened the door to show her out. "And if you find Peggy Pearson at home, you can tell her from me that if she reports for duty at one o'clock tomorrow, I'll forget about today and won't ask her for a doctor's certificate. Between ourselves, of course."

Feeling rather reckless now, Maggie took a taxi to Olton Street, and then told the man to wait. A woman who looked as if she had been both drinking and crying answered her knock.

"I'm not buying anything," she told Maggie, looking her over suspiciously. "And I don't want that caper about what washing powder I use or what magazines I read."

"It's nothing like that. Are you Mrs. Pearson? Well, I want to talk to your daughter Peggy."

"I might have known. What's she been doing?"

"Mrs. Pearson, I don't know her. But she wrote a letter to my father. And she may be able to tell me something I badly need to know. It's all quite private and personal."

"You'd better come in." And Mrs. Pearson led the way into a room that looked like a corner of a secondhand furniture store. It had a horrid smell. And Maggie could only sit about three feet—if that—away from Mrs. Pearson, who was not really old, probably only in her forties, but looked hopelessly crumpled, stained, defeated. Trying to find her father, she arrived at this woman, this room, this street, together representing the first step in her search; and she felt half frightened, half depressed.

"Mrs. Pearson, I'm Maggie Culworth," she heard herself saying. "I work for my father, who has a bookshop in Hemton. Without telling anybody where he was going, he left the shop at lunchtime on Monday. Afterwards I learnt at the bus station that he took a bus to Birkden. This morning a letter came for him, written by your daughter." Then she checked herself. "But I ought to be talking to her, not to you."

"Well, you can't. She isn't here. While I was out last night, visiting my friend Mrs. Muston, her ladyship comes back from the Lyceum, packs her suitcase and goes off to Birmingham. I know that because she left a note on the kitchen table telling me she'd gone to Birmingham. That's all—not another word. I don't know where she is, who she's with, what she's doing. *Me*, her own mother."

"Oh—how maddening!" But Maggie was thinking about herself, not about the deprived and insulted mother.

Mrs. Pearson must have sensed this. "I don't know what sort of a father you've got, but I know my own daughter. And if you're thinking she's gone off with a man his age—nearer sixty than fifty, I'll bet—you can think again."

"But I never—" Maggie gasped.

"She can be silly about boys," Mrs. Pearson cut in sharply, "like most of 'em now. But she wouldn't look twice at a man old enough to be your father."

"Oh, do stop it. You're just wasting time and temper. Of course she didn't go off with him. I'd never dream of suggesting such a thing. Besides, as I told you, she wrote him this letter." She fumbled around in her bag. "Here it is. You can read it."

Mrs. Pearson not only read it but read it aloud, very slowly, giving it an ominous air that made Maggie want to snatch the letter away. " 'Dr. Salt came here to ask me about Noreen and from what he said I think I was wrong what I told you about her. And now there is trouble so look out but I am in a hurry to write this so can't explain.' " She waited a moment before handing back the letter, stared hard at Maggie, then said, still using an ominous tone, "Well, you can see what that means."

"No, I can't," Maggie told her impatiently. "If I could, I wouldn't be here. Do *you* know what it means?"

"I know this. She went off to Birmingham—she has friends there and then there's my sister—to get away from this trouble she mentions. I don't say she was right—she ought to have waited and then asked me what she ought to do—but it all begins to make sense."

"Well, it doesn't to me. Who's Noreen, and where does she come into it?"

"You don't know?"

"Oh, really!" Maggie could have slapped her. "Of course I don't know."

"Well, your father does, doesn't he? Peggy wrote that letter to him. She says she told him something about Noreen. It's there in the letter, isn't it?"

"Yes, it is, Mrs. Pearson." Maggie was making a great effort to control herself. "But you see, I'm looking for my father. And if your daughter's gone away, then I'll talk to this Noreen."

"You can't. She's been missing for the last three weeks."

"Oh, no!" It was a cry of dismay, not a contradiction. "Are you sure?"

"Well, she had a room here. She walked out one night and never came back. Dr. Salt knows all about it. He was Noreen's doctor. Ours as well."

"Then I'll go and see Dr. Salt." Maggie got up, glad to be

going. "And if somebody tells me *he's* missing, I'll start screaming. Do you know where I can find him?"

"No, I don't. I used to see him at his office, but he's finished down there. He's leaving Birkden." Clearly Mrs. Pearson enjoyed making these announcements.

Maggie muttered something about finding him in the telephone book, then hurried out, hoping she had done with Mrs. Pearson forever.

3

The man who opened the door was smallish but rather bulky and was probably about forty-five. He was wearing an old corduroy jacket over a dark-blue sport shirt. He had that fine dusty sort of hair, but darker and bristling eyebrows. Behind him a phonograph was making a tremendous sound, so that she had to shout and felt foolish. "Good afternoon. Are you Dr. Salt?"

He nodded. "No longer in practice, though."

"I don't want to consult you as a doctor," she shouted. "It's about Peggy Pearson and somebody called Noreen."

He nodded again and then, instead of replying, he opened the door properly and waved her in. As soon as he had closed the door behind her, he hurried past her to turn off the phonograph.

"Scherzo of the Bruckner Seventh Symphony—Klemperer and the Philharmonia," he said solemnly. "But do sit down. This isn't a bad chair." He removed a pile of books from it. "There you are. I'm about to move on and I'm trying to decide which books and records to keep. Tricky business. Going to take me longer than I thought." He removed two record cases from a large armchair, sat down, and began lighting a pipe. "Now then. What about Peggy Pearson and Noreen? Or first, what about you?"

"I'm Maggie Culworth. I don't live here but in Hemton—"

"Bookshop—High Street?"

"Oh, you know it. I'm so glad. Yes, that's my father's shop, and I work there."

"Been in a few times. Downstairs chiefly—secondhand department. Talked to your father, and I seem to remember a comfortable middle-aged woman—"

"Yes, Mrs. Chapman." Maggie was still feeling glad. After the Lyceum and Mrs. Pearson, this seemed so sensible and cozy. "Probably you've never seen me because I'm often working in the little office at the back. But anyhow, you've met my father, and it's because of him I'm here, Dr. Salt." She explained carefully what her father had done on Monday, and then went on: "As you've met him, perhaps you can understand why we're so mystified and worried. He's always so cautious, so conscientious, so reliable."

"He would be, yes," said Dr. Salt. "Not the kind of man to go off and leave you all worrying about him."

"That's just it. Well, then this letter came for him this morning. And as you're mentioned in it, I don't see why you shouldn't read it." He seemed to take in the letter almost at a glance; he was obviously an exceptionally quick reader. Then he looked at her, nodded and handed back the letter. "I ought to tell you," she said hurriedly, "that I tried to find Peggy Pearson at the Lyceum Cinema, but she wasn't there. Then I went to see her mother, who told me that Peggy rushed off to Birmingham last night—"

"Away from the trouble she mentions in the letter?"

"That's what her mother seems to think. But she's a muddled sort of woman, and she wasn't in last night and so didn't hear what Peggy had to say. Dr. Salt, does any of this make any sense to you?"

"Yes," he replied cheerfully. "Most of it."

"Thank goodness! Can you tell me?"

"Certainly. But I can't tell you how your father comes to be involved. So we'll leave that for the moment. I saw Peggy Pearson yesterday afternoon at the Lyceum to ask her some questions about a friend of hers, Noreen Wilks, who used to be one of my patients. Peggy believed that Noreen had gone to the south of France with her boyfriend. I told her I didn't believe this. On the morning of September twelfth I signed her application form for a passport. That evening she went out at the usual time and never came back. Now just after I had left Peggy, I think she was threatened by an unpleasant young man, who afterwards paid me a visit here. I also think she ran into the office a few yards away, and there she hastily wrote that letter to your father. He probably saw her on Monday afternoon, and she told him she thought Noreen had gone abroad."

"And now she's telling him that you didn't think so," said Maggie hastily, if only to prove she wasn't a complete fool.

"And something else equally important. Read the second sentence."

"'And now there is trouble so look out but I am in a hurry to write this so can't explain.'" Maggie looked at him. "The unpleasant young man?"

"I think so. You realize, of course, Miss Culworth, that Noreen Wilks is the central figure here."

"She isn't to me," Maggie told him bluntly. "I don't care about Noreen Wilks; only about my father. That's natural, isn't it?"

"Certainly. But it may not be good enough." He gave her a sharp, bright look. It was rather startling, because most of the time he looked so lazy and sleepy. An odd man. She couldn't decide if she liked him or disliked him. "It's possible," he went on, without any hardening of tone, "you may have to take an interest in Noreen Wilks."

"You think my father came here to ask about her?"

"He may have had other things to do, but we know he did that. And now he seems to be missing. And we might say that Peggy Pearson is missing too. And I know that Noreen has been missing for the last three weeks. Too many people missing, don't you think, Miss Culworth?"

"I do. I also think you'd better call me Maggie."

"Certainly, Maggie."

"Now could you please explain about this Noreen Wilks?"

"Shortly," he said, getting up. "But first, can you drink China tea—very good China tea—without milk and sugar?"

"I can and I often do. So if you're offering me some, I'd love it."

He picked his way through the muddle, but turned before he reached the door leading to the kitchen. "While you're waiting, Maggie, I wonder if you'd mind looking round to see if you can find, first, the autobiography of John Cowper Powys—biggish and, I think, brown binding—and secondly, Mahler's Fifth Symphony, played by the Boston, two records in an album."

Maggie didn't know where to begin, there was such a clutter of books and records all round the room. It was a maddening room if only because before this Salt-made earthquake it must have been both comfortable and charming. Above the white shelves, now cleared of books, were some colored lithographs and a few bold foreign posters. The curtains at each end had been chosen by somebody who had an eye for color and design. There were several Chinese pots, yellow, apple green, dark red, along the tops of the shelves. There were glimpses of good rugs, though now rucked and dusty, between the piles of books and records. It was all a dreadful mess now, of course, but she felt she could have loved this room before Dr. Salt began to think of leaving it, when everything was in its place. She was also ready to bet almost anything that some woman had helped him to furnish and decorate it. She found the Mahler album, but gave the Powys up as a bad job. And when he came back with the tea tray, she told him so. "It must have been staring you in the face," she added.

"That's what happens," he told her. "Once you don't see something, you keep on not seeing it." He handed her a rather large but delicate cup, without a saucer. "It happens all too often in my profession. We miss what is staring us in the face."

44

"Thank you for this tea," said Maggie after a silent interval. "It's delicious." Then, after some hesitation: "I've been telling myself what a charming room this must have been before you began pulling yourself out of it. And I couldn't help feeling that a woman must have had a hand in it originally."

"My wife. She died three years ago. Leukemia."

Deciding in a flash not to say she was sorry or make any apology, Maggie said, "It was a good marriage, wasn't it?"

"Yes. We were very happy. Perhaps we used up our ration. Do you like Birkden, Maggie?"

"I hardly know it. But I don't find it interesting. It's the wrong size, neither one thing nor the other. I spent five years in London. Then I came back to Hemton, which is small and sensible and still attractive in spots. I can take Hemton, I can take London, but not a town like this, too big and yet not big enough. And as you're leaving it, I imagine you don't care for it much."

"I don't—no. It was all right when there were two of us. But now, having got rid of my practice, I'd like to get out as soon as I can. Go a long way, if possible. But I'm not going until I know what happened to Noreen Wilks." He said this very quietly, in his usual rather sleepy tone, but Maggie knew at once that he meant exactly what he said.

"Tell me about her. Was she somebody . . . rather special for you, Dr. Salt?"

"As a person, not at all. She was rather prettier than most, but I've had dozens just like her in and out of my surgery. Thoughtless, silly, though not vicious in any way. But she was important to me as a patient because she was suffering from a type of kidney disease I'm particularly interested in. Hoped to specialize in it once. Might still have a try. I'd hit on a treatment that was keeping her going nicely. If she missed it for a couple of weeks, she'd soon run into a screaming hypertension and after that she'd be fighting for her life. She knew this. I'd given her a thorough fright about it." He explained then, as he had to Superintendent Hurst, how he had made Noreen promise to

45

see a doctor, showing him the brief report on her case that she always carried in her bag, wherever she might be. "I don't think she went abroad," he concluded. "And any English doctor would have got in touch with me—or Dr. Baldwin, who now has my practice. He's heard nothing, and neither have I. And she's been missing now for three weeks."

"So—what do you think?"

"I could be wrong," he said slowly, "but I think she's dead." He kept silent for a few moments. "Have some more tea, Maggie."

"Thank you." While he was filling her cup, she said hesitantly, "Dr. Salt—I suppose I've no right to say this, but I can't help feeling that you haven't told me all you know."

"Yes, I have. All I *know.* The rest is so much guessing, some of it pretty wild. And of course, your father doesn't come into it. He's quite new in the picture."

"Yes, but there's the unpleasant young man who seems to have frightened Peggy Pearson and who came to see you, you said. Where does he come in? What did he want? Or am I being too curious?"

"I might think so, Maggie, if it weren't for one thing. Your father's somehow involved in this."

"I know." She blinked hard. "Though I can't imagine how or why. But I'm sure now he *is.*"

He nodded, then drank some tea and lit his pipe again, using what seemed to be an outsize gas lighter. He smoked and said nothing for what must have been about a minute, while Maggie controlled her impatience.

Finally, "Who do you have at home with you?"

"My mother. And I'm not going to tell her any of this. My brother, Alan, who's several years older than me, not married, and lectures on physics at the university—Hemtonshire, I mean, of course."

"Ah—clever chap?"

"Very clever in some ways. Idiotic in others. Hasn't really

46

quite grown up. But I'll tell him everything, of course. He might be a great help."

"Would you like to leave it to him?"

"Certainly not." She was indignant. "Besides, I can spare more time."

He waited a moment. "Because your father's somehow involved in this Noreen Wilks business, it doesn't follow that you ought to be. No—listen to me, Maggie. You still have a choice. Either go home now and try to forget about Noreen—and me. Or help me to find out what happened to her, in the hope you might discover where your father is and what he's doing. I believe, though I can't prove it, that there's a definite connection. And I could do with some help, from both you and your brother."

"Then that's settled," she said impatiently.

"Not quite. We may have to take the lid off Birkden. What we find inside may be very unpleasant. It might even be dangerous."

"Dr. Salt, I'm disappointed. I didn't think you'd be the sort of man to exaggerate like that."

"You were right then, wrong now."

"We're in Birkden, not Chicago or New York."

"You're years out of date, Maggie. You're now in a distant suburb of New York and Chicago. I'm not talking for effect. I never do. I've spent seven years as a GP here in Birkden. I know what goes on. But not all. Not enough." And he almost shouted this, surprising Maggie, who told herself again what an odd man he was. "And now I ought to see a man, and, if you're going to help, then you might learn something by coming with me. I'll ring up to make sure he's there."

"Then I'll clear away the tea things." And then, when she saw the kitchen, he surprised her again. Instead of being a horrible mess of unwashed dishes and cutlery and moldy this and smelly that, it was cleaner and tidier than their kitchen at home. Hastily she began washing and drying the tea things.

"He's there. Let's go." He was so curt that she wondered if he resented her being in the kitchen. Did men feel things like that? She went out, wondering. He was certainly very much a doctor and yet quite unlike any other doctor she'd ever met. As she waited for him to lock the door, she noticed the card he had pinned on it: *L. H. Salt.* "What do L. H. stand for?" she asked him as they went to his car.

"Lionel Humphrey," he told her gruffly. "And now just forget 'em. Call me Salt when you're tired of doctoring me."

"Okay, Salt," she cried a bit too heartily, to cover her nervousness.

He neither smiled nor seemed offended. Probably he didn't care a damn what she—or for that matter anybody else—called him. He seemed the oddest mixture: one minute sleepy, simple and rather sweet; the next minute hard and ruthless. Either too busy driving or thinking hard, he didn't talk, so she had plenty of time to wonder about him as he drove through a number of side roads, by-passing the center of the town, and finally arriving at a part of it strange to her. It was a dingy and tumble-down region, most of its buildings looking as if they were waiting to be demolished.

FOUR

1

Dr. Salt stopped the car near a barred entrance, which had above it a neon sign, not switched on yet, that said *Buzzy's*. When they got out, he found a narrow doorway, not far from the club entrance, and he led the way up some rickety wooden stairs. At the top there was some sort of office, hardly bigger than a hanging cupboard. Looking important in it was a thin, spectacled youth, like a rather older version of Reg Morgan. "To see Mr. Duffield?" he inquired primly. "Have you an appointment?"

"Yes. I'm Dr. Salt."

"Of course—you telephoned. This way, please."

The room beyond was larger but so narrow that it looked as if it had been made out of a corridor. There was no outside window at all—it had three very bright electric bulbs with green shades hanging from a high ceiling—but a sheet of glass ran the whole length of the left wall, while against the opposite wall was a very long table, higgledy-piggledy with cigar boxes, bottles, glasses, plates, an enormous pork pie and some cheese, two vases filled with dusty artificial flowers, a green telephone and a red telephone and a pile of directories. Maggie was able to take in all this because they had to wait a minute or two for Mr. Duffield, who then came in, wiping his hands and face on a very large pink towel, through a doorway at the other end of the room. He was wide and fat and bald, with an enormous face on which his features merely seemed to be huddled together in the middle.

"Hello, Buzzy," said Dr. Salt. "Miss Maggie Culworth—Mr. Buzzy Duffield."

"Pleased to meet you, Miss Culworth." Mr. Duffield, having got rid of the towel, shook hands with her; she felt it was like having her hand wrapped in meat. "It's a pleasure. It's a privilege. *Bzzz.*" And if he made this bee noise all the time, no wonder he was called Buzzy. He was shaking hands now with Dr. Salt. "Doctor, it's a treat to see you. It's lovely—lovely." He turned to Maggie. "Five to one he's never told you what he done for my brother. Saved him when he was nearing death's door. In Australia now—fit an' well—an' never more miserable in his life. Never satisfied, Arthur isn't. *Bzzz.* Dr. Salt here could make rings round the lot if he wanted to, Miss Culworth. I call you Miss Culworth—y'know, bit of class—but you call me Buzzy. Promise."

"All right, Buzzy."

"Mind you, that's no privilege. This town's full of twerps I wouldn't spit on that call me Buzzy—when I'm not there. *Bzzz.*" He looked at Dr. Salt. "Now you're here, doctor, I'll tell you something. When I invited you to a big classy French dinner at the Queen's—anything you wanted—y'know, just before I got Arthur off to Australia—an' then you wouldn't wear it, I was hurt. Honest to God, I was deeply hurt. *Bzzz.*"

"I'd too much to do, Buzzy. Saw too many people—all day and half the night. Just wanted to be quiet when I was off duty."

"I'll bet, I'll bet. Here—what we drinking? Miss Culworth?"

"Isn't it rather early? Oh, well. A gin and tonic, thank you, Buzzy."

"If you'd like anything fancier, just name it. I've got everything. Doctor?"

"A little Scotch, thank you, Buzzy. Neat—if it's good."

"The best—twenty-one years old. Like mother's milk—if you happen to be born a tiger. Look, doc, why don't you help yourself while I attend to Miss Culworth? Over there, if you don't mind. You can pour me one while you're at it. *Bzzz.* So now you're packing it in, doc. A lot of people are going to be sorry."

"Not many. A few, only a few, Buzzy."

"You're dead right, of course. Only a few. You said it. Most of 'em wouldn't notice if a wooden dummy was taking their temperatures. They're only bloody wooden dummies themselves. *Bzzz.* Here's your gin an' tonic, Miss Culworth, an' you'll have to excuse me if my language an' expressions get a bit fruity."

"Buzzy, I spent five years as a secretary in a stockbrokers' office in the City. You ought to have heard some of them. But tell me—why do you have this window thing, here along the wall?"

"So I can see what's happening in my club. The dance floor's down there. Any trouble, I can spot it. *Bzzz.* Come in later one night—any night except Sunday—when it's all lit up down there, and you're looking through a window at a monkey house. Got another room the other side—six one-arm bandits, one roulette table and another for pontoon. Not classy here, y'know. Not enough money, town this size. Not even a license, though some of our bitter lemon drinks behave as if somebody had gone an' put gin in 'em. An' don't ask me how it happens. I'm just old Buzzy, the one they wouldn't give a license to. All right, Winston boy, what d'you want?' The prim, spectacled youth was looking round the door.

"It's Charlie, Mr. Duffield. On the blower, from Northampton." He still sounded prim. "Do I put him through?"

"No. What's he want?"

"He's got eighty-five transistors. Jap jobs. He'll take four-ten each, he says."

"Not from me, he won't, Winston boy. They must be all hotter than a baker's flue. Tell Charlie not to be silly. *Bzzz.*"

"Yes, Mr. Duffield." The door closed.

Buzzy waited a moment, then looked from Maggie to Dr. Salt. "What about that one? I ask you. Winston. Winston Sandby. Born in our finest hour. *Bzzz.* I pay him ten quid a week and he's here from ten in the morning till all hours, doing the accounts and the books and taking messages on the blower and behaving to me as if I was Chairman of Barclays Bank. Doesn't smoke, never takes a drink, never tries to get one of the girls up here. He isn't human. Winston. Can you beat it?"

Before either of his visitors could say anything, the red telephone rang. "Buzzy here," he told it. "What's new? . . . What, again? Then tell him to stay away and keep away. *Bzzz.* No, listen. Get Whitey to tell him—y'know, all sinister, like they do it in the pictures. Oh, and you, Whitey and Joe had better report here a bit earlier tonight. . . . I don't know, but I might have something special for you to do—or one of you. *Bzzz.* Yes, and I only hope you don't feel as tired as you sound. Like ringing up a bloody old men's home. *Bzzz.*" He left the telephone, swallowed his whisky, then lit a cigar. "You heard what I said to Fred then? One of my boys. I suddenly had a hunch. I get hunches. Sometimes they pay off, sometimes they're sheer flaming lunacy. So now, doc, what's worrying you? Or is it Miss Culworth?"

"It may be both of us, Buzzy. First of all," said Dr. Salt, "who's an unpleasant young man with reddish hair, dark glasses and a leather jacket, who thinks he's an American gangster?"

Buzzy thought for a moment. "His name's Russ. Came from Coventry. Worked for me for a few weeks, but he had some wrong ideas. A villain. Been inside. Not going to give you any trouble, is he, doc?"

"He might."

"Well, now look. I've got some hard boys working for me that could take him apart—and anybody he goes around with—just for a light workout. *Bzzz.*" Then he gave a hoarse little laugh and looked at Maggie.

"You heard me then, Miss Culworth? To hear me talk you'd think this was Chicago or Detroit and young Winston out there was cleaning a Tommy gun. Me, talking like that—born an' bred here in Birkden! All right, I run a couple of betting shops, a cheap nightclub; I'm a promoter; I've done a few deals on the swift and shady side—but I'm no American gangster. Yet you noticed the way I talked? And we all do it. What's the matter with us?"

"Oh, I suppose it's films, television, paperbacks," said Maggie. "All the trends."

Dr. Salt nodded his agreement. "They're turning us intő a slow-motion shabby America. This must have been a decent little provincial town once."

"And not so long ago neither," said Buzzy. "Not more than a market town, when I was a nipper here. Real farmers coming in with their red-cheeked, fat-arsed wives and daughters, wishing nobody any harm. Then—*bzzz*—just before the war, during the war, just after the war, industry moves in—and all of a sudden we're a big town. We make shoes, we make hats, we make nylons and Terylenes and whatnot. We have the United Anglo-Belgian Fabrics—"

"Stop there, please, Buzzy. At the Fabrics. It's one reason why I'm here, to ask you about them. They run a club, don't they?"

Buzzy contorted his features, already too small for his face, so they almost seemed to vanish. "They do, doc. But they won't have me in. Too common. I know about it, though. Ask me an' I'll tell you."

"Young girls from the town go there sometimes, don't they?"

"That's right. Special parties. Party girls, these kids are. They feed 'em to their Belgian directors and big buyers from the

States and South America. *Bzzz.* I have two girls working here who used to go, before they got too hard and tough. They like 'em young and fresh up there—same as vegetables. And I'd say they're wrong, even if they're only out for the old goona-goona."

"So would I, Buzzy. Young girls are for boys. Men should have women. But it's chiefly the idea that fascinates these fellows—taking something that doesn't belong to them."

"But does a party girl have to go to bed with somebody?" Maggie asked.

"Oh, no. She could just keep on teasing 'em. *Bzzz.*"

"Buzzy, I met Sir Arnold Donnington yesterday morning. We were both visiting the police. I didn't like Sir Arnold, but I can't see him attending these parties."

"*Him?* He wouldn't admit they existed. He fines school kids two quid for necking. *Bzzz.* He's a bluenose if there ever was one."

"Yet he's the big boss at United Fabrics."

"That's right. But the old dolchy-veety up there at the Fabrics Club is run by the sales director, Tommy Linsdale. And he likes the gay life, Tommy does. I know him. He used to bet with me now and again. He and a fancy piece he's keeping, they run the parties. *Bzzz.* She finds the girls. He brought her here one night —slumming. A classy handsome piece—and about as soft and tender as a sheet of high-duty alloy. Jill something—I forget what."

"Would it be Jill Frinton?" said Maggie.

"That's her. You know her, Miss Culworth?"

"No, not really." She glanced at Dr. Salt, who was staring hard at her. "I was serving in the shop one Saturday afternoon, and she came in with a man. She bought one book and asked for another we hadn't in stock, so she ordered it and gave us her name and address. And there are two reasons why I remember her name. I once had a dreadful fiasco of a holiday at Frinton. The other reason is that my brother Alan happened to be in the

54

shop that afternoon, and he couldn't take his eyes off this Jill Frinton. We teased him about it afterwards. She's tall, dark, very smart—and I suppose very attractive if you like that type." She couldn't resist looking inquiringly at Dr. Salt, but he wasn't having any.

"But why the Fabrics Club, doc? If you're thinking of living it up before you go, I can't oblige you there. But you can have anything you want here at my club. Buzzy's is all yours. *Bzzz.*"

"Thanks, Buzzy, but I like a quiet life. I'm asking questions because a young patient of mine is missing. Noreen Wilks. She's not been heard of since September twelfth. And I think she went that night to a party at the Fabrics Club."

"Noreen Wilks, did you say? I'll ask around. Some of my boys and girls might know something. Excuse me." He pushed past them, shouting, "Winston, make a note." When Winston opened the door, he was told to stay where he was. "Make a note for when Fred, Whitey and Joe get here. I want to ask 'em about a kid called Noreen Wilks. Been missing for weeks. Might be a brass, I don't know, but she doesn't sit at home watching the telly and mending her drawers."

They could hear but not see Winston. "They don't wear drawers."

"A lad who looks like you oughtn't to know what they wear. *Bzzz.* Oh—an' make another note. Russ—you remember him? Well, I want to know what he's doing now. One of the boys'll know." Buzzy shut the door. "You heard that, doc? Might be some help. Doing my best. *Bzzz.*"

"Thanks, Buzzy. By the way, who'd be paying Russ to make a nuisance of himself? He must be working for somebody."

"Anybody who wouldn't want him to sweat for his money. Otherwise, you've got me. I can't think who. But I'll ask around. You heard me telling Winston. *Bzzz.*"

"In a day or two," said Dr. Salt, rather dreamily, "it might get rough."

"If it does, doc, let me know. *Bing bang.* If Russ or anybody just promises you some trouble, tell him from me to expect a punch-up. But it isn't likely, is it?"

"That's just what I was going to ask," said Maggie.

"It's extremely likely. Somebody wants me to clear out of Birkden—the sooner the better—simply because I'm asking questions about Noreen Wilks." Dr. Salt looked at Maggie and then at Buzzy. "Somebody doesn't want any questions about Noreen Wilks. I'm serious, Buzzy. I might have to ask you soon for a little protection."

"You'll get it, doc—pronto."

"Maggie, do you want to tell Buzzy why you're here?"

"Yes. Buzzy, my father came to Birkden on Monday—and we don't know where he is or what he's doing—and this is so unlike him. I know one thing, though. He asked a friend of hers where Noreen Wilks was."

"And I think Russ told this girl, Noreen's friend, to shut up and clear out—"

"And she shot off to Birmingham last night, without telling her mother why she was going or where she was going. I suppose I could tell the police—"

"Don't make me laugh. I'm getting too fat. *Bzzz*. But I'll start my boys and girls asking questions—tonight."

"I saw Superintendent Hurst yesterday morning, Buzzy, and told him about Noreen Wilks. Do you know Hurst?"

"Known him since he was on the beat. He's all right, Bob Hurst is, doc. Wouldn't plant evidence on you—none of them games. *Bzzz*. But he hasn't got to be superintendent by showing his independence, if you see what I mean."

"What's the chief constable—Colonel Ringwood—like?"

"Well, if they just had kit inspections in the police, he'd be good. As it is, he's wasted on us, the colonel is. The only thing you couldn't pinch from under his nose would be his official uniform. *Bzzz*. You won't get any action from him unless you turn yourself into a horse. Another drink, Miss Culworth—doctor?"

"No, thank you, Buzzy." She looked at Dr. Salt, who was shaking his head and getting out of his chair, which was low and sagging.

"Well, watch it, doc. Birkden isn't a very nice town anymore. *Bzzz.* What's your next move now?"

"I thought we might pay a call at the Fabrics Club. But you know nothing about it, Buzzy."

"I can tell you one or two things that might help. *Bzzz.* It's run by an aftershave-and-talcum nance called Donald Dews. On the company pay sheet as assistant personnel officer. They get away with bloody murder, these big combines. He looks and sounds like a powder-puff twerp, but don't kid yourself—he's as wide and crafty as they come. I know that much because a barman up there—Tony—used to work for me, and just after he went he came back once or twice for a natter. *Bzzz.*"

"That's all, is it, Buzzy?"

"No, there was something else. I'm trying to remember the name. Might be useful. Tony said the real hard character round there—on the admin at the works but kept an eye on the club —was—half a minute—it's a funny name—son—son?"

"I think there's an Ericson—"

"No, I've got it. Not Ericson—Aricson. Same thing but not quite. Tony said he was the real hard character round there— Aricson. *Bzzz.* Well, Miss Culworth, pleased to have met you. Hope you find your father all right. And any time you want to sit here and watch the monkey house—or do a jiggle yourself —I've a good little four-piece band. Just walk up these back stairs."

"Thank you, Buzzy."

"It's a privilege and a pleasure to see a nice class of people round here. 'Cause I'll tell you frankly—I won't lie. Most of my customers are either silly twerps or sheer bloody riffraff. So long, doc. Come again."

As she went rather cautiously down the rickety stairs, Maggie decided that although Buzzy was a kind of monster, she liked him and would trust him in an emergency. She also decided to stop being grand and aloof about Birkden just because she had lived and worked in London. She might soon come to hate Birkden—already she could easily imagine herself doing that—but she could no longer talk and behave as if it was simply a dull place full of dull people.

"What do we do now?" she asked as they reached the street.

"Talk in the car." This was sensible, but Maggie rather resented his curt manner. She realized, however, that Buzzy's gin and tonic had contained more gin and less tonic than she was used to, and that anyhow this had been earlier than her usual drinking time. Probably Dr. Salt could down a stiff whisky, however old, at any time without feeling a desire for a cozy mellow chat.

"You can do one of two things," he began in the car. "Go home and talk to your brother. Or come back to my place and do some telephoning from there."

"Can I be of any use if I stay on?"

"Yes. But you must persuade your brother to join us."

"I want to. I feel if I go home and try to explain, he'll think it's all my nonsense. If you do it, he won't. Also, I want to keep my mother out of this."

"My place then." He started the engine. "And we'll talk when we get there. It isn't six o'clock yet. Lot of traffic about. I don't like talking and driving."

He seemed almost unfriendly now, not calling her Maggie as he'd done earlier, and she began to wonder if she didn't really rather dislike him. On the other hand, without working it all out, she felt certain she would never find her father without a lot of help from Dr. Salt.

"Will your brother be home yet from the university?" he asked her. They were now among the books and records again.

"No, it's too early."

"Then I suggest you ring up all the Birkden hotels and ask about your father. You'll find them in the classified directory."

"That's what I thought," she replied tartly.

He ignored this. "Has he any friends in Birkden he might stay with?"

"I asked myself that, yesterday morning, and decided he hadn't. I do know about my father, Dr. Salt."

"Do you?" His tone wasn't sharp but amiable, rather sleepy. "What about Noreen Wilks? No—no, Maggie. I'm not trying to score a point. The truth is, we know far less about people than we think. Sometimes their very closeness hides more than it reveals. By the way, has your father a passport? Yes? Well, ask your brother if it's still there."

"Yes, Dr. Salt. Any further instructions, Dr. Salt?"

"I sound like that, do I? Sorry, Maggie."

"What shall I tell Alan we're going to do, if he does join us?"

"Pay a visit to the Fabrics Club."

"He'll be all for that if there's a chance of seeing Miss Jill Whatsit—Frinton—again."

He stared at her, but then, just as she thought he was going to tell her not to be too light and airy about this business, he merely nodded.

"All right, then," she said. "I'll start phoning. What are you going to do?"

"I'm going to have a bath."

"Well, my God!"

"Can't get any hot water in the morning. And if I light a pipe and just soak, I may get an idea or two."

FIVE

1

Either he required an incredible amount of smoking and soaking or he deliberately kept out of the way until she had admitted Alan and had begun her explanations. Just as she expected, Alan was skeptical and obviously thought she was being influenced by something dreamed up by a crackpot.

"I must say, Dr. Salt," Alan told him, about seventy-five seconds after she had introduced them, "so far as I can understand it, this all seems a bit thick." His manner wasn't hostile, but neither was it friendly.

"It's not a bit thick, it's a lot thick," said Dr. Salt, in his amiable sleepy style.

"I tried all the hotels," Maggie interposed hastily. "They don't know anything about my father. And Alan found his passport at home."

"In any case," said Alan, "can you see him going to the south of France? He hadn't enough money anyhow. Besides, he just wouldn't. Why shouldn't he have asked a few questions about this mysterious girl—your ex-patient—"

"Noreen Wilks." Dr. Salt seemed to like repeating her name,

rather slowly and grimly. Already it was beginning to irritate Maggie. Blast Noreen Wilks!

"Noreen Wilks," said Alan. "Why shouldn't he have asked a few questions about her and then gone on to do something else?"

"What? Where?"

"Well, of course, I don't know. But I don't see that Maggie and I have to bother about this Noreen Wilks."

"No, you haven't, but I have. You don't care about Noreen Wilks; I don't care about your father. Very well, let's leave it at that."

"No—please," cried Maggie urgently. "I'm sure there must be some connection. Alan doesn't understand yet—"

"What don't I understand?" He gave Maggie a glance, then looked at Dr. Salt.

"I want to leave Birkden as soon as I can," said Dr. Salt. "But I'm not going until I know what happened to Noreen Wilks. She was a patient—an unusual patient—and I still feel responsible for her. You can understand that, can't you, Culworth?"

"Yes, of course, but—"

"Never mind the *buts* for the moment. Listen to this. Noreen Wilks left her lodging on the evening of September twelfth, dressed for a party, and never went back. She's never been heard of since. Early on the morning of the thirteenth, Derek Donnington, only son of Sir Arnold Donnington, head of United Anglo-Belgian Fabrics and Birkden's Mr. Big, shot himself. The official verdict was 'Accidental Death,' but we can ignore that. Well, that might be a coincidence. It might be another coincidence that when your father arrives on Monday to ask about Noreen, he suddenly disappears. It might be another coincidence that the cinema girl he saw, and the one I questioned yesterday, cleared out in a panic last night. It might be still another coincidence that the young man who warned me to leave Birkden was the one who said something to her. Now I don't know what happens in physics, Culworth, but in medicine

61

we don't like as many coincidences as that. Finally, I'll tell you what I believe, though I've no proof. While I don't suppose for a moment that anything very serious has happened to your father, I believe Noreen Wilks is dead."

Alan raised his right eyebrow and took his pipe out of his mouth as if to examine it—one of his donnish tricks. "Isn't that going much too far?"

"Possibly. It's just possible that she's been to a doctor who's never got in touch with me. It's just possible her condition isn't as serious as I thought it was. Perhaps Noreen and your father are laughing their heads off somewhere—"

"I'm sure that isn't true," Alan said sharply.

"You believe it isn't. So do I. And I also believe Noreen Wilks is dead. Now I'm going to ask a few questions at the Fabrics Club. You're welcome to come with me. You may notice things that I miss."

"We might as well, Alan," said Maggie. "I'm certain now Daddy came here to inquire about Noreen Wilks. And after all, that's what Dr. Salt is doing. And what else can we do?"

"I don't know." Alan looked unhappy. "But we've nothing to do with this Fabrics Club. Aren't we going to look silly—"

Dr. Salt bounced out of his chair. "Let's look silly, then. I haven't cared a damn for years about looking silly. Are you coming or not?"

"I am," Maggie told him.

"I've got my car. I'll follow you." Alan didn't sound downright sulky, but obviously he was still skeptical. "Do you know where it is?"

"I've never been there, but I know vaguely where it is," said Dr. Salt. "And I'll drive fairly slowly."

When they were in his car and moving off, Maggie said to him, "I know you don't like talking when you're driving, but perhaps you don't mind listening. I want to explain about Alan. He's not really against you. The point is, he's just come from his university and lecture room and physics lab, and he's suddenly plunged into all this, and so far he hasn't—sort of—absorbed any of the atmosphere. He's still in his particular world where you don't expect anything *strange* to happen to anybody."

"Except the Bomb," Dr. Salt muttered.

"I know. I've argued with Alan and some of his friends about that. There's a kind of innocence about them in some ways. Perhaps because they've always been in school or college, never where people are thinking about money all the time. He often makes me feel years older than he is."

Dr. Salt made a grunting noise. Apparently he didn't care how old any of the Culworths were.

"Actually, Alan's four years older."

This time he didn't even grunt. Not interested.

"And anyhow, I can't altogether blame Alan," she went on, determined now to make him show some interest. "You know, Dr. Salt, you do pile it on a bit. Every time you say 'Noreen Wilks,' you make it sound as if you thought she'd been mur-dered."

"Do I? Sorry!"

"Oh, I know you don't mean to. Why would anybody—"

"I'm driving," he cut in ruthlessly.

Furious with him, and feeling compelled to do something, she looked back to see if Alan was following them. He was. Then she stared ahead at the darkening streets of Birkden, almost expect-ing them to begin looking quite different. But they refused to look sinister and mysterious. Birkden wore the same face it had worn when she had come in by bus a few hours ago—only a few hours, though now she felt as if she had spent days with Dr. Salt.

2

They were passing semidetached homes and larger houses in their own grounds, softening the edge of town and country. Soon they were moving alongside the vast bulk of the United Fabrics works—she remembered then that the firm had moved

63

almost into the country some years ago—and at the imposing entrance Dr. Salt stopped to ask a man on duty there the way to the club. His directions took them up a road that might still have been almost a country lane. They turned into a drive and parked in a wide space, where there were only a few other cars, not far from a lighted doorway.

"Now what?" said Alan rather grumpily as he joined them.

"We go in," Dr. Salt told him. "I can do the talking."

"It doesn't look very busy," said Maggie.

"Early yet," Dr. Salt said. "Anyhow, it may be one of their quiet nights. And so much the better."

He led the way in. There was no porter just inside the door —Maggie had expected one because she had been to several private clubs with Hugh—but there was a place where a porter ought to have been, so perhaps he wasn't on duty yet. Dr. Salt did not hesitate, but went forward and opened a door into soft lights and soft music. It was a cocktail bar, charmingly lit, and decorated and furnished in an unfussy modern style, rather Scandinavian. There was plenty of space in front of the curved bar counter, where the white-coated barman and his array of bottles took most of the light, but all round the walls were low tables and rather low chairs and banquettes, variously upholstered in what were probably the most magnificent specimens of United Fabrics' fabrics. Nobody was sitting at the tables, but three people, two smart young men and an even smarter girl, were standing at the bar. The muted violins, the melancholy clarinets that had been taped somewhere in New York or Los Angeles went on and on, as they did now all over the world, saying that life and love were rather sweet, but that nothing really mattered very much. Maggie thought she heard Dr. Salt muttering curses on them.

Now the three at the bar could be overheard. One of the young men was saying that somebody was projecting the wrong image.

"You and your images!" cried the girl wearily. "Do you mind?"

"Come off it, ducky. As if you didn't know what it was all about."

"Do I? Since when?"

"Since you were about fifteen, I'd say."

"And you'd be quite wrong, Alec." This was the second man. "But where the hell's Kate?"

"Don't say I didn't warn you," said the girl. "Every time she starts doing her face, she begins thinking about something else."

"Do we know what?"

"As a matter of fact, you don't," the girl told him. "Because even I don't."

"Let's go in, then," said Alec. "George, if a Miss Tiller asks for me, tell her we've gone in. I've already signed for her." The three were now moving slowly toward a door on the left of the bar. "They're very sticky about that here."

"And quite right too," said the other young man. "God knows what would be blowing in!"

Maggie knew very well that this was not aimed at her and her two men. The young man had never noticed them. But the remark did not make her feel any better. In these surroundings, still wearing her shop clothes, and after taking one look at that girl, she felt small, shabby, dreary. As Dr. Salt went slowly towards the bar counter, she sat on the edge of the nearest chair, beckoning to Alan to sit down. But he persisted in leaning against the wall, just inside the doorway, and in glaring at nothing in particular, feeling—as she knew without any doubt—a perfect fool. That was simply because he knew he had no right to be there and might be ordered out at any moment. But the whole snooty place wasn't telling him that his face and hair were wrong, his clothes and shoes wrong, that he was just a miserable little drear; which was what it had been busy doing to her. She now watched and listened to Dr. Salt, who was leaning against the bar counter and had been lighting his pipe. He might be—indeed, he obviously *was*—a maddening man, but there was one thing about him: he didn't seem to care a damn.

"My name's Salt," he told the barman very carefully. "Dr. Salt."

"Oh yes." The barman was fairly young and had a crew cut; his face seemed wider across the jaw than across the forehead. Maggie had been against him from the first glance.

"Are you Tony?" asked Dr. Salt.

"No. Tony's not here any longer."

"Oh, what a pity!"

"Most people don't think so. I took his place."

"I see." Dr. Salt sounded vague and rather stupid. "Though I don't really know Tony. He was mentioned to me by a friend of mine."

"Is that so? Well, I don't think you're a member, are you?"

"Oh, no, not at all." Dr. Salt gave a little laugh that Maggie had never heard before and instantly disbelieved in. "Though I don't know why I said 'not at all,' because either one would be a member or not a member—one could hardly be partly a member. No, I'm not."

"I got it the first time. Well, I can't serve you a drink unless you're a member."

"I don't want a drink."

"What do you want, then? And are those two with you?"

"Yes, friends of mine. Miss Culworth. And Dr. Culworth, of the University of Hemtonshire." Dr. Salt sounded idiotic. "They're just waiting for me. And I'd like to speak to your manager—Mr. Dews, isn't it?"

"Yes. Does he know you?"

"I'm afraid not. Hardly anybody knows me."

"I doubt if he'll see you."

"One of us could try, couldn't we? That is, if he's here to-night."

"Yes, Mr. Dews is here."

"Where, may I ask?"

"In there." The barman indicated a door in the wall to the right of the bar.

Dr. Salt looked as if he were about to move in that direction. "Oh, well, perhaps if I knock, and then ask nicely . . ."

"He wouldn't like it."

"Hates being disturbed, does he?"

"If he's busy, he does. And most times he's very busy. Has all this place on his hands. No joke, I can tell you. I wouldn't change jobs with him." The barman glanced to his left. "Oh—you're lucky. He's coming out. Oh, Mr. Dews," he called. "This is Dr. Salt, and he'd like a word with you."

"But of course—of course." Mr. Dews came tripping, rosy and smiling, into the brighter light illuminating the bar. He wore a charcoal-gray suit, black suede shoes, a dusty-pink tie, and his hair in bronzed waves. A pretty youth probably about forty-five; he gave Maggie the creeps even across the room.

"I'm Donald Dews, Dr. Salt. And if you want to see me, here I am. Shall we sit down, or do you prefer to stand? I've been sitting down in my office, so I'm quite happy to stand. But why don't we have a *drink*?"

"I'm not a member."

"Oh, poor man—you've been *warned*, have you? We just have to be strict here. But after all, I do *run* the club and now you're my guest—"

"I'm not alone. Come on, you two."

Reluctantly Maggie and Alan moved forward and met the other two about halfway to the counter. Dr. Salt, who now seemed to talk and behave like somebody else, sounded quite fussy and self-important as he introduced them. "Miss Maggie Culworth, Dr. Alan Culworth of the University of Hemtonshire

67

—Mr. Dews. They live in Hemton and—believe it or not—they're here—I mean in Birkden, of course—trying to find their father, Mr. er—"

"Edward Culworth," said Maggie.

"Mr. *Edward* Culworth," said Dr. Salt, looking grave and sounding fatuous. "They don't know where he is."

"Really—and ought they to? I mean is there something *wrong* with him?" Mr. Dews twinkled from Maggie to Alan.

"No," said Alan bluntly. "Let's forget it."

"Then *do* sit down, everybody. At least we can have a quick little drink. Miss Culworth?" He was now leading them to a table, and by the time they were all sitting down he knew what they wanted to drink. "George—a gin and tonic, two Scotches and water, and the usual for me." He looked round the table. "Campari and vodka. Have you ever tried it?"

"I could never live up to it," said Dr. Salt.

"Now you're being *satirical*, Dr. Salt. But don't you like our bar, Miss—er—Culworth?"

"It's delightful."

"We think so. And you should have seen it when I first took over, three years ago. Like a miners' canteen. I nearly went out of my tiny mind. Cigarette, anybody? Oh—thank you, George. Well, cheers, dears!"

As they drank, Maggie looked across the table and saw that Alan's eyes, dark at any time, were now black with resentment and misery. And she still felt small, drab, dull, and she was angry with Dr. Salt, disappointed in him too. He should never have brought them here. And anyhow, he seemed to be behaving like an idiot, as if this Fabrics Club had gone to his head.

"Well, now, what can I do for you, Dr. Salt? Do you want to become a member? We have two doctor members, but they're connected with the works."

"Who are they?"

"Dr. Bennett. You must know *him.*"

"Oh, yes. One of Birkden's bastions. And the other?"

"A Dr. Lemmert. He's fairly new."

"I think I've heard the name, Mr. Dews."

"Now I must tell you—and I know it's all very tedious and tiresome—that you have to be proposed and seconded by two United Fabrics people on the executive level. But then you must know some of them, Dr. Salt."

"I'm afraid I don't, Mr. Dews." He produced an apologetic little smile. "My practice was well below the executive level. However, I don't want to join the club. I'm leaving Birkden."

"Lucky you! Not that I see much of the place, toiling here the whole time. But how can I help you, then? There must be *something*."

"There is, Mr. Dews." Dr. Salt had now an air of earnest simplicity that set Maggie wondering. "It's a little medical problem I ought to tackle before I leave Birkden. I'm trying to trace a patient of mine—a young girl called Noreen Wilks—and I'm told she used to come here."

"Yes, of course. I remember Noreen. Quite a pretty girl, though not very smart, not very bright—rather common, really. But I haven't seen her for weeks, you know."

Dr. Salt nodded. "Nobody seems to have seen her since September twelfth, Mr. Dews. But on that night, I believe, she came to a party here."

"Did she? I can't remember. There's so much to-ing and fro-ing here, as you can imagine. But we can soon find out if she did, Dr. Salt. You see, party or no party, everybody who isn't a member must be signed in. It's our strictest rule, doctor—absolutely cast iron. And of course, little Noreen isn't a member. So if she was here that night, she'll be in the book. And we must look and see, mustn't we? I hope this isn't too boring for you, Miss—er—Culworth. Excuse me. George, have you the book or have I?"

"It's here. Coming over." The book he brought to the table was about two feet square, rather thin, and bound in limp blue leather.

"Now here we are—the sacred book." Dews opened it. "What date did you say, Dr. Salt?"

"September twelfth."

"September twelfth . . . September twelfth. This is it, and as you quite rightly said, we had one of our dreadful parties that night. Look—all those impossible names. Customers, of course. Not that the parties really *are* dreadful—they're quite good as parties go—but of course it's a frantic amount of work for poor me. And it's all a lot of *salesmanship*, really—rather sordid, don't you think? Well, now, I can't find a *trace* of little Noreen here. But please do check the list yourself."

And Dr. Salt did, very carefully. "No, Mr. Dews. Her name's not here."

"Definitely not, is it? I'm so sorry, doctor. Evidently Noreen hadn't been invited that night. And you do understand, don't you, that I've nothing *whatever* to do with all that? I'm simply a kind of *slave* who has to make sure that the people who *are* invited—and the members, of course—are provided with sickening amounts of food and drink. But there it is. Noreen wasn't here. Perhaps she'd already run off with somebody. She always seemed to me rather a flighty little thing."

There he stopped, because somebody had arrived. She was an impressive smart type, wearing a rather severely cut suit, but of soft fine wool, darkish yellow, and a lighter yellow scarf. And then Maggie remembered her from that afternoon in the shop. This was Jill Frinton.

Mr. Dews had jumped up. "Jill darling, you're the very person we want—"

"Hold it, Donald darling," said Miss Frinton, crisp and dry as a biscuit. "Do you have a message for me, George?"

"Yes, Miss Frinton." The barman found a note and read from it. "Mr. Linsdale's secretary told me on the phone I was to tell you, if you came in, that Mr. Linsdale will be ringing you at home tonight from New York."

"Thanks, George." She came towards their table. "Well, Donald darling, why am I the very person you want?"

"I'll explain in a moment, darling. But first, let me introduce Dr. Salt—Miss Jill Frinton. Oh, I'm so sorry, Miss Culworth. This is—"

"We've met before somewhere, haven't we?" said Miss Frinton, cutting in sharply.

"Yes. In our bookshop at Hemton," said Maggie. "This is my brother, Alan, who also happened to be in the shop that afternoon."

"Oh, well, you wouldn't remember," Alan began.

"Yes, I do." She awarded him a dazzling smile. She wouldn't miss a trick, this one, Maggie told herself. Poor old Alan. Now what?

"You see, Jill darling," Dews told her, "Dr. Salt's been inquiring about your little Noreen Wilks—"

"Not mine. I'm not having that."

"Do be cooperative, dear. We're all trying to do our best to help Dr. Salt. She was one of your assorted bits and pieces. And Dr. Salt says she's been missing since September twelfth, one of our party nights. But she didn't attend our party that night because her name's not in the precious book."

"You've looked, have you, Dr. Salt?" A sympathetic tone and smile for him.

"Yes, Miss Frinton. A dead end here, I'm afraid." He sounded sad, defeated.

"Oh—poor man! I'm sorry." Did she exchange a brilliant glance with Dews? Anyhow, Maggie could have slapped her.

"Miss Frinton, I wonder," Dr. Salt began, with an appealing look, "if you'd be kind enough to allow us to call on you later this evening—say, about nine o'clock? I promise not to take up much of your time. It would be a great favor."

"If you think I can be of any help, Dr. Salt—why, of course. I'll have to be there anyhow, to take my New York call. Nine

71

o'clock will be splendid. I live at 6 Cadogan Mansions—it's a big newish block of flats on the Hemton Road. And anyhow, I'm in the phone book. Nine o'clock, then."

"Thank you so much. And thank you for the drink and for being so helpful, Mr. Dews. Maggie, Alan—let's go."

Dr. Salt said nothing to her and Alan until they reached the cars. "No talk now, please," he said briskly. "I want you to dine with me. Usually I cook for myself, but now there isn't time. We're not going to eat any of that hotel muck. I know a little place where they do nothing but simple grills, but they do them very well. I hope you're hungry. Alan, keep close behind, as you did coming here. I'll drive slowly. It's not an easy place to find."

3

He drove back into the town and stopped in a short street not far from the center. The place looked like an ordinary house and not at all like a restaurant, though it had a small sign saying *Pete's Grills.* Maggie had a wash and did her face in a bathroom on the first floor. Then she found the men sitting at one of two tables in a small room at the back. The other table was occupied by two fat men and a fat woman, who seemed to be eating, drinking, talking and roaring or screaming with laughter all at the same time. Pete was an oldish man with one arm and one eye and an enormous leathery face, rather like a retired pirate. He seemed to be a friend of Dr. Salt's.

"What fillet steak I've got isn't worth the money," he told them in a curious hoarse whisper, as if he had lost part of his voice as well as an eye and an arm. "I'd be robbing you. I've a chump chop or two—never without—but if you want to make me happy, as well as yourselves, you'll ask me for three of my Special Mixed Grills. A green salad and a touch of cheese afterwards—eh?" Now he concentrated on Maggie. "I've no license, young lady—wicked, isn't it?—but it just happens that last time

72

he was here Dr. Salt left a bottle of Burgundy behind. Must have clean forgotten it."

"Hurry up and open it, Pete, and let it breathe," said Dr. Salt. "And if Maisie's baked any bread, rush it here with plenty of butter."

"Can do," Pete whispered. And off he went.

"Knew him years ago, in Penang," said Dr. Salt. He seemed to be closing, not opening, a subject of talk. He slumped back in his chair and did not seem inclined to say anything else. Perhaps he was thinking about Penang.

Maggie saw that Alan was beginning to wriggle, as he nearly always did when he was feeling embarrassed. "What's the matter, Alan?"

"I was thinking about that visit of ours to the club. Surely that was a complete dead loss, wasn't it?"

"I don't know." Though, of course, she felt that it had been. "And after all, you saw the Frinton girl again, didn't you? Come on. I noticed you. Your eyes were sticking out of your head."

"No, they weren't. And anyhow, she was laughing at us. I'm sorry, Dr. Salt, but she was—and so was that pansy manager, Dews."

"Then perhaps our visit wasn't a complete dead loss," said Dr. Salt mildly. "In point of fact, it was highly successful."

They both stared at him. "I must say, I don't see that," said Maggie.

"You will when I talk to Miss Frinton. We shall make some headway tonight, you'll see. Ah—Pete. Bread and wine—not a bad first course." Pete had wheeled in a trolley. Maggie watched him, fascinated; he was quicker with one arm than most waiters were with two. She was hungry and the home-made bread was delicious. She realized that Dr. Salt did not want to talk about the club and Noreen Wilks and their lost father, so she asked him when he had been in Penang, though she couldn't remember where Penang was. At least, she felt, this would head off Alan, who was in one of his rare awkward moods, probably because he had been made to look foolish in the presence of the dashing, handsome and detestable Frinton girl.

By asking questions throughout the meal (which was good), she was able to keep Dr. Salt talking and Alan quiet. She learned that Dr. Salt, immediately after graduating, had served in Burma, and had then lived and worked in the New Territories, Hong Kong, in North Borneo, Penang and Singapore, and that this practice in Birkden, which he had now done with after seven years, was the first he had ever had in England. And at the end of the meal she was still wondering if he was stupid, clever or just odd.

SIX

1

They had timed it nicely. It was only a minute or two after nine when Jill Frinton smilingly drew them into 6 Cadogan Mansions. She had changed, of course—she *would*—if only to make Maggie feel shabbier and drearier; and now she was wearing a long, high-necked, Chinese-style housecoat, mostly green but with a faded-red pattern on it, that would probably enslave Alan and blunt Dr. Salt's wits, if he really had any. Maggie was ready to hate her, but had to admit to herself that just as somebody to look at, this was an uncommonly handsome and attractive girl. She was very dark in a brilliant kind of way, and she had the bold but not bony features seen more often in drawings for expensive advertisements than in actual photographs. And —probably all set to make them look silly again—she was quite pleased to see them and, of course, damnably pleased with herself.

Maggie had also to admit that either Jill Frinton or some United Fabrics designer, probably another man she had on a string, knew what to do with a flat. The fairly large sitting room was done in soft yellows and browns with a few sharp accents of vermilion and black. The wages of sin—blast her—had paid off nicely here.

"Very pleasant indeed," said Dr. Salt, smiling at her. "You have excellent taste, Miss Frinton."

"Thank you, kind sir. But do sit down, everybody. Miss Culworth—a drink? Brandy? Whisky?"

"Do you mind if I don't?" said Maggie, sweet and false. "I seem to have had so much tonight—and I'm not used to it."

"Sometimes I wish I wasn't. Well, you men—whisky?"

Dr. Salt said he would like a little whisky and water. And of course poor old Alan, who would have accepted wormwood from those fair hands, would have some too. And also, of course, now he followed her to the drinks table, to fetch and carry, or just to be closer to one of those dazzling smiles. Maggie looked at Dr. Salt, rather a lump in a very low chair, and, to her surprise, he winked at her. He really was the oddest man.

"Yes, it's a charming room," said Dr. Salt. This was after the drinks had been poured out and the four of them were sitting down. "And I'm very grateful for this chance of a talk. I shan't be staying very long, by the way."

"Neither will I," said Maggie. Alan said nothing; no doubt he was ready to stay all night.

"Then we mustn't waste any time, must we?" said Miss Frinton, with one of her smaller smiles. "I must warn you, though, Dr. Salt. You won't learn very much more from me than you did from Donald Dews and George, the barman."

"That's all right," said Dr. Salt, in his amiable sleepy manner. "I didn't do badly out of them."

"You surprise me."

"Me too," said Alan. "When do we begin making the headway you mentioned?"

"No, Alan." And Maggie frowned at him.

Miss Frinton looked amused, but said nothing.

"When you've practiced medicine as long as I have," Dr. Salt began, still amiable and sleepy, "and among Chinese and

76

Malays and Indians for years, you learn to be observant. And I'm afraid those fellows at the Fabrics Club are a pair of clumsy clods."

Here he had to stop because Miss Frinton produced a genuine little shriek of laughter. "Oh, I'd love our Donald darling to hear you say that. He thinks he's so clever and subtle."

"Well, he isn't. It was a terrible performance," said Dr. Salt severely. "An insult to anybody's intelligence. I'm surprised at you two Culworths. Where have you been? A man marches into a club bar. He's not a member. Nobody has to bother about him. He inquires about a young girl—also not a member, just an occasional guest. Instead of saying, 'We don't know and don't care. Good night,' they serve drinks and produce the club book and fall over themselves being helpful. Why?"

"Yes, of course—when you think about it," Maggie began.

"Well—why?" Alan cut in, not convinced.

Maggie glanced at Jill Frinton and saw that she was staring speculatively at Dr. Salt, the whole look of her quite different now.

"They were giving a performance, Culworth," Dr. Salt told him. "And it was terrible." He looked at Jill Frinton. "They must have thought I was half-witted. To begin with, they were very clumsy liars. Now I've had to listen to a lot of lying. And I never watch faces. I look at hands and listen very carefully to the tone and tempo of speech. When they're deliberately lying, most people can't maintain a steady tempo. When the big lie comes, either they hurry a little or slow down. There's a change in tone too, though you may have to listen hard. With the early lies there's a faint faint note of apology, a distant whine. With the later lies, when they feel they're getting away with it, there's a faint faint note of triumph; the impudence begins to show. Dews and his barman were so obvious, I could have yawned in their faces. Now let's see what really happened tonight in that bar. I'm not boring you, am I, Miss Frinton?"

"You know damned well you're not."

"You're beginning to show off, though," said Maggie.

"No doubt I am, Maggie. I'd forgotten how a man has to guard against it, talking to good-looking women. However, you might remember, Maggie, that two hours ago you were beginning to think I was a complete ass. No, no—let's leave that. Now—what really happened in that bar. As soon as I said who I was, the barman had to take his mind off me for a moment, to remember what he'd been told to do. He had to press a bell with his foot, a bell that rang in Dews's office to tell him I was there. I didn't see him press the bell, of course, but I could just hear it ringing in Dews's office. Dews needed this signal so that he could telephone you, Miss Frinton. When he'd done that, he came into the bar. Now he had to do two things. He had to detain me there until you came. He had also to show me the club book and the list of guests for the party on September twelfth. I couldn't find Noreen Wilks there. That proved she hadn't gone to the club that night."

"Well," said Jill Frinton defiantly, "what's wrong with that?"

"First that he should want to show me the book at all. Why this rigmarole for somebody who wasn't even a member? Secondly, I wasn't being shown the original page. It's a book on the loose-leaf principle. What I was shown was a new page with Noreen Wilks left out. All the other names were there, of course. It was very well done, but I'd just time to notice that the ink was a little fresher than that on the following page. I already knew they'd started lying. After that performance with the club book, following the build-up they'd given to the club rule about guests having to be signed in—remember?—I was certain Noreen Wilks had gone there that night. That may not interest you, Culworth, but it does me. So I couldn't agree that the visit to the club had been a complete dead loss."

"Sorry I said that," Alan told him. "But I still don't see why there was all this elaborate detaining business because of Miss Frinton. I don't see where she comes into it."

"No doubt she'll tell us, shortly," said Dr. Salt dryly. "But I think her job was to act as a beautiful clincher. If I seemed rather doubtful, it would be Miss Frinton's turn. Perhaps she'd invite me here, give me a few drinks and encourage me to talk —they know she's good at that; it's part of her job—and that would be the end of the Salt nuisance. As it was, I appeared to have accepted the performance, so her intervention was hardly necessary. Still, she could take over if she thought it worthwhile—"

"Yes, yes," cried Maggie eagerly. "I felt there was something false and wrong then—I really did. But I was being so stupid about you, Dr. Salt."

"You're not the only one, are you, dear?" said Jill Frinton wryly. "A lot of us weren't being very clever, were we?"

Maggie ignored this. She was still looking at Dr. Salt. "It began—I mean my being stupid—when you insisted upon introducing Alan and me so solemnly, both to that barman and to Dews, even mentioning our father."

"I wanted to see how they'd react."

"But they didn't. They weren't interested."

"The barman elaborately wasn't. But Dews felt sufficiently confident to do a little turn—elfish and whimsical." He stopped, glanced from Maggie to Alan and added curtly, "I think your father called there on Monday. No, no—one thing at a time." Now he gave Jill Frinton a hard look. "Well, Miss Frinton— going to bluff it out?"

"No, Dr. Salt. You win. I've spent too much time with salesmen and buyers. I've forgotten about really clever men." She waited a moment, then suddenly burst out fiercely. "But why do you have to start churning up everything? Why are you bothering about that silly little bitch Noreen Wilks?"

"She was my patient. She's missing. And she'll die soon, if she isn't already dead." Briefly he gave her his medical reasons for believing this, then went on, with a cold ferocity that seemed to Maggie at once surprising and terrifying: "This is a matter of life and death, Miss Frinton. Something quite different from

79

arranging parties and pimping for businessmen. I'm going to find out what happened to this girl if I have to turn Birkden upside down and inside out. I'm leaving soon and I haven't time to play games with people like you and that clown Dews. I don't care how you earn your slimy living—"

"Drop that, Salt," Alan cut in angrily. "Now you're going much too far."

"You tell me that when you've found your father, Culworth. Where is he? What's happening to him? And what do you know about Birkden? Don't interrupt or we'll get nowhere. I'm going soon and you can console Miss Frinton after I've gone." He stared at her. "Now then—stop lying. *Where is Noreen Wilks?*"

"Believe me, Dr. Salt—please believe me. I don't know." She was shaking her head and seemed to be finding it difficult to speak. "I'll tell you all I do know, even though it may mean I'll be out of this place and looking for a job in a few days." She picked up her glass and, finding it empty, held it out to Alan. "Get me a drink, please—whisky with a lot of soda. My throat's too dry; I can't talk properly." After Alan had taken her glass, she looked at Dr. Salt and tried to smile. "I'm sorry, but you'll have to wait."

"I can wait," Dr. Salt told her. "But not long."

Maggie was now beginning to feel sorry for this Frinton girl. As for Dr. Salt, he now seemed a terrifying, ruthless man, and she could hardly believe that only a few minutes before, he had winked at her.

2

"Now I'll tell you all I know and the exact truth," Jill Frinton began, her manner and voice easier now that she had swallowed most of the drink Alan had given her. "Noreen Wilks came to that party on September twelfth with Derek Donnington. I didn't want her there. As far as I was concerned, she was a little nuisance. She didn't want to entertain the guests. She was having an affair with Derek. They just wanted to eat, drink, dance for a couple of hours and then go off to make love somewhere. And don't ask me where they went, because I haven't a clue. But I just wished she'd go away and stay away. I was afraid that Derek's father, the great Sir Arnold, would learn about this affair and blame me and the club. He never wanted the club, loathed the idea of parties there, and it was Tommy Linsdale—he's the sales director—who talked him into it. I might add that Tommy's been away—in America—since early September, and this hasn't made it any easier for me. I might also add—and just remember this, Dr. Salt—that I've never exchanged more than a dozen words with Sir Arnold Donnington. He didn't like the look of me, and I didn't like the look of him. No wonder that poor little Derek was a bit wild and very silly, and that the girl, Erica, still is."

"Donnington has a daughter, then?" said Dr. Salt.

"Yes. Two years older than Derek. And a pest. We're lucky she isn't here this minute. She has a crush on me at the moment, and when she's half stoned, she can't keep away. But let's get back to Noreen Wilks and that party. She and Derek left together. I know that because I saw them go and it was a welcome sight. She may have been sober, but I'm sure he wasn't." She hesitated a moment. "All right. This is where I may be tossing my job out of the window." She looked around, ending—and lingering a little—with Alan.

"We can keep anything she says to ourselves, can't we, Dr. Salt?" Alan looked even more appealing than he sounded.

"You can. Probably I can," said Dr. Salt, "though I imagine she won't be telling us very much."

"That's not because I don't want to, Dr. Salt. It's because I don't really know anything. I can only guess. I don't even know for certain that Derek Donnington shot himself a few hours after they left the club. It *may* have been an accident, as they said it was at the inquest—"

"They'd have said he died smelling roses, if Donnington had

suggested it," said Dr. Salt. "I've no doubt whatever the boy committed suicide."

"Neither have I," said Jill Frinton. "And I think he took Noreen Wilks home—*his* home—and that his father found them together and there was a hell of a row. What happened then is anybody's guess. But I think that as soon as he knew what Derek had done, Sir Arnold got Noreen away somehow. He had to do that or there'd have been a hell of a scandal, real sensational Sunday-paper stuff: the *dolce vita* of the industrial Midlands—drunken wild parties given by United Anglo-Belgian Fabrics—working girls debauched to entertain foreign buyers—"

"Well, isn't that just what was happening?" This was Maggie, who hadn't meant to interrupt her but couldn't restrain herself any longer.

Jill Frinton might not have been able to handle Dr. Salt, but she was not standing any nonsense from Maggie. "Life isn't a bookshop, dear."

"I've not always been in a bookshop."

"And it isn't a sensational Sunday paper either."

"But wasn't it part of your job to round up attractive young girls for these parties? No, Alan—you shut up. I'm asking her—and I happen to know it's true."

"Yes—terrible, isn't it?" Jill Frinton, who had the eyes for it, glared at her. "Taking them out of Birkden back streets, a few stinking pubs and greasy dance halls, and letting them wear pretty clothes and taking them where they had civilized food and drink and company—terrible! All right, they may have had rough passes made at them, a wrestling match now and again—my God, I've had some of them here—and they may have occasionally crept into bed for a five-pound note, instead of being fumbled and tumbled in a back street—terrible, terrible! But do you know what's it's *like*, being a working girl in Birkden?"

Dr. Salt got in first. "I ought to," he said dryly, "after seven years as a general practitioner in one of its poorest districts. But let's keep to the point. You think that Sir Arnold Donnington —terrified of a scandal that would involve him, his family, his firm—took steps at once to make sure there wouldn't be one. Noreen Wilks had to disappear immediately. No questions had to be asked. The lid was on firmly. And that's where I come in —um?"

"Yes, Dr. Salt. I was told last night—not by Sir Arnold, who wouldn't want to recognize my existence—that a nosy little doctor might be asking questions about Noreen Wilks. This Dr. Salt was leaving Birkden, anyhow—and perhaps a bit sooner than he thought—so if he did turn up at the club all we had to do was to persuade him he was wasting his time."

"And you fooled him, all right, didn't you?" said Maggie acidly.

"Look—don't you start crowing too soon," cried Miss Frinton. "I saw by the look in your eye at the club that you thought him a bit of an idiot. You can't deny it. All right, he's tough, clever and probably quite ruthless—and I've given in, God help me! But what about you and this nice brother of yours? What about your father? Do you think he's going to let you off? All he cares about is knowing what's happened to Noreen Wilks. Soon he may be just as tough, clever and ruthless with you people."

"I don't know whether you're flattering me or insulting me," said Dr. Salt mildly. "But I think we can drop the subject. What I want to know now is this. Who gave you and Dews your instructions last night?"

"I can't tell you that."

"You mean you won't—not you can't."

"I mean I've gone as far as I dare, Dr. Salt."

"And in the circumstances," said Alan, "I think that's reasonable."

"You would, wouldn't you?" Maggie was angry with him.

Dr. Salt ignored this Culworth exchange. "Now then, Jill—" he began.

She cut him short. "Oh—I'm Jill now, am I? A soft sell, this time."

"Don't count on it," Dr. Salt told her. "The fact is, I believe Jill *is* your name—and that Frinton isn't."

"Well, my God—really!"

"It's too much part of the persona—the mask, the character —you've been carefully establishing. All very different from Birkden. Frinton. Snooty. The exclusive resort. Miss Jill Frinton. Table for Miss Frinton. A call for Miss Frinton. RSVP Jill Frinton, 6 Cadogan Mansions. Very good. Too good. So I say it isn't your real name."

"And I say," said Alan angrily, "you're being offensive, Salt."

She gave him a grateful little smile. "But he's right, of course, the artful devil! My real name's Irish—one of those that suggest, if you're a girl, that either nobody can have you or everybody can." She looked at Dr. Salt. "All right, make it Jill. But I'm not going to tell you anything else. I can't afford to."

"You can't afford not to, Jill," said Dr. Salt. "Yesterday morning I talked to Superintendent Hurst at police headquarters. I'm going to see him again tomorrow. Now it's true that Hurst believes it's a privilege to be living in the same town as Sir Arnold Donnington. But within his limits he's an honest man. He knows already he must now make some inquiries about Noreen Wilks. I shall have to tell him that I know she went to that party on September twelfth. But I don't have to tell him —unless you make me—how I found out. I don't have to complain about the Fabrics Club—"

"All right," she said wearily. "You win again. It was Aricson who spoke to us last night."

"And who's he?"

"Officially he's public relations. Tommy Linsdale calls him 'the troubleshooter.' How he does most of his troubleshooting, I don't know. I've really had very little to do with him. He doesn't often come to the club. I fancy he dislikes me, and I know I dislike him. He's a cold, calculating type, though he has a fairly attractive wife and two children. You're not going to talk to him, are you?"

"Of course I am. Tonight, if possible. It's only about half past nine. I'll see if he's at home. What's his telephone number?"

"It's in the little red book there." Jill seemed defeated. "But have a heart, Dr. Salt. You don't have to tell him you're ringing him from here, do you?"

"No," said Dr. Salt on his way to the telephone. "I've no hard feelings, Jill. If I can keep you out of it, I will." He picked up the little red book, but then the telephone rang. Automatically he answered it. "A call from New York for you."

"Don't put the receiver back yet," she said hastily. "I'll take it in the bedroom." She hurried out and a few moments later he replaced the receiver and moved across to be closer to Maggie and Alan.

"No questions. There may not be time. If Aricson's in, I'm going to see him. You'd better come with me, Maggie. I want you to stay here with Jill, Alan. Maggie and I won't come back here—might spoil something. I don't expect to be long with Aricson, so I'll take Maggie back to my place. If you're not there by eleven, I'll run her home. You can tell Maggie anything she ought to know—I mean, really, anything *I* ought to know—in the morning. Maggie, if you'd rather not go with me to see Aricson, I could drop you off at my flat on the way—"

"No, I want to go with you," she told him sturdily. "Don't forget you said my father called at the club on Monday. Besides, he came to Birkden to ask about Noreen Wilks."

"You come along, then. If he isn't in, then I'll simply run you home. Yes, Alan?"

"Jill may not want me to stay on here."

"We shall soon know."

"I'll be glad to talk to her. But as a possible friend." Alan mumbled this, obviously embarrassed. "And not as a member of the Noreen Wilks investigation team. I think she told you all she knows—and it wasn't easy—and just remember, both of you, that so far we've had everything from your point of view, not hers."

"Oh, Alan, can't you see—"

"No, Maggie," Dr. Salt cut in sharply. "Alan's quite right."

"Well, at least," said Maggie in a fierce quick whisper, "he might as well know she's the mistress of this man who's telephoning from New York—Tommy something—Linsdale."

"And now he does know, doesn't he?" Alan told her. "But you don't have to sound so damned vindictive, Mag. It's nothing to do with you."

"It has if you—"

"Hold it."

"One day," said Jill, who seemed to have recovered her earlier manner, "somebody will pretend to be phoning from New York and really will be in the next room. I'm trying to tell you how clear it was—without being a bore. Oh—Dr. Salt, *must* you ring up Aricson?"

"Yes, I must. I want to leave Birkden as soon as I can. So I have to press on." He had dialed now and had the receiver to his ear. "Is that Mr. Aricson? This is Dr. Salt, and I'm wondering if I might come and see you for a few minutes. . . . Well, yes, it *is* rather urgent. Let's see—no, I'll be calling in ten minutes or so. Thank you." He looked at Jill and grinned. "I nearly slipped then. I was just about to ask him where he lived."

"Well, why not, if you're going to call on him?"

"Because if I'd got his number from the directory, I'd be also looking at his address. If I asked him for it, then I hadn't been using the directory but somebody's private list of phone numbers. The question then would be whose?"

"You really are trying to cover up for me. Thank you, Dr. Salt."

"And thank you for the drink, Jill. Ready, Maggie?"

"Why do you think he left us together?" said Jill as they settled down with their drinks. "Does he imagine there are still a few useful bits and pieces you might coax out of me? Because there aren't, and if there were, you couldn't."

"I'll tell you exactly what I said to him when he suggested I should stay on here. I said I'd be glad to talk to you, but as a possible friend, not as a member of his investigating team—and that I thought you'd told him all you know. I also reminded both of them that so far we'd had everything from their point of view, not yours."

"Quite right. You're a friend already—not just a possible one. Now tell me something. Am I slipping—I mean knowing about men—or did he take you in too?"

"You're not slipping. He took me in, all right. I could hardly speak to him in that club bar, I thought him such a fool. Not that I haven't met anybody like him before. I attended a conference last summer, and a chap there—a well-known physicist— drifted around looking like an imbecile, but as soon as I started talking to him, he made rings round me."

"A lot of the men I've met lately try to make rings round me —mostly with their arms—but our Dr. Salt's a new type to me. But that's enough about him. And if you so much as mention Noreen Wilks, I'll tell you to go. Talk about yourself."

"It's a dull subject, Jill. I'm thirty-three, a lecturer in the physics department of Hemtonshire University, unmarried, live with my mother and Maggie and my father when he isn't missing. Outside my work, I'm chiefly interested in moths. And don't giggle—they can be fascinating. I'm a bit cleverer than I look, but no intellectual giant."

"Girl friend?"

"Not at the moment. I've had a few, of course. There's plenty of sex running loose in universities. They all have to prove they're so damn broad-minded. By the way, who was the big, red-faced, sloppy man you were with when you visited my father's bookshop?"

"The man who rang me up from New York—Tommy Linsdale."

"Oh—that one. Are you in love with him?"

"If it's any of your business, Alan—no, I'm not. But I'm rather fond of him in a kind of cozy-boozy way. He's a fake—but then, so am I. He puts on a show as a rough, tough, hard-driving salesman, American style, and he must be good at his job, otherwise Donnington, who doesn't really like him, wouldn't keep him on and pay him so well. But underneath all that roaring and bounce and drinks-all-round he's about seventeen and terrified when he finds himself sober. But he was kind to me, after I thought unkindness had set in forever. Really I owe him a lot —all this gracious living we're sampling, for instance. And don't think you're not impressed by it, because you are. Just as you were struck by my appearance when you saw me in your shop. If I'd looked as I did just before I came to Birkden, you'd have given me one glance and then have gone to find a moth. Oh, I know—I'll save you the trouble. My beautiful eyes, my charming nose, my delicious mouth—*they're* what you noticed at once, perhaps couldn't forget for days, weeks—"

"Months," said Alan. "And it's true. I couldn't forget them, though I couldn't really remember them either."

"And I still say, my sweet-talking friend, that if I'd looked as I did just before I came to Birkden, when I hadn't the money to spend on my appearance, you'd have given me one look and forgotten me for the nearest moth—*any* moth."

"And I still don't think so," said Alan. "Where were you before you came here?"

"The great big city, dear—yes, London. And I'd had one of those affairs—one of those huge, disastrous, take-all-the-bloom-off-a-girl affairs—"

"Like Maggie."

"I'm not surprised, now you mention it."

"She'd three years of it. Her chap was married."

"I haven't even that excuse. Mine wasn't—and was taking damn good care he never would be. And I couldn't run fast enough to give him everything I'd got. And when some particular man wants it, what a girl's got seems precious and wonderful to her. And when he doesn't, she begins to wonder what the hell she thinks she has got, anyhow. This stinker took it all—yawned —vanished. It lasted a couple of years, but that's just about what happened."

"Then what?"

"The Retreat from Moscow in a West Hampstead bed-sitter with scrambled eggs and sniffles, gin and aspirin. Then a girl I knew told me about Tommy Linsdale and United Fabrics— she'd had a night out with him—so I spent my savings on a suit, hat, shoes and various aids to beauty, arrived here with about nine pounds in the world, and insisted upon seeing Tommy. I got a job in his sales department, and was soon doing all its more raffish female jiggery-pokery. I acted as hostess on those occasions when no wives and daughters were present. Then—parties at the club, more intimate parties here—"

"Does this flat belong to Linsdale?"

"No. All these flats are owned by the Birkden Development Trust, and *that's* controlled by United Fabrics. And if they decide they don't like me, then I'm out."

"Perhaps it would be better if you *were* out."

"Don't be silly."

"Do you enjoy going to bed with Linsdale?"

"Oh—shut up."

"And what about these girls you round up for the parties?"

"You heard what I said about them? I'm still saying it." She sprang up, flushed and angry. "I took enough from Dr. Salt and your sister. If you're starting now, I'm not having any. You'd better go."

He was up too, and now he moved closer to her.

"Oh, no, you don't," she warned him.

"Don't what?"

"Try to start necking. I'm not in the mood. This may not look like a wrestling ring, but that's what it's been all too often. Now either we sit down and talk—and that means no unpleasant questions or good advice—or you must go."

His long arms shot out and she found herself firmly held by the upper arm, so firmly that she didn't attempt even a wriggle. "There isn't going to be any wrestling or necking, Jill. I shan't touch you again—not tonight nor any other night—until you ask me to. I'm a serious type." He released her and stepped back. "I didn't come here for a night out."

"And you didn't come to meet me either. Oh, blast!" The doorbell was ringing. She went to answer it.

Alan heard a girl's voice: "Darling, it's only me."

Then Jill: "My God—it would be you, wouldn't it?"

"Somebody's with you. I'm jealous. Let me in, let me in, let me in!"

The girl who came hurrying in ahead of Jill was in her early twenties and had a long, narrow face that somehow seemed too loose. She wore an expensive fur coat over a black sweater and the usual faded blue jeans. She stared at Alan with her mouth open. "Oh—a *man*. Well, that's all right, darling—if you *must*."

"Alan Culworth—Erica Donnington." Jill was curt and cold.

"A solemn square, I'd say, though not bad-looking," Erica told her. "But, darling, you know me—I couldn't care less." She was obviously an excitable, neurotic type, and she looked and sounded about half tight. "Darling, can I help myself to a simply enormous gin and tonic?"

"If you haven't had too many already."

"Jill darling, they were all so *filthy*. I followed a girl into that loathsome Buzzy's Club—you know, the one run by that fat buzz-buzz man. They're not supposed to serve real drinks there —just lemon and orange muck—but if they know you they'll slip you something in a flask. And the gin there is really very peculiar. I think old buzz-buzz must make it himself." She had now provided herself with a drink that was as much gin as tonic. She took a hefty swig of it. "Now this is *quite* different."

"You're an idiot to go to that place."

"I told you why I went, only she turned out to be awful—a real untouchable." She went nearer Alan, who was sitting down again. "Now I'll tell *you* something."

"Go ahead, Miss Donnington."

"Oh, don't be such a square. Call me Erica—the whole town does. Some other towns too. Well, you must be wondering why Jill's being so rude to me. Haven't you noticed? You must have. The reason is I'm in love with her and she's not in love with me."

"Sit down and shut up, Erica." Jill sounded severe but not nasty.

"What's your name? Alan? Well, Alan, has this ever happened to you? You love somebody—and—you love somebody but—well, *she* doesn't love you?"

"Not up to now," Alan told her. "I've probably been too conceited. But I can see now that it *might* happen." He looked at Jill, who quickly frowned and shook her head. He felt she was warning him against saying anything worth listening to, here in the presence of Erica, who had now flopped into a chair. Jill was eying her with obvious distaste.

Well, somebody had to say something. "Erica, is Sir Arnold Donnington your father?"

"Yes—and that's a scream, isn't it?"

"Is it?"

"Don't you know him?"

"No, I don't."

"Do you know anybody?"

"About five hundred—perhaps six hundred people."

"Where, for God's sake?"

"Mostly at the university. I lecture there."

"I'll bet you do. I nearly went there, to please my father, and

then I thought why should I? He never tries to please me."
Erica pulled a lock of hair down over her nose and then blew
it away. "What are you doing here? Trying to make Jill while
Tommy Linsdale's away?"

"No, he isn't," said Jill sharply.

Erica waved the hand holding the gin and tonic and spilled
some of it. "Don't interrupt, darling. Aren't you attracted to Jill?
Most men seem to be. What's the matter with you?"

"Nothing, I hope." But then the phone rang.

"Yes, it's Jill darling, Donald darling," she replied with ominous mock sweetness. "No, silly Dr. Salt isn't here. Silly Dr. Salt
gave us all one look and saw clean through us. . . . Oh, no, you
don't. It wasn't just me. He gave me an exact account of what
you and George thought you were doing—and weren't, if you
see what I mean. And another thing. If you think of any more
little games, leave me out from now on. . . . You're damn right
I'm frightened. I'm out of my depth and the water's cold. Dr.
Salt isn't the kind of man I know how to handle. . . . Aricson?
Don't believe it. Dr. Salt is calling on him this minute. The best
thing we can do, Donald dear, is to keep as quiet as mice. Bye
now!"

"What—what's all *that* about, darling?"

"Club business. You wouldn't be interested."

"Who's this Dr. Salt you all keep talking about?"

"Who are *we?*"

"Well, you're one, darling, and my father's another. I could
hear him on the phone before I went out last night, and he was
Dr. Salting it like mad. Who is Salt? Where is Salt? I could do
with another doctor. I'm tired of boring old Bennett. Why don't
I send for Dr. Salt?"

Jill laughed, then suddenly checked herself.

"Not funny—or what?" Erica turned to Alan. "Do you know
him?"

"We've met. And I don't think I'd try sending for him. Anyhow, he's given up his practice here."

"Well, why is there suddenly all this yapping about the man? What was Jill saying to Donald Dews? Why should my father bother about him? My father— Oh, hell, it doesn't *matter!* Does it? And *don't* tell me now—I'm going to the loo."

As soon as Erica had gone, Jill swept across to Alan, put a hand to his cheek and whispered, "If you look as if you're staying on, she'll go quite soon. But if you go, God knows when I'll get rid of her. So—you stay."

"Thanks for the compliment." But he put a hand up to cover hers.

"I know. She's just a pest. But don't forget. I've gone and touched you—our way of asking—so you can wash out your solemn vow."

So Alan stayed on.

SEVEN

1

Aricson lived in one of those houses they had passed on their
way to the club. A tall, fair girl—obviously some kind of Scandinavian—with a smile empty of all meaning admitted them and
led them across the hall to the sitting room. Maggie felt it was
like walking into an advertisement. The room was just like that,
completely and nicely furnished, just enough of everything,
and somehow looking as if it were waiting for a photographer;
and so were the Aricsons, who might have been carefully se-
lected models, dressed and then posed during the last half hour.
Mrs. Aricson, dark and rather haggard, was wearing blue velvet
pants and a sort of Paisley jacket and was doing needlework.
Aricson had got into a casual-living rig for the evening and was
examining an illustrated magazine through rimless glasses. He
was one of those fair, clean-cut Scandinavian-cum-American
types Maggie had often seen in London, both in and out of the
office—somehow impressive, a trifle sinister, but never quite
real as people.

Dr. Salt, she realized at once, was back in his role of the

humble man trying to please. He apologized for calling so late, apologized for bringing her, and appeared almost ready to apologize for his very existence. Mrs. Aricson was very gracious, but declared at once that she must talk to Elsa, who was new and still had much to learn. Mr. Aricson was gravely-courteous-but-with-a-twinkle, and seated them as carefully as if they, too, might be photographed shortly. No refreshments were offered. Maggie couldn't imagine any in this room; they were in a furnish-your-home and not a whisky advertisement.

"Well, now, Dr. Salt—what's the trouble?" Rather as if he were the doctor and his visitor a patient. And in spite of his name and the general atmosphere, he spoke without a trace of any alien accent and must have been born and bred in England.

Dr. Salt stared at him quite hard. Maggie knew at once he had jumped out of his humble-man part. "Mr. Aricson, where is Noreen Wilks?"

But if he thought he could startle Aricson into making some admission, he was quite wildly wrong. "I'm sorry, Dr. Salt, but I haven't the slightest idea."

"You know who she is?"

"Oh, yes. I saw her several times with Derek Donnington. Is she one of your patients?"

"She *was.*" Dr. Salt then explained what Noreen was suffering from and why he was worried about her. "And you see, Mr. Aricson, she's never been heard of since she attended that party of yours on September twelfth."

"Not a party of mine, Dr. Salt. You mean one of the UF parties at the club, don't you? Remember, I'm not responsible for them. I ought to be—as PR man—but Tommy Linsdale, who's senior to me, insisted on taking them over. If he's away—as he was on September twelfth—Jill Frinton, one of his assistants, is in charge. But I understand that Noreen Wilks didn't attend that particular party. Have you checked at the club?"

"I did that, earlier tonight." He added nothing, though Aricson obviously expected more.

Forced to speak, Aricson said, "Well, didn't you find she hadn't been there that night?"

"No, I found that she had."

Maggie saw at once what a clever stroke this was. No matter what he replied, Aricson would have to abandon his lofty detachment and occupy a weaker position.

"Are you sure?" Aricson's surprise was nicely done. "I ask because I rang up Dews and he said he would look at his book, and then he told me she couldn't have been there."

"Why did you ring him up?" said Dr. Salt softly.

"Why shouldn't I?"

"Well, look at it, Mr. Aricson. You're not responsible for those parties. And you're certainly not responsible for Noreen Wilks, are you?"

"Of course not."

"Then why suddenly ring up Dews to ask if she was there, at a party, three weeks ago?"

If Aricson knew he was now being compelled to occupy a still weaker position, he gave no sign of it. But Maggie realized that the two men were fencing hard now.

"There's no mystery about that, Dr. Salt," he replied quietly. "It was a Fabrics Club party, and after all, I am in charge of UF public relations. I also happen to be very conscientious. All right?"

"I'm afraid not—no. On September twelfth a girl goes—or doesn't go—to a party. Where do public relations come in?"

Aricson gave him a thin smile. "Now you're forcing my hand, aren't you, Dr. Salt?" He looked at Maggie, perhaps to give himself more time. "I don't understand your interest in this, Miss—er—"

"Culworth—Maggie Culworth." She hesitated, but then out of the corner of my eye caught a nod from Dr. Salt. "You see, Mr. Aricson, we don't know where my father is, and he's not the

96

sort of man to leave us worrying about him. I know now he came to Birkden on Monday to ask about Noreen Wilks. And Dr. Salt thinks he may have called at your Fabrics Club on Monday, just as we did tonight—I mean to ask about Noreen Wilks."

"I'm sorry, Miss Culworth, but all this is quite new and strange to me. I know nothing about your father, or anybody called Culworth, I do honestly assure you." And if he wasn't being sincere, then, Maggie felt, he was certainly a marvelous actor.

"I believe you," said Dr. Salt, taking charge again. "But what's in the hand I'm forcing? What have Noreen and that party to do with your public relations?"

"In my opinion—and strictly speaking—nothing."

"Then why, after all this time, suddenly ask Dews if she was there?"

"Because I work for Sir Arnold Donnington," said Aricson carefully. "He's UF as far as this country is concerned. And I may say I admire him. He's an exceptionally fine type of big industrialist. He's also unusually public-spirited, cares about this town, works hard for it. What will happen, Dr. Salt, when you leave Birkden?"

"Nothing."

"You're too modest. But if you took Sir Arnold out of Birkden, the place would start falling to pieces."

"I've sometimes thought that wouldn't be a bad idea. But you're ready to do anything for Donnington because you admire him—um?"

"I do admire him, but I also want to keep my job. And he can be demanding. But UF pay me so well that now I have to hang on and daren't let go. It's a new kind of tyranny you may not have noticed, Dr. Salt. It's tyranny by overpayment. You're paid more than you're generally thought to be worth in the market. You live up to your income. You have to keep your wife and children in the style to which the advertisers tell them they're accustomed. Now you're clamped in. And that can make a decent, easygoing man suddenly hard and unscrupulous."

Dr. Salt was lighting his pipe. "I see. Very interesting," he said between puffs. "But why tell me?"

"I thought you'd like to know how and where I stand."

"Almost a warning—um?"

"Oh, no, not that. Miss Culworth, you'll have to excuse all this."

"Oh, but I find it fascinating."

"I doubt that, but do believe me when I say I know absolutely nothing about your father. Now where were we, Dr. Salt?"

"You'd just given me a warning that you said wasn't one. But why bother to tell me how you're situated?"

"Because now I see you're a clever man; not some interfering, self-important little GP, but a clever man who's behaving stupidly."

"Possibly. But why?"

"That party on September twelfth was no ordinary club party —and for one very good reason. That was the night young Derek Donnington had an accident cleaning a gun. All right, he shot himself, committed suicide—but don't try saying that in public or you'll run straight into trouble. That's why I think you're behaving stupidly, because whatever you do or say, you're heading for trouble. It all hangs on Sir Arnold, of course. You see I'm being perfectly frank with you. The only son he had blew his brains out that night, so he's jammed the lid on it. I don't blame him—and you oughtn't to."

"I'm not blaming anybody, Mr. Aricson. I'm merely asking one question. What became of Noreen Wilks?"

"I don't know. And to tell you the truth, I don't care. Whatever arrangements Sir Arnold made—probably for her to clear out immediately—he didn't bring me in. I admit that's unusual —it's part of my job to attend to things for him—but I can't help it, that's how it was. And I'm ready to swear any sort of oath you want that I know no more than you do about Noreen Wilks."

Dr. Salt waited a moment. "All right. I believe you. Do you believe him, Maggie?"

"I don't want to, but I'm afraid I do."

"Quite so. There you are, Mr. Aricson. We don't want to believe you, but we're afraid we do."

"I'm glad I could satisfy you. Well—" And he made one of those preparing-to-rise movements that so often lift callers out of their chairs.

"Please—if you don't mind, just another question or two. Now I don't see Donnington asking our friend Donald Dews to fake his book."

"No, Dr. Salt. I did that."

"I thought you did. But why?"

"I'd had my orders to discourage you."

"I know that. But I still ask why."

"Oh, come off it, man." Aricson's patience had suddenly vanished. "I've explained what happened that night. Then the boy's suicide was wrapped up and put away. So the last thing Sir Arnold wants is somebody like you going to the police and then round the town, asking questions. And of course I agree with him. No questions—no scandal."

"You've missed my point," said Dr. Salt, not taking the same impatient tone but suggesting an inexhaustible store of patience. "I know that you and Donnington are afraid of scandal —though I'm neither a reporter nor a policeman. But what is this scandal you're afraid of?"

"Don't ask me. I've told you all *I* know."

"You mean I should ask Donnington."

"Don't be ridiculous. He wouldn't listen to you. He wouldn't even admit his son had died from anything but an accident. He'd threaten you with an action for slander."

"Maggie, we ought to go," said Dr. Salt, almost rolling out of his chair. He was a very untidy getter up and sitter down, though not really fat. "Mr. Aricson, thank you for seeing us. I can't pretend to know what you're talking about." He motioned

Maggie to go ahead of him towards the door and then spoke over his shoulder. "You seem to be protecting yourselves against a scandal that isn't there. I mustn't let something out, although there isn't anything. You're helping Donnington to keep the lid firmly down on nothing." They were now crossing the hall. "There can't be anything wrong, but it mustn't get out. Well, I'll try to accept all that—though it may take some doing —if you'll just ask Donnington, on my behalf, one simple question." He turned and looked hard at Aricson. "Just this. *Where is Noreen Wilks?* Good night."

2

They were back in Dr. Salt's flat, back in the muddle of books and records again, drinking his very good China tea. He had offered to run her straight home from Aricson's. He thought she was tired, and she was, but it was only just after ten, her mother would still be up, and she hated the thought of answering a lot of questions—and with no mention of Noreen Wilks—before either having a night's rest or talking to Alan. So while Dr. Salt was making the tea, she had telephoned home to say that she might be late, and had found her mother more angry than fretful. She had been to the police and though they had not been rude exactly, they had refused to take her seriously. If husbands who had been away for only two and a half days were to be considered officially "missing," police stations would soon be like lunatic asylums. And she could not persuade them that Edward Culworth was quite different from the sort of men they had in mind. And what did Maggie think she was doing? To which Maggie replied that she was only in Birkden for her father's sake and was doing the best she could. And she wasn't quite sure *what* Alan was doing; and that, at least, was no lie.

"Do you think I'm right," she asked Dr. Salt over the teacups, "to keep this Noreen Wilks thing from my mother?"

"Yes, Maggie. If your mother had been the kind of woman

you could tell anything and everything, you wouldn't be asking that question. It answers itself."

"All right, then. But mind you," she went on, rather defiantly, "I'm positive there wasn't anything—y'know, sexual—between him and Noreen Wilks."

"I'm not positive, but I'm inclined to agree with you. I don't really know your father—"

"He's a very conscientious, hard-working, modest, shy bookseller."

"Quite so. And Noreen was young, even for her age. No, it's something else. Perhaps he knew her parents—or one of them. By the way, did he come into Birkden fairly often?"

"No, I don't think so. Once or twice a month, perhaps. He didn't like Birkden. I think he came here specially on Monday to ask about Noreen Wilks. But what made you suspect he went to that Fabrics Club?"

"The behavior of the barman and Dews when I so carefully mentioned you Culworths. The barman went blank on it. Dews, who vastly overrates himself as a smart liar, thought he could be cheeky with it. 'Really—and ought they to? I mean, is there something wrong with him?' " Dr. Salt quoted, almost capturing Dews's impudent manner and tone. "Bouncing it—for a giggle with the barman after we'd gone."

"What a good memory you have! I couldn't have recalled exactly what he said, and how he said it."

"Unless I keep my wits about me, Maggie, I'll be wasting valuable time. It's my belief your father went to the Fabrics Club sometime on Monday, after he'd talked to Peggy Pearson at the Lyceum. What happened after that, of course, I don't know. This explains something that had been puzzling me before you arrived, this afternoon. I couldn't understand how these Fabrics people—in or out of the club—could be on the alert so quickly. The answer is I didn't start it yesterday morning. Your father started it on Monday. Then *something happened*—"

"To my father?" Maggie cried apprehensively.

"Involving your father—yes. Nothing terrible—don't worry."

"How do you know it isn't?"

"Because somebody like Dews wouldn't dare to cover it up. He'd be terrified. But he knows something we don't know about your father."

"My mother said she went to the police tonight and they just wouldn't take her seriously."

"She can't expect them to. You and she know this isn't like your father, but they don't. However, I'll be talking to Superintendent Hurst tomorrow, and he's not going to laugh me off."

"The shop's closed tomorrow afternoon, anyhow. Can I come and see you? I must know what's happening—and I'm certain now my father's mixed up in this Noreen Wilks business. I won't be a nuisance. And perhaps there's something I could do." She gave him a long, appealing look.

"Have another cup of tea? Good. Yes," he said as he took her cup, "I'll be glad to see you. I may be badly in need of a witness soon. Things may hot up. It may be one man against a town. And anyhow, I'm not naturally a hermit, a solitary, and I can feel lonely. I'll expect you about half past two, Maggie."

"Thank you." She said this both for the tea he was offering her again and for the invitation. "I don't really like talking about Noreen Wilks. I can't help disliking her—because of my father and also somehow she gives me the creeps. But did you really believe Mr. Thing—Aricson—when he said he didn't know what had happened to her?"

"Yes. He really doesn't know. I'm sure of that. But there's something else. I could just catch a flicker of it. *He doesn't want to know.* I'll swear to that, Maggie. He's a type who naturally wants to know—to be in on everything—but not this time. He's closed his mind and put a padlock on it. But that doesn't mean I can go ahead and find out what happened to Noreen. One way or another he'll try to stop me."

Maggie finished her second cup and put it on the tray. "I

know why that girl gives me the creeps. You talk about her as if she were dead."

He nodded. "I think she is."

She suddenly felt she wanted to be at home and in her bed. "Perhaps I could go now. Or do you think I ought to ring up Alan at that woman's?"

"I'm against that, Maggie. Give him a chance."

"A chance? What—to fall in love with a woman like that?"

"He might do worse."

"Who with? A call girl?"

"She's not as tough as she pretends to be," said Dr. Salt. "I'm prepared to bet she's here because some man treated her badly elsewhere—probably in London."

"Does that mean she has to behave like a tart and a—a procuress?" Had she given herself away by flaring up like that? Did Dr. Salt's quick look mean anything?

Apparently not. "It might do your brother no harm to make a fool of himself. Besides, she might be useful to us."

"Oh, rubbish! I wouldn't trust her a yard. I must go, Dr. Salt. All of a sudden I'm feeling really exhausted. Too much has happened today. And I don't *enjoy* it—as I believe half the time you do."

If he had started arguing, she felt she would have screamed. But he didn't; and though he looked quite amiable, he never said a word, not even when, about halfway home, she began crying in a small, miserable, idiotic way, and a few words of comfort would have been welcome. He just drove in silence, a cold pipe in his mouth, probably thinking and thinking about the wretched Noreen Wilks.

EIGHT

1

Dr. Salt breakfasted off a large cup of coffee and a small slice of brown toast, which he covered with butter and honey. When he had finished it was nearly nine o'clock. He lit a pipe and went outside to take a look at the morning, which even in Birkden was autumnal, beautiful, melancholy. A young man called Gooch, who lived on the second floor but was often away, taking orders for electrical fittings, joined him outside the front door.

"Morning, Dr. Salt. When are you leaving us?"

"Soon. Early part of next week, perhaps. I've one or two things to clear up."

"Disposed of your flat?"

"Yes. A couple waiting to move in as soon as my stuff has gone."

"Nice people?" asked Gooch hopefully.

"Not nice, not nasty. Dummies. No, that's not fair," Dr. Salt added with some haste. "Only met them twice. They may be all right."

"Glad to be leaving Birkden, aren't you?"

"Well, after seven years I've had enough of it. Though I don't suppose it's any worse than twenty or thirty other towns about the same size."

"That's what I tell Joan—my wife—but she can't wait to get out of it. Always at me. You know how women are."

"Biologically, yes. Otherwise, I don't. Unless I really know them, of course."

"You don't think they're all alike?" Gooch sounded astonished.

"Certainly not. It's the men who think women are all alike who are really all alike."

"You surprise me, doctor. But I must go and earn a few pennies. Bye now."

Dr. Salt sent several puffs of smoke after the hurrying Gooch, and then went indoors to telephone his acquaintance Sergeant Broadbent, at police headquarters. "Two things, please, sergeant. I believe Superintendent Hurst is coming to see me here about five o'clock today. Could you confirm that, please? The other thing is this. Could you possibly find out for me if an ambulance called at the Fabrics Club sometime on Monday evening? And if it did, then where did it go? I'd like you to call me here as soon as you conveniently can—Birkden 52317. You've got all that? Thank you very much, Sergeant Broadbent."

He cleared and then washed up his breakfast crockery and cutlery, slowly, absent-mindedly, but quite efficiently. He picked up several bills, took them to his desk at the far end of the sitting room, made out the checks they asked for and addressed the necessary envelopes. Then he stared at the room's muddle of books and records and decided he could do nothing about it, not this morning. The telephone rang and it was Sergeant Broadbent.

"The super'll come round about five this afternoon, Dr. Salt. And I've given him your address. I didn't tell him about your ambulance inquiry. But anyhow, it's negative. No ambulance was called for the Fabrics Club or anywhere near it on Monday evening. That's certain. Does it surprise you?"

"No. In the morning nothing surprises me. But now and then, late in the evening, I'm occasionally surprised."

"You're a bit of a one, aren't you, Dr. Salt?"

"No. But many thanks, Sergeant Broadbent."

"Don't mention it. But perhaps you'd like to tell me now what that inquiry was in aid of—eh?"

"You wouldn't be interested. It was just a vague idea. But thank you again."

After putting down the receiver, Dr. Salt made no other movement for a minute or two. He was trying to remember the name of the other doctor, junior to Dr. Bennett, that Dews had mentioned. Then he recalled it—Lemmert. Hastily he looked for it in the telephone book, and was much relieved to find it there. He didn't want to talk to Dr. Lemmert in the factory clinic, under the same roof as Aricson and Sir Arnold Donnington. With equal haste he dialed the number he had found in the book.

"This is Dr. Salt," he told the girl at the other end. "I want to see Dr. Lemmert. It's rather urgent but it won't take long, and I can be with him in five or ten minutes."

After a short delay, the girl said Dr. Lemmert ought to be leaving almost immediately but that if Dr. Salt, who mustn't keep him long, went round at once, Dr. Lemmert would see him. The girl's tone suggested that Dr. Salt should consider himself a very, very lucky man. He saw her as a soulful brunette whose large dark eyes would never lose a chance of dwelling upon her wonderful Dr. Lemmert. And he was quite right; she was.

Dr. Salt had never seen Dr. Lemmert before, and after one quick look he decided that it would be all right if he never saw him again. Dr. Lemmert was a tall, thin, youngish man with a long nose and not much forehead or breadth to his head. Most youngish doctors were either hearty and almost back-slapping or were inclined to be pompous. Dr. Lemmert was high in the pompous class. Dr. Salt decided at once on a brutal attack.

"After they sent for you at the Fabrics Club on Monday night," he said, staring hard, "what did you do with your patient?"

"I beg your pardon—"

"You said your time was precious and now you're wasting it —mine too," Dr. Salt continued, severely. "His name's Culworth. He's a bookseller in Hemton. I'm a family friend. His daughter's coming to see me this afternoon. That's why I'm here. Now then, Dr. Lemmert, what about him?"

Dr. Lemmert's pomposity, together with his recent adoption by United Fabrics, glasses of sherry with old Dr. Bennett, and perhaps the devotion of dark-eyes in the next room, left him wide open to this frontal attack. If Dr. Salt had cleared his throat, looked apologetic and asked a timid question or two, Dr. Lemmert would have had time to make up his mind and then tell his visitor not to talk nonsense but go away. Caught off guard, he hesitated, and this was fatal to any chance of a complete denial.

"Well?" And Dr. Salt was still staring hard.

"He met with an accident not far from the Fabrics Club, in the grounds of that large empty house—"

"The old Worsley place?"

"Yes. Some concussion. I didn't like his heart. And as soon as he was conscious, he was obviously under great emotional stress. Complete rest—sedation, of course." And Dr. Lemmert's voice, already down to a murmur, faded away.

"But no ambulance?"

"It saved time to make use of one of the company's vans—"

"Bollocks," said Dr. Salt. "It saved something, but not time. Where did you take him?"

"Where he has been having the best possible care."

"I didn't think he was tied up in a cellar. But I want to know where he is."

Dr. Lemmert had now recovered from the original assault.

"He's under proper medical care, Dr. Salt. The company have accepted financial responsibility, even though he had no right to be wandering about those grounds. He's my patient, not yours, and I see no reason why I should tell you where he is—especially as he's made considerable progress during the last two days. And now, if you'll excuse me—"

"Just a minute, Lemmert. I won't press you to tell me where he is. I can soon find out. And when I do, his daughter will be with me. But if there's any hanky-panky—and I can tell it a mile off—you and the nursing home will be in a hell of a pickle. You didn't send for an ambulance. You haven't tried to notify anybody. You've now refused information demanded on behalf of his family. So if you or the matron give him one unnecessary shot of anything, to keep him dopey and quiet, you're over your heads in trouble. I'll do you this favor, Dr. Lemmert. I'll find him myself, so you can tell Aricson or Donnington it wasn't your fault. But try any funny business from now on, and you'll wish you'd never heard of United Anglo-Belgian Fabrics. Good morning."

He went out so quickly that he bumped into the soulful brunette, just behind the door. She gave him a look of utter disgust, this man who had been bullying wonderful Dr. Lemmert. "Good-bye, dear!" he called cheerfully.

2

Back in his car, he did not drive off at once but filled and lit a pipe while deciding he ought to pay another visit to 45 Olton Street and Mrs. Pearson. Moving cautiously along the wretched length of Olton Street, which a number of very young children were trying to use as a playground, he thought, not for the first time, that a people who accepted their Olton Streets, generation after generation, without throwing a few bricks when three million pounds were spent on two houses in Downing Street, probably deserved what they got. Mrs. Pearson, though not dressed to receive company, was glad to see him.

"Peggy's written," she said as soon as they were settled in that small, smelly front room. "She's staying with her auntie in Birmingham till she gets a job, and she's trying for one at a picture palace—she didn't say which but of course there's lots in Birmingham and she's had experience, Peggy has. And she ran away 'cause a very nasty young chap told her to keep her bloody big mouth shut and slapped her face and kicked that tin box she puts the half tickets in. She thinks it's to do with Noreen Wilks. Is that right, doctor?"

"I think it is, Mrs. Pearson. But you can tell her from me that if she wants to come back, she can—not this week, perhaps, but next."

"I'll write and tell her that, Dr. Salt. You say she'll be all right, do you? Then I'll write this morning."

"You do. Now—about Noreen. Have you been through her things?"

"I haven't laid a finger on 'em, doctor—not a finger. I've been expecting her back every day, so I haven't touched nothing. There's two letters come for her since she left, and I done nothing except put 'em behind the tea caddy in the kitchen. I didn't tell that sergeant who come asking questions, 'cause I didn't like the look of him and it's none of their business. Shall I fetch 'em for you, Dr. Salt?"

"Yes, please, Mrs. Pearson."

"Wait here, then. Won't take me a minute." She left him staring at nothing over his pipe.

"Well, I must say," she cried on her return, "I've never seen you looking like that before—right down in the mouth. I used to tell my friend Mrs. Muston that you were always so cheerful it did me good just to go and see you. And Peggy used to say the same."

"You were patients then, Mrs. Pearson. But if I was looking

miserable, I'm sorry. I was thinking—and they weren't very cheerful thoughts. The truth is, I'm convinced that Noreen Wilks is dead."

"Oh, no!"

"Yes. And that's why I'm here, Mrs. Pearson. I can't leave Birkden without finding out exactly what happened to Noreen Wilks. It's no use keeping letters until she comes back. She isn't coming back."

"I knew it, I knew it," said Mrs. Pearson, beginning to cry. "I've known it somewhere inside ever since that night. I said as much to Peggy, and she laughed at me and said Noreen was having a high old time at the seaside in France. Oh, the poor little thing! You're sure, are you, doctor?"

He nodded, then regarded her gravely. "But I have to prove it, and that could be a tricky business. Do you trust me, Mrs. Pearson?"

"Dr. Salt, you're the only man I've known for a long time I would trust—the only one. Oh, I feel so upset. Just excuse me a minute."

When she came back from the kitchen—and the bottle in the cupboard—she was still carrying the two letters, and now he held out a hand for them. "You must give me those letters, Mrs. Pearson. If they are what I think they are—and the police got hold of them—some nice people I know might soon be very unhappy."

"I'm sure you know best, doctor." And she handed them over.

"And now I want you to go up to her room, search her things carefully, and if you find any letters or notes she's kept—and I'm certain you will—then please let me have them. They may be very important."

"All right, if you say so." She made a hurried move, but then stopped in the doorway. "Do you think it happened that night —September twelfth?"

"That night or early next morning—yes."

"Well, do you think she was suddenly taken ill and just died

—or did somebody kill her? I mean—you don't think she might have been *murdered*, do you, doctor?"

He held her fearful stare steadily for a moment. "I don't say you haven't a right to ask that question, Mrs. Pearson. But it's just possible I might run you into trouble if I answered it. All I've told you this morning is that I believe Noreen Wilks is dead. And if you'll hand over any letters—anything in writing she kept—I'll take the responsibility."

"Yes—yes, I'll do that. I don't even want 'em about here." And off she went.

He looked at the two unopened letters, both addressed in the same neat hand and bearing the Hemton postmark. Slowly, very reluctantly, as if he hated doing it, he opened and then read the letters. It would be wrong to say he gave a sigh afterwards—definite sighing seems to have gone out—but his breathing was heavier and seemed to have something melancholy in it. And when at last he put the letters into an inside pocket, he found that the pipe still in his mouth was cold.

Five minutes later Mrs. Pearson returned. She had powdered her grief-stricken face so thoroughly that it was now a lilac shade. "These are all I could find." She pushed about a dozen letters at him. "Usual place—tucked away below her stockings and undies. I haven't stopped to read 'em. I know we're all supposed to be so bloody curious—but I don't want to read 'em."

"Neither do I." He stuffed the letters into a side pocket and then got up. "But I must find out all I can about her. Thank you, Mrs. Pearson."

She stopped him just as he was opening the street door. "Dr. Salt, if she really *is* dead, what am I going to do with all her things?"

"Better hang on to them for a while, and then do what you like with them."

"Yes, I suppose so. I mean, poor Noreen hadn't anybody, had she? No relations—nobody."

"She had one, I think. Whether he'd want some little thing belonging to her, I don't know. Probably not. Thank you again, Mrs. Pearson. And tell Peggy she can come back if she wants to —anytime next week, I think."

3

After he had read the letters that Mrs. Pearson had found for him, Dr. Salt made a list of local nursing homes—and it was quite short—that he and Maggie would have to visit. Feeling then it was time to attend to his own affairs, he put in an hour's good work sorting out the books, refusing himself the luxury of dipping into those he was doubtful about keeping. So it was nearly twelve when he heard a ring at his door.

"Hello—are you Dr. Salt?" The girl was wearing a mink coat over a black sweater and blue jeans, no hat but a lot of hair that needed washing, and was an expensive slut with a long, loose face and body.

"I am. Who are you?"

"Erica Donnington. Well, let me in, for God's sake. We can't just stand here. And if you want to call it a professional visit, okay, go ahead. I'll pay you whatever we pay silly old Dr. Bennett."

"Not necessary." He stood aside and then followed her into the sitting room.

"My God. I thought my room was a mess, but as a jumble this is really fab. How can you be a doctor and live like this?"

"I can't. I don't. I'm leaving, so I'm sorting things out."

"Where do you suggest I sit?"

"Wait." He took some books out of a chair. "Try that. And now you know where, you might tell me why."

"Why what?"

"Why you're here. You can't consult me professionally even if you do pay me whatever you pay silly old Dr. Bennett."

"Oh, don't be so square, Dr. Salt. I think I'm going to be

disappointed. I believe you're just another doctor. Of course, it was just curiosity, after what I heard last night. But I'll explain all that over a drink. Gin and tonic, please. Plenty of gin and not too much tonic. And even if you're breaking all your rules, for God's sake give yourself a drink too. I hate drinking alone."

He gave her rather a long, hard look, nodded without smiling, then went into the kitchen for the gin and tonic and a little neat whisky for himself. He could hear her moving around the sitting room. Having made a fuss about where she should sit, now she wasn't sitting. He took his time over the drinks, wondering how to deal with her. His natural inclination was to be sharp and hard with a type like this, but he realized that he might learn more if he appeared to be sympathetic.

"You were saying you were curious, after last night, Miss Donnington." She had her drink now.

"Erica—do you mind? Otherwise, you'll soon be asking to look at my tongue or my eyeballs."

"Only for cash down, Erica. But what happened last night?"

"Oh, I'm not sure. I was half stoned anyhow. I nearly always am now. Not in the morning—at night, I mean. You don't look very clever."

"I know." He lit his pipe very carefully and then looked at her blankly, as if he might never speak again.

It worked. "Has anybody ever told you I'm queer?"

"Nobody's ever told me anything about you, Erica."

"Well, I am. And now it's Jill Frinton. I'm crazy about her and I don't care who knows it. So, being half stoned, of course I had to see her last night, though I knew damned well she didn't want to let me in. She'd got a new boyfriend there—one of those tall, dark, handsome devils—who was eating her with his eyes."

"Ah, yes. Alan Culworth. What was happening?"

"What do you think? Not when I was there, of course, but they soon got rid of me. An hour or so afterwards I went back. No lights. And his little car was still there. They were in bed or on it. You can imagine what I felt. Talk about *jealousy!* I went screaming round the countryside, doing eighty most of the time, for two hours, trying to work it off. It was *hell*. Still is."

"I see, Erica. Sorry about that. But where do I come in?"

"Oh, well—I heard Jill telling Donald Dews on the phone how clever you'd been. Then I said, oh, I'd overheard my father saying something about you on the phone. And I was—I was wondering, why was everybody suddenly Dr. Salting it like mad? And—incidentally, do you *have* to stare at me like that?"

"No. It's a bad habit some of us doctors have picked up. If your father's Sir Arnold Donnington, I met him on Tuesday morning—with Superintendent Hurst."

"Um—mm. I'll bet you didn't like him."

"I might have if he hadn't so much weight to throw about."

"Does he? He's so square it hurts. We—well, no wonder Derek and I started—kicking things around."

"Perhaps he gave your brother too big an allowance."

"Are you trying to be funny? You don't know much, really. Father kept poor Derek—he kept my poor brother very short. Especially after he'd been sent down from Oxford. If it hadn't been for me, Derek would have—you see, I have some money, thank God, that came from my mother. Otherwise, Derek would have been wondering how to pay for a few double Scotches. Where did you get that idea from—that Derek had plenty of money?"

"Vague rumors, Erica. Talk among the peasantry. About taking a girl to the south of France. And having a flat or some place of his own in or near Birkden."

"Oh—for God's sake. Rumors! Oh, Jesus—no. If *he'd* had—if Derek had had a flat of his own, they'd have had to be giving 'em away. I don't know—I must say, I *don't* know what Jill was talking about, *your* being so clever. Clever! I don't see—but perhaps you're one of those people who aren't very bright in the morning. Is *that* your trouble?"

"I think I am—yes," said Dr. Salt thoughtfully. "But of course

I'm sorry if you're disappointed. By the way, I met Mr. Aricson last night. What about him?"

"He *is* clever, up to a point. But I don't like him—and he doesn't like me. Though, of course, I don't see much of him. I just mean—well, you know, I don't like men. And—his wife isn't attractive. Not like Jill, who's *madly* attractive, both to you men and somebody like me. Didn't *you* fall for her? And don't tell me you're too old. I've seen men a lot older than you in Jill's flat, just sitting up on their hind paws and *begging*."

"Well, I don't do much of that, Erica."

"No one—it's always—look, for God's sake, *are* you going to give me another drink?"

"No, I'm not. For two reasons. First, I'm running short of gin—and I'm mean. Secondly, I'm busy. So some other time, please, Erica.".

"No, thank you," she said, getting up. "And I might as well tell you, I don't think you're clever—and I also think you're rather a miserable little sod. D'you mind?"

"Not in the least," Dr. Salt told her cheerfully. "And now—bugger off."

This startled her. "Is that the way you talk to people?"

"Only if they call me a miserable little sod."

"Oh, shut up!" She was hurrying out now. "And anyhow, you don't know what my life's like. You can't begin to imagine. Silly bloody clown!" She banged the door behind her.

Dr. Salt stood at the window watching her hurling herself into the cream Jaguar and then listening to her go roaring off. His face was heavy and frowning, but not with anger. Then he realized that he was beginning to feel hungry. He took the two glasses into the kitchen, where he decided to scramble some eggs.

NINE

Maggie was busy in the shop most of Thursday morning, dividing her time between the little back office and the front room, where she did her best to take her father's place, even though she neither knew nor cared about books in general as he did. Moreover, she was worried about her father, about Alan, and in a confused sort of way about this odd Dr. Salt. Where was her father? What had happened to him? And what had he to do with Dr. Salt's Noreen Wilks? As far as Alan was concerned, the situation was clear enough—no mystery there—for it was obvious he had gone and fallen at once for that artful bitch Jill Thing. He had come down late, looking washed out, and though they had had the time and opportunity only to exchange a few words before she had had to leave for the shop, and nothing had been said about his Jill, Maggie knew at once he must have spent about half the night making love to her. And Alan was a serious character, not likely to grab some sex because it could be had, and if there was going to be much more of this Jill work, he might soon be in horrible earnest, while she was bouncing around again with salesmen and buyers. And if it hadn't been for Dr. Salt, Alan would never have set eyes on this blasted Jill again.

So one minute she was ready to like Dr. Salt, so clever and helpful and attractively odd. Then the next minute she would decide that she was furious with him, that she didn't like him at all, that he was only using the Culworth family, in a cold-blooded and quite ruthless fashion, to help him find out more about his wretched Noreen Wilks, and that he might be an unusual man, but that didn't mean he was either attractive or friendly.

She tried to explain some of this to Bertha Chapman during a brief elevenses in the office. But it was all too complicated and she cut it short by telling Bertha she was seeing Dr. Salt again that afternoon and that he might have found out something about her father. "On the other hand," she concluded rather miserably, "I feel he's quite capable of telling me that he hasn't given us Culworths another single thought. And it's now all such a mysterious tangle that if he won't help me, I'll feel absolutely bewildered and lost. It's as if Birkden, which I used to sniff at and despise after London, has suddenly turned into a dark jungle. Yet somehow I believed Dr. Salt yesterday when he told me he didn't think anything very dreadful had happened to Daddy. Oh, Bertha—it's all so mystifying and maddening."

Bertha gave her a look. "I can see that, dear. And how much of all this are you telling your mother?"

"Hardly any of it. Only that I've met a Dr. Salt who thinks he might be able to find out about Daddy. Just because he's a doctor, Mother believes me. I feel a bit mean and rather guilty, keeping back so much from her."

"No, you're quite right, Maggie dear. I know that if I were in your place— Oh blast! I'll have to go. So will you, I think. There's a run on us just because it's half-day closing."

"I'll have time for a quick lunch," said Maggie as they went out to the front shop together. "We'll go to the Primrose, Bertha."

They hadn't much time because it was ten past one when they reached the café, and Maggie would have to take the Birkden bus and then be at Dr. Salt's by half past two. And though she was still ready to be furious with him—getting Alan entangled like that—she was also determined not to be a minute late, feeling in some obscure fashion that if she wasn't there on the dot he might vanish, like a magician in a fairy tale. But over some tomato soup and woolly plaice, she was able to tell Bertha how she and Alan had begun to think, in the Fabrics Club, that Dr. Salt was an absolute fool, and how they soon had to change their minds and felt silly themselves—at least she did.

"Did he crow over you then—Dr. Salt, I mean?"

"No, he didn't, Bertha. But then I don't think he cared what we felt. On the other hand, I must say that when I suggested I ought to see him today, he told me at once to come at half past two."

"That's being a doctor, isn't it? Making exact appointments—sharp—bang-bang-bang! What does he look like?"

"Not specially odd and original—though he *is*. Rather ordinary until you take a good look at him. He had a wife—and obviously he adored her—and she died. And I don't know whether it's that or a lot of less important things all adding up, but he makes me feel he doesn't like it here anymore and wants to get back—oh, I don't know—to places thousands of miles away, to where he was before he came to Birkden. And he's only waiting now to find out exactly what happened to this Noreen Wilks."

"Perhaps he was in love with her, Maggie."

"I wondered about that, but I soon saw that he wasn't at all. She was his patient. And rather special, not because he was fond of her but because she had to have this special treatment for her kidney disease. She'd been missing three weeks. Nobody seemed to care. So he decided to care. And he's not only very sharp and clever but also—I'd say—very obstinate."

"Do you think he's interested in you, Maggie dear?"

"Not a bit. And as soon as Daddy's found, I shan't be interested in him. But without him I wouldn't know where to look, what to do. Birkden's quite different from what I thought it was, and Dr. Salt understands it—and I don't." Maggie got up, rummaged in her bag, then dropped some silver on the table. "Pay for me too, Bertha darling. I must fly."

"Of course you must, dear. Don't keep this fascinating Dr. Salt waiting."

"He's not fascinating—don't be silly. I'm going."

"If he isn't, then let me go instead," cried Bertha, who worried less about voices raised in public than Maggie did. On her way out, Maggie believed she could even hear Bertha laughing. And a fine time this was to begin shouting and laughing in public!

2

Dr. Salt surprised Maggie at once by looking quite different than he had the previous day. Instead of the sloppy old clothes, now he was wearing a neat dark-gray suit, a white shirt and collar, a tie of the deepest shade of crimson. He said nothing about it, so she didn't, at least not until she was back again in the muddle and mess of his sitting room.

"Oh, dear!" she cried in genuine dismay. "This looks worse than ever today. And with you now all so neat and carefully dressed up. I couldn't live a day with this ruin of a room. It's so *depressing.*" Her tone and look challenged him to deny it.

"I know, I know." He was mild, almost apologetic.

"I might as well tell you, Dr. Salt," she began, taking advantage of this meekness, "that I'm furious with you today. No, I'm serious. Alan must have spent half the night with your Jill Frinton or Murphy or whatever her name is. And now he probably thinks he's in love with her. Which means that no matter what happens from now on, it'll be all wrong. Either she'll soon laugh at him and go back to her fat businessmen, or she'll be serious about it too and they'll want to get married, and then a fine old mess that will be."

"How do you know it will, Maggie?"

"Oh, don't be ridiculous. Can you see her living on what poor Alan earns? In a few months she'd be back in that flat and the Fabrics Club or trying to make some other tarty arrangements."

"I'm not sure about that," he cut in rather sharply. "But let's discuss it some other time."

"I'm only telling you why I'm furious with you for bringing them together, Dr. Salt. Have you found out anything else? Or have you spent the morning trying to decide between gramophone records?"

"I've almost finished with the records now," he told her, again quite mildly. "And in fact I haven't listened to one this morning. I've been too busy, Maggie."

By answering her like that, he made her feel ashamed of her angry tone and scornful emphasis, though she doubted if he had done this deliberately. She realized that he was one of those rare people who always take their own tone, who don't raise their voices if you have raised yours, who don't automatically return anger for anger, scorn for scorn, who don't behave as if talk were a desperate tennis match. As Hugh always did, for one. Though, of course, Dr. Salt was older, had probably never been spoiled as handsome Hugh had been by his mother and sisters, and had undoubtedly seen a lot more of life, all kinds of life.

"Nothing new about my father, I suppose?" she asked, small and humble now.

"Yes, it was mostly concerning him." He went to his desk. "I've a list of local nursing homes here. You and I are calling on them this afternoon. I'd have done it myself, but I want you with me—as his daughter. Incidentally, that's why I'm dressed like this—to impress matrons or manageresses. You see, I'm almost sure we'll find him in one of these nursing homes."

"I don't see why we should, not yet, but is he—do you think —very ill?"

"I'm sure he isn't," he told her cheerfully. "Though he may have to keep quiet for a day or two. But I've a spare room, and I'll be responsible for him. So not to worry, Maggie."

She stared at him, then shook her head so that she wouldn't let go and begin crying. "We'll go as soon as you like, of course. But it seems so extraordinary—I mean how did you find out about him? I wish you'd explain before we do go."

"Well, it was a long shot—but not entirely in the dark. I told you last night that I knew *something* had happened that had involved your father. And that fellow Dews at the club was fairly transparent. He's an impudent liar, but not a really tough one. Now if your father had been killed or even seriously injured—or if, injured in any way at all, he'd been at that moment upstairs in one of the club bedrooms—and they have a few— then Dews wouldn't have taken that easy cheeky line. He hasn't the guts. But if he knew something about your father and somebody else had taken the responsibility, so that he hadn't to worry, then that's exactly the line he would take. I'd really got as far as that by last night, you may remember."

"Yes, I do remember now. And you're making me feel very silly and stupid—and ungrateful."

"Then don't, Maggie. Remember, you're emotionally involved, and I'm not. And I'm only trying to explain, so that you'll be ready to face the nursing homes."

"I know. Please go on."

"I felt sure your father had called at the club and had probably asked some very awkward questions about Noreen Wilks. Now not far from the club and sharing the same grounds is a large empty house, the old Worsley place. And I asked myself what would have happened if your father had been knocked out or had met with some accident in or near that house, between it and the club. He couldn't be left there unconscious— that was too risky for various good reasons. He'd be taken to the

121

club, probably into Dews's office. Dews would call one of the two doctors he mentioned to me, Bennett and Lemmert, both of them members and both having some connection with the factory. And I felt sure he'd choose the younger man, Lemmert. So I saw Lemmert, a pompous young ass, this morning and bounced him into admitting he'd attended your father at the club on Monday night. He also told me your father was suffering from slight concussion, some heart trouble—"

"Yes, his heart isn't very strong."

"And that he was obviously under great emotional stress. What I think happened then—though I can't prove it—is that Dr. Lemmert called Aricson, or got Dews to do it for him, and that Aricson then talked to his big boss, Sir Arnold Donnington, who then gave some orders—"

"But why all this fuss about my father—unless, of course, he was dangerously ill."

"He wasn't. That's not the point. He was important because he'd been asking questions about Noreen Wilks, and then, probably not satisfied, had gone nosing around in or near the Worsley house. That's why they didn't send for an ambulance to take him to hospital. And of course we knew he wasn't in hospital or you'd have been notified. Dr. Lemmert arranged for him to be taken in one of the company's vans to a nursing home, where he's been kept under sedation—at the company's expense. Incidentally, I'm fairly certain that Lemmert has given him the kind of care and treatment any other doctor would have given him. Don't imagine there's been any dirty work at the nursing home. We'll find that he's been properly looked after. But after being bounced into admitting so much, our Dr. Lemmert dug in and refused to tell me which nursing home it is. When we find it, I may need you—his daughter—to back my demand that I now take charge of the patient and bring him here. I won't move him, of course, until I've examined him and made sure it'll do him no harm. So now, let's go, Maggie."

"I'm ready." But as she left the room with him, she said,

122

"There's just one thing. This great emotional stress Dr. Lemmert mentioned to you—has it something to do with Noreen Wilks?"

"Yes, it has, Maggie."

"Or do you just think it has?"

"No, I know it has. Now—where's my bag? Must have it, and I nearly forgot."

They were in the car, though not moving yet, when she spoke again. "Can you tell me why you know for certain my father's in such a state about that girl?"

"Not now, Maggie. Let's find him first."

The car was moving now, and though she longed to ask more and sharper questions, she kept silent, remembering how he disliked talking when he was driving. Cutting through the relief she felt because she knew what had happened to her father, who couldn't be far away, was the disturbing thought that this man who was so distressed about Noreen Wilks, somebody she'd never heard of before yesterday, was himself a kind of stranger. She half dreaded meeting and greeting him, and then reproached herself for entertaining any such feeling and being disloyal to her father, whom she still loved as she had done when she was a child (and as she no longer loved her mother), and being disloyal at the very time when she was on her way to find him.

There was another and much smaller thing, really quite silly, that worried her. She was beginning to feel now that she couldn't talk easily to Dr. Salt—couldn't question him, apologize to him for being so stupid, thank him properly—just because—and oh, it was all so silly—she couldn't decide what to call him. "Dr. Salt" was too formal; he didn't like his Lionel and Humphrey, and certainly they didn't suggest him; and though he had told her simply to call him "Salt," she didn't take to the curt chaps-at-the-bar sound of that; so what was left? There was, of course, the old initial trick, but "L.H." suggested a junior executive talking to his managing director. No, she'd have to

123

invent a name for him. That was, of course, if she was going to do much more talking to him, and there was no obvious reason why she should, not now that he had found her father for her. Or nearly had.

3

They found him at the third try, in a street like the one that Dr. Salt lived in, but on the other side of the town. Mrs. Coleman, who owned and managed this nursing home, admitted at once that Mr. Culworth was one of her patients. She was very tall and thin, had blue hair and three enormous old-ivory teeth, and might have been a ladylike witch.

"I gather," she said, after taking them into her little office, "that you have already spoken to Dr. Lemmert."

"I have," said Dr. Salt briskly. "And I've told him that I'm taking over the case—at the request of Mr. Culworth's family. That's true, isn't it, Miss Culworth?"

"Yes, Dr. Salt," said Maggie, looking at him and not at Mrs. Coleman, who was really rather frightening.

"I'll have a look at Mr. Culworth. If I think he can stand a short journey across town, I shall take him to my place."

Mrs. Coleman made a hissing noise, as if about to call a demon cat, but then it appeared that she was merely feeling embarrassed. She was the victim of her respect for doctors. She knew that Dr. Lemmert hoped she would be able to keep Mr. Culworth there, but now here was another doctor, older and clearly a more powerful character, telling her he would take Mr. Culworth away. "Surely, Dr. Salt," she stammered, "all this is—well, very irregular, isn't it? I mean to say—"

But Dr. Salt cut in ruthlessly. "It's been very irregular from the first, Mrs. Coleman. Full of hanky-panky and hocus-pocus. Dr. Lemmert may possibly have covered himself, but you could soon be in a pickle. One wrong move now, and you may find you'll have to turn this nursing home into a boardinghouse. A respectable citizen, probably after being knocked out by a United Fabrics employee, is rushed here, kept under sedation, his family not notified—"

"But—but—but—" Mrs. Coleman was so obviously alarmed now that Maggie couldn't help feeling sorry for her. "Dr. Lemmert told me—quite distinctly told me—he would take all responsibility—*all* responsibility."

Dr. Salt said nothing. He picked up his bag and stared hard at the unhappy Mrs. Coleman.

"Very well, Dr. Salt," she said meekly. "I'll take you up to Mr. Culworth's room."

Dr. Salt looked at Maggie. "I'm afraid you'll have to wait, my dear. I must make sure your father can stand the excitement of being moved and seeing you. If you'd rather go—"

"No, of course not. I must wait."

"Be careful, then, if and when I bring him down. Embraces, kisses, tears—all right. But no questions, no reproaches, remember."

"Do you take me for a complete fool?" she began hotly.

"No, I don't, Maggie. But don't forget you'll be under some emotional stress." Then he smiled—it was a real smile, not a grin—and it almost startled her. "I really am trying to do my best for the Culworths. It's not all Noreen Wilks. Right, Mrs. Coleman—lead on."

Maggie sat waiting in a mental muddle that was even worse than the physical muddle in Dr. Salt's sitting room, which she remembered denouncing with some embarrassment now. Even if he *had* taken her for a complete fool, and she realized he hadn't, he had every excuse because she kept behaving like one, suddenly shouting at him when he was doing everything possible to help her. Without him she would have been hanging about Birkden, wondering what on earth to do next.

She had just finished reproaching herself when Mrs. Coleman came back. Free of Dr. Salt, Mrs. Coleman was her grander self again. Maggie was only another young woman, and Mrs. Coleman had no respect for young women. Maggie saw this at once as soon as Mrs. Coleman entered.

"Dr. Salt has examined your father, Miss Culworth," she announced from some remote height, perhaps an icy peak in the Andes, "and has decided he can be moved at once. Of course, I accept no further responsibility. The case is now entirely out of my hands. You understand that, Miss Culworth?"

"Of course. What's happening now?"

"I believe that Dr. Salt is helping your father to dress." Now behind her desk, Mrs. Coleman moved some papers about in a vaguely important manner. "And as I'm busy here and may have to make some private telephone calls, Miss Culworth, I must ask you to wait for them outside in the hall."

"Certainly. Good afternoon." And off Miss Culworth went, to hang about the hall, which was painted a sad brown and had a smell of ether or something and cottage pie or something. It had a lift by the stairs, and after a couple of minutes or so she heard the lift coming down and braced herself to meet her father. But it was only a fattish middle-aged nurse, who stepped out, looked at her severely and said, "Quite useless you waiting. Mrs. Gore doesn't feel up to seeing anybody this afternoon."

"I'm not waiting to see Mrs. Gore. I don't know Mrs. Gore."

"That's what you said the last time. And then you tried to get into her room."

"Oh, don't be silly."

"Manners," said the nurse sharply. "I shall speak to Mrs. Coleman." And she made for the office, her back quivering with indignation.

This ridiculous encounter made Maggie feel for a moment what some admired new novelists and playwrights seemed to feel all the time—that things in general were slipping out of all reasonable control, that rational cause and effect had been mysteriously suspended, that life was drifting into idiocy and chaos. And then while she was still entertaining such thoughts and still staring in the direction of the office door, she heard her name cried from the stairs. Dr. Salt was slowly coming down, carrying his own bag and her father's suitcase, and behind him, with a hand on his shoulder for support, was her father, hollow of eye and cheek, shockingly older.

"Oh, Daddy!" And then she was crying, close to him, and he seemed to be crying a little too. And Dr. Salt left them together, going ahead to put the bags into the car, and then she helped her father, who was very shaky, like a very old man, out through the front door, down the steps towards the car.

"Mustn't talk much yet, Dr. Salt says, Maggie."

"I know. Just don't bother about it, Daddy."

"Different from the other chap, this Dr. Salt," he said with an obvious effort. "Friend of yours—is he—Maggie?"

"Yes—yes. And he'll look after you."

"We'll have you taking it easy in the back, Mr. Culworth," said Dr. Salt. "I'll drive slowly so that you aren't bouncing about."

He did too, and before they arrived at his flat Maggie found that her father had fallen asleep.

4

After Maggie had spent about ten minutes restoring some of the books to what she hoped were their original piles, Dr. Salt came back. "Your father's in bed and quite comfortable, and you can go along now and have a word with him. But you mustn't stay, Maggie, and I'll explain why." He gave her a long, serious look.

"Well, go on." She was rather short with him because she couldn't help feeling she ought to have been fussing over her father and not sorting out Dr. Salt's books.

"He won't rest properly until he's told his story. He's not up to telling it to you—or your brother. He's emotionally involved with you. Now, he isn't with me. Moreover, I've let him know that his story won't come as a surprise to me because I'm acquainted with some of it already. So he wants to confide in me first, and then, when his mind is easier and a mild sedative has sent him to sleep, he wants me to explain to you and Alan. This is his idea, not mine, but medically I approve of it. So after you've had a word with him, Maggie, try to phone your brother, tell him what's happened, and ask him to come here as soon as he can. There's nothing urgent and desperate about it, but the sooner he joins you here, the better. All right?"

"Yes, I suppose so." Then, ashamed of her dubious, grudging tone, she continued: "Yes, of course it is. Poor Daddy—he must be feeling terribly guilty about something. Well, I won't stay more than half a minute, then I'll try to phone Alan, do some more tidying up and make some tea. Or couldn't I make it now and take some in for you both?"

"Do that, Maggie. He's in the little spare room and it's through my bedroom. And don't imagine it's full of books, records and assorted junk, because it's neat and clean as a pin. Tea then, quick as you can, girl." And he went off to rejoin her father while she began threading her way through the books and records towards the kitchen.

After filling the largest cup she could find for her own share, she took the tray through Dr. Salt's bedroom, which contained a huge double bed that cried out for another woman to share it, and deliberately made a noisy approach to the spare room, so that any embarrassing confidences might be halted.

"Tea—tea," she cried as she entered. "And it's very good tea too—just the kind you like, Daddy."

He produced a rather tired smile for her. "Wonderful, Maggie. But haven't you given yourself any?"

"About a pint, in the biggest cup I've ever used. I'll be drinking it while I'm trying to get Alan on the phone. You know what a business *that* can be." She was all very gay, but it was rather a heartbreaking pretense. Her father looked better than he had in the nursing home, but it was still as if about fifteen years had fallen on him during the last four days.

128

"And your mother, Maggie—what about her?" There were those extra fifteen years in his voice now.

"Well, naturally she's been very worried. But I've explained to her that Dr. Salt was helping us to find you. She doesn't know him, of course, but she perked up at once just because we had a doctor on the job now."

"Dr. Salt says I ought to be able to see her in the morning—but there are difficulties."

"Nothing that Maggie and I can't settle," Dr. Salt cut in cheerfully. "Leave that to us. And now you pop off, Maggie. You've work to do."

"I know, I know. And what an orderer-about *you* can be! Well, Daddy—" And she pressed her cheek to his, and he clung to her for a moment, then she hurried out before she began bawling again.

There was the usual fuss about finding Alan at the university and getting him to the telephone. As soon as he heard her voice, he began grumbling, telling her she knew very well he hated being rung up there.

"Oh, shut up, Alan. This is important. Dr. Salt's found Daddy, and now he's here, in Dr. Salt's flat."

"What happened to him?"

"I don't know all the details yet. But Dr. Salt wants you to come here as soon as you can. Daddy's telling Dr. Salt the whole story, and then he wants Dr. Salt to tell us."

"Why can't he tell us himself? There seems to me a lot too much Dr. Salt in all this."

"My God, you really are the end, Alan." She was furious. "Daddy's here because Dr. Salt found him for us, when you and I hadn't a clue. Where did you think you were going to find him —in Jill Thing's bed?"

"Turn that up, Mag."

"Well, you turn up your 'too much Dr. Salt.' Daddy's still very shaky—and looks awful. After all, he was knocked out and then taken to a nursing home and filled full of dope. He's in a highly emotional state and must explain to somebody."

"What about us, then? You're his daughter. I'm his son."

"Oh, don't be so stupid. I keep telling you he's still weak and shaky, and so he doesn't feel ready yet to explain everything to us. But he has to tell *somebody*, to get it out of his system, and the obvious person is the doctor who's now looking after him— Dr. Salt. So what time can you be here?"

"About six, I suppose." Alan's voice still had a grumbling tone.

"All right, then. I'll tell Dr. Salt. And I warn you, Alan, that if you're hostile or sulky, I'll be furious. You may be against Dr. Salt—chiefly because he made your Jill Thing look silly—and I'll admit his mixture of the offhand and the bossy doesn't charm me, but the fact remains that in one day he's found our father for us, when we'd have been wandering around for weeks with our mouths wide open. So for God's sake, try to look and sound a little grateful. He's a lot cleverer than we are. And if he suddenly decided he'd had enough of us, we might find ourselves still in a mess."

"Why should we?"

"Because there's still this sinister Noreen Wilks business— and Daddy's up to his neck in that, don't forget. And there's Mother. She'll have to be told something, probably tomorrow. Dr. Salt can do it. Can we? I'd be bad and you'd be worse. So just try to forget Jill Thing for an hour or two, and be nice to Dr. Salt."

"Right, Mag. Do my best. Must go now."

Maggie tried to finish her tea, but now it was cold, and she returned the giant cup to the kitchen. Then she set to work again on the toppling piles of books and records.

TEN

1

It was about five o'clock when the three young men walked in. Twenty minutes earlier, Dr. Salt had returned from the spare room, carrying the tea tray, and had told Maggie that her father had told his story and had then needed only one mild pill to send him to sleep. "I doubt if he'll wake up much before breakfast time," Dr. Salt had continued. "When he'll probably feel hungry. He wants to sleep now, to take a rest from reality. I won't tell you his story until your brother comes. He *is* coming, isn't he? Good."

"I'll only ask you this," Maggie had said. "Is it—something really disgraceful—shocking?"

"It didn't give me a shock," Dr. Salt had said cheerfully. "And if you're the sensible girl I take you to be, Maggie, it won't give you one. I can't answer for your brother. You've been tackling the books and records, haven't you? I'm getting damnably behindhand. So let's keep at it."

Having just piled some special records on his desk, at the far end of the room, they were still standing near it when the three young men, having found the front door open, walked in at the other end. Maggie felt afraid as soon as she saw them. One, who seemed to be the leader, wore dark glasses and a leather jacket. Another, very big but quite young, was wearing a dark-blue sweater, dirty flannel trousers and what looked like gym shoes. The third was much smaller and rather older; he had a tight black suit and a thin and beaky face; pale and vicious. Maggie knew at once they were horrors. Even before anything was said, she took a step nearer to Dr. Salt.

"Well," said the one with dark glasses, "if he hasn't got a bird. Made it yet, doc?"

"And while I've seen better," said the big one, coming farther in, "I've seen worse. So if you're looking for anything young and fresh—what about it, birdie?"

"He'll never be any use to you," the black-suited one sneered, as he too came forward. "Too many bloody books." And he aimed a kick at the nearest pile and demolished it.

Maggie cried out and put a hand on Dr. Salt's arm.

"It's all right," he told her quietly. "Take it easy, Maggie." Then he moved to open one of the drawers in his desk.

"You won't be told, will you, Dr. Salt?" said the one with dark glasses. "And you can't say I didn't warn you. Remember, you're redundant now, so you can be roughed up a bit."

"I don't think you'll do anything to me, Russ," Dr. Salt told him, quite coolly, almost pleasantly.

"I'm afraid we'll have to. These boys love it. And they don't like your attitude. You see, doc, though you don't like Birkden, you won't leave it when you're told. But your bird can take off."

"Aw, Russ boy—don't I have any playtime?" This was the big one.

"She isn't going," said Dr. Salt, rather sharper now. "But you are. For two reasons."

"Shove your reasons," said the black-suited one. He turned to the one called Russ. "Let's shut him up."

"Not yet," Russ told him. "Let's see how he talks his way out of this. Go on, doc. Two reasons?"

"Yes. The first is, I've an appointment here with Superintendent Hurst at five o'clock. And it's a minute or two past five now. So he'll be here any time now."

"That's your story. And I think it's a load of crap. Anything else?"

"Aw, for chrissake, Russ—let's knock the shit out of him." And the big one came nearer.

But Dr. Salt, who had taken something out of his desk drawer, now moved around to stand in front of Maggie. "The other reason is this," he said, sounding not at all frightened and even rather amused. "It looks like a water pistol. But in point of fact, it's filled with telluric acid. A little idea of my own—I'm thinking of patenting it. Telluric acid not only burns the skin but also stains what's left of it a dark purple. Now three of you can obviously overpower me. But *one* of you—the first man—will have a face like a squashed black grape. And I advise him to keep his eyes tightly closed. Naturally I've never tried this stuff on the human eye, but I'm afraid the result will be very unpleasant indeed. Of course, it won't be easy to rush me with your eyes shut." He moved forward, well in front of the desk now. "You have your dark glasses to protect you, Russ. So if anybody's going to risk it, then it ought to be you."

"Him or nobody," said black-suit. "Not me."

"Nor me." This was the big one. "I didn't reckon on this packet."

"He could be bluffing," said Russ slowly.

"Okay, Russ. Have a go—an' see."

"Mind you," Dr. Salt told them in a brisk and cheerful manner, as if giving a lecture. "The acid might easily burn through the frame of the dark glasses, then the eyes wouldn't be protected. In any case, Russ, your cheeks, nose, mouth—especially the mouth—will be badly burned."

"I hate to see this patronizing sod get away with it," Russ cried. "Look—we could rush him with our hands stretched out, covering our faces."

"An' what happens to our hands, for chrissakes?"

"A sensible question," said Dr. Salt. "I'd hope to hit four out of your six hands. And those four wouldn't be picking anything up for a good many weeks—probably months. I don't know what you two are being paid for this—I'm leaving out Russ now —but I think you'll be badly out of pocket."

"An' so do I," said black-suit. "You think you're bloody smart, Russ, but you'd be smarter if you got some proper info before doing a job."

"Right," said the big one. "You said it would be dead easy."

"I'm afraid he's been deceiving you. Don't forget—for twenty years I've had to look at things that would make you boys go and vomit."

"An' I'll bet you have, at that. The deal's off, Russ."

"You stop an' play with him," said the big one. "Not me."

There was a knock. "Come in, Superintendent," Dr. Salt called cheerfully. Then a large middle-aged man filled the doorway. "Sorry I'm late, Dr. Salt," he began. "Hello, who are these?"

"Callers," Dr. Salt told him.

The superintendent looked them over. "And not invited neither, if you ask me. Villains or layabouts. Well?" he bawled at the one in the black suit.

"We're not doing nothing, Super. Honest."

"Are you charging them, Dr. Salt?"

"No, no."

"Sure? All right, if you say so." He cleared the doorway for them, then shouted, "Outside! Sharp as you can. And straight home. *Go on.*" They left hurriedly and he closed the door behind them. "You don't want to be soft-hearted with that sort, Dr. Salt."

"Superintendent Hurst—Miss Culworth. You all right, Maggie?"

"Now I am. But I must sit down. My knees were like jelly when you were talking to those three."

134

"Sit over there." He turned to the superintendent, who had now come closer. "No, I don't want to charge them. And not because I'm soft-hearted, but simply because I don't want to be kept hanging about as a witness."

"Would you have burnt their faces or hands?" Maggie inquired. "I mean if they'd attacked you."

"Not with this I wouldn't. It's a water pistol I took from a small boy at my surgery a week or two ago." He squirted a little water at the floor. "Must try to remember to return it to him. Well, Superintendent, I must find a chair for you."

"Don't bother, Dr. Salt. We had this appointment, so I looked in, but I'm not staying."

Dr. Salt frowned at him. "I've been busy since we last met. And everything that's happened points one way. I'm certain now that Noreen Wilks never left Birkden, that she's dead and that her death was no accident."

"Now, now, now, Dr. Salt, I told you to leave it to us, didn't I? If you've been busy trying to find out about this Noreen Wilks, then I'm afraid you've been wasting your time. No, just a minute. Can I use your phone?"

"Of course. But I wish you'd listen to what I have to say."

"I'm trying to save your breath, Dr. Salt. And your face, perhaps." He was now at the telephone, dialing. "Superintendent Hurst here. Anything come through for me from Comdon Bridge yet? Yes, Wilks inquiry. Well, you might give them a tinkle. It was a Sergeant Driver who was looking into it for me. No, I'm coming straight down myself."

He looked across at Dr. Salt as he put down the receiver. "Will you be here the next hour or two? Right, then. As soon as I have this information I need, I won't just phone you, Dr. Salt, I'll come back here and tell you straight to your face exactly what we know about your Noreen Wilks. No, no, I don't want any argument. And I don't think you will—very soon. But I'll be back—I'll be back. And don't bother, I can let myself out." And he bustled off.

"And that's that," Dr. Salt observed darkly. "I don't dislike Hurst. He's a good, honest bobby. But he's looking too pleased with himself. And if I know his type, that means he's getting himself into something damn stupid."

"I'm thinking about you, not him. You're really entitled to feel pleased with yourself. I thought you were wonderful with those three horrors," she continued rather shyly. "You're very brave, aren't you?"

"Not at all. No bravery required. Just cheek. But that reminds me. I must ring up our friend Buzzy. By the way, would you like a drink?"

"I would, but I think it's too early."

"No, that excitement makes it later. I think you need one, Maggie. Doctor's orders. Help yourself to a drink while I'm calling Buzzy."

While she was finding the gin and tonic in the kitchen, she could hear him at the telephone. Apparently Buzzy wasn't there. "All right, then, Winston. Give him a message from me, Dr. Salt. Tell him I've had that chap I mentioned the other day —Russ—round here making a nuisance of himself again. So I'd be obliged if Buzzy could have him run out of town. . . . Yes, that's it—*seen off*. And I'll be here for some time if Buzzy wants to call me. Thank you, Winston."

He was attending to the pile of books that had been kicked over, when she returned with her drink. "We'll get on with this until your brother comes," he told her. "We can also be thinking about dinner. I don't mean cooking it but planning it. Something good that doesn't take too much time and fiddling about. That means the Far East is out. But one day I'll cook you a Chinese dinner that'll astonish you, Maggie."

Still squatting among the books, he looked up and gave her a wide grin. Hardly knowing what she was up to, she said, "I hope so, Salt," and bending down quickly, she gave him a brief light kiss somewhere just below his right eye.

"I still can't see," said Alan as soon as the three of them had settled down, "why my father couldn't have waited and then told us himself." And he gave Dr. Salt a defiant look, for which Maggie could have slapped him.

"Try using your imagination," said Dr. Salt. "Start by imagining yourself a man in his late fifties, far from robust, bewildered, worried, loaded with a guilty secret like a rucksack full of lead. Right?"

"Oh, Alan—I did explain," Maggie began.

"Next, you're knocked out and then wake up all dopey in a strange nursing home. Before you can make sense of anything, you're out again. But you're just as full of worry and feelings of guilt as you are of sedatives. Finally, you're taken out of this nursing home by another doctor—and your daughter's with him."

"And he must tell somebody," cried Maggie, "but he can't face telling you or me—not yet. Alan, you're deliberately being stupid."

"All right, then," said Alan, impatient rather than convinced. "Let's say it had to be done this way. Go on, Dr. Salt. What's the great and terrible secret?"

"Well, it won't be one to you—or to Maggie—but I want you to remember that it is one to him. And might be to your mother if she ever found it out. And you two can't afford to take it lightly, not only for your parents' sake but also because it could easily become entangled with a murder—"

"Oh, no!" And as Maggie, horrified, cried out, she couldn't help feeling that somewhere, at the back of her mind, she had known this all along.

"Is that a fact or just your opinion?" Alan looked and sounded skeptical.

"So far, just my opinion," said Dr. Salt quite mildly. "But

during the last two days, as Maggie realizes even if you don't, several of my opinions have turned into facts."

"And if they hadn't, Alan, we'd still be wondering what had happened to our father. What's the matter with you?"

"Nothing, Mag. I'm not trying to be offensive. I just thought the murder thing a bit much, that's all."

"Quite so. And I'm not taking offense, Alan. Now then," Dr. Salt continued briskly, "I'm leaving out all details, accusations or excuses, mental lights and shades, and just giving you what you want—the facts. During the war, as you know, your father was some sort of clerk, with the rank of sergeant, in the RAF. He fell in love and had an affair with a girl in the WRAF. She was a young and childless widow whose husband, a rear gunner of a bomber, had been killed early in 1940. Her name was Catherine Wilks. I came to know her fairly well because she ended up as a patient of mine. She only died a year ago—cancer. She had a daughter, Noreen, and from the first your father regarded her as his child."

"So that's it," cried Maggie. "And I think I've really known it all the time. Haven't you, Alan?"

"No, I haven't. I've been divided between thinking there was nothing at all in this Noreen Wilks thing or that she was his girl friend. I discussed it last night with Jill, though, and she was dead against the girl friend theory."

"And she's really my half-sister," said Maggie, remembering how she had resented this Noreen Wilks character that Dr. Salt had kept dragging in all the time. Now she looked at him. "I'm sorry. Go on."

"When your father settled in Hemton after the war, Mrs. Wilks came to Birkden and finally got a job at United Fabrics, which was then beginning to expand. I don't know if this was his idea or hers. I don't know if the affair went on or whether he simply felt responsible for her and the child. My guess is he'd still feel responsible for her even if he knew—or guessed—she was having affairs with other men. And I'd say she was. He couldn't spend much time with her. She must have been quite attractive up to her last few years. And I'd say she was one of those rather vain, shallow but good-natured women who enjoy men's attention and then don't like to refuse them anything. Probably your father lost all interest in her—they can't have had much in common—but of course he felt deeply responsible for Noreen. He gave Mrs. Wilks a regular allowance, of course, and that can't have been easy."

"Alan, that's why we've always thought he was so ridiculously cautious and careful about money—almost mean."

"I know, I know," Alan told her gruffly. "You're not the only one who's working it out."

"Then when Mrs. Wilks died and Noreen was on her own, he felt even more responsible and worried harder than ever. I know that because I've read several letters he wrote to her that arrived after she was missing. I called on Mrs. Pearson, her landlady, this morning, and she handed them over to me, along with some notes from her boyfriend that Noreen had kept."

"Well, I don't see why you should have read those letters my father wrote to her. Does he know?" Alan's tone seemed to Maggie unpleasantly hostile, and she felt fearful of what might happen next.

"No, he doesn't know, Alan. And I don't propose to tell him." Once again Maggie marveled at the way in which Dr. Salt, unlike almost everybody she had ever known, was able to avoid returning hostility with hostility, for he spoke quite mildly.

"Then, if you ask me, I think you've been nosy and officious." And Alan gave him a hard, challenging look.

"Alan—no!"

"It's all right, Maggie. I'm sorry you think that, Alan. But I want you to remember this. I'm not interested in your father's private life, except that, for the moment, I consider him my patient. What I really *am* concerned about—and if it's boring to hear this again, just put up with me for a moment—and what keeps me here in Birkden when I want to get out of the place, is simply the answer to one question: What really happened to Noreen Wilks? That's what I want to know, and it's what I'm going to find out, even if it means reading other people's letters and taking a few assorted risks."

"Were those three horrible young men part of it?" Maggie demanded.

"Of course. It was Russ's second attempt to frighten me out of Birkden. Look, Alan, there's more in this than you seem to understand."

"He doesn't want to, that's why," Maggie cried. "That girl, Jill—"

"Shut up, Mag. Jill doesn't come into this."

"She does. Of course she does. She's one of that lot—"

"Let it ride, Maggie," said Dr. Salt. He regarded Alan gravely. "I'm sure that Noreen Wilks is dead. And I'm almost sure now that she was murdered. But let's get back to your father. When she didn't reply to his letters, he wrote to Peggy Pearson. She rang him at the shop on Monday morning, telling him she thought Noreen didn't come back from the Fabrics Club party on September twelfth because she'd gone to the south of France with her boyfriend. Peggy didn't know who this boyfriend was, but your father did—Noreen must have told him. He was young Derek Donnington, who shot himself early in the morning of September thirteenth. So what had happened to Noreen, missing for three weeks? Your father couldn't find Peggy or her mother, so finally he went to the Fabrics Club. He got no sense out of them, as you can imagine, so then he decided to search the big empty house, the Worsley place, which shares the same grounds as the club. It was dark by that time. Before he got to the house he ran into the man who was looking after it—and was also half drunk, your father thinks. They exchanged some angry remarks. Your father tried to push past the man, who coshed him. I doubt if it was a heavy blow, but your father wasn't wearing a hat, he hasn't a thick skull and, anyhow, he isn't a robust type. He went out like a light and stayed out. We can guess the rest. He was taken into the club; Dews sent for Dr. Lemmert, who afterwards spoke to Aricson, who in turn— though I can't prove this—told Sir Arnold Donnington what had happened. Then your father was rushed off to a nursing home, with the firm or Donnington himself ready to pay all expenses. And if you want to know why, I'll tell you. This man —your father—wasn't just a casual trespasser. He was some- body *who was asking questions about Noreen Wilks.* Therefore —no hospital, no police, no public fuss." He stopped to light his pipe.

Alan looked dubious. "What you're really asking us to believe is that Noreen Wilks may have been killed, and that somebody high up in United Fabrics may be involved. And I must say, I can't wear it. I'll agree there's something queer and fishy about this Noreen Wilks thing—Jill knows that, and what happened at the club last night was very suspicious—but it seems to me you're jumping wildly to conclusions, Dr. Salt."

"I agree there doesn't seem much real proof yet," said Mag- gie, glancing apologetically at Dr. Salt before she looked at Alan again. "But I've seen a lot more of this mysterious business than you have, Alan, and so far Dr. Salt's been right every time. Last night—and this morning—we hadn't the ghost of an idea where Father was, but Dr. Salt found him. It may be some kind of intuition."

"No, it isn't, Maggie," he told her. "It's just that I'm used to watching people very carefully and listening intently to them, and then drawing my own conclusions. And I've also spent years dealing with people who aren't so obvious as we are. That's all." Now he looked at Alan. "But there isn't as much wild jumping to conclusions as you think. I've collected plenty of my own kind of evidence, though so far it wouldn't be worth tup- pence as legal proof. If I haven't given it all to you two, that's because I'm waiting to give it to Superintendent Hurst when he comes back."

"Do you want us out of the way then?" asked Maggie, hoping hard that he didn't.

"No, I want you here. I need witnesses. And if Hurst objects —and he easily might—I'll make a fuss. But I propose to keep your father out of it."

"Oh, thank goodness!"

"That's what I say, Mag." Alan wagged a finger at her. "So don't forget and then drag him in yourself. Better just keep quiet."

"And I think it's about time you kept quiet," she told him indignantly. "Ever since you came you've behaved as if Dr. Salt had gone and lost Daddy and not found him for us. You don't know half of what's happened, where Dr. Salt has been and what he's done since you saw him last, and then you stalk in here and say you don't believe this and you doubt that—as if you were some pompous silly old judge. And that's all you have done so far." And she nearly added something about his precious Jill, but checked herself in time.

She was instantly rewarded. Alan gave her one of his rare sweet smiles. "You're quite right, Mag. I've been a bit much. Would you like an apology, Dr. Salt?"

"No, thanks, Alan. Apologies don't work. By the time people have made 'em, they're beginning to resent you all over again. Hello—this must be Hurst. Could one of you clear another chair for him?"

3

Maggie knew at once that Superintendent Hurst was feeling very pleased with himself. As soon as he had been introduced to Alan and given a chair large enough for him, he looked as if he might be about to start purring. "Now, Dr. Salt, before I tell you what we've done, I wish you'd repeat, word for word, what you said about Noreen Wilks when I called earlier. D'you mind?"

"Not at all. I told you I'm certain now that Noreen Wilks never left Birkden, that she's dead and that her death was no accident."

"Thank you, doctor. That's what I thought you said. You've been making your inquiries, I suppose, and they've brought you to that conclusion—eh? And a very serious conclusion, I think you'd agree—eh?"

"Of course. And I hope you'd like me to explain how I arrived at it."

"Not till you've heard the result of our inquiries. Because we haven't been idle, you know, Dr. Salt. You'll remember I promised on Tuesday morning we'd start making inquiries. These included informing all the police in our area, borough and county that the girl was missing. Now—do you happen to know Comdon Bridge?"

"I know roughly where it is, that's all."

"Quite so. Between here and Birmingham—and nearer Birmingham. Oldish town but all industrial—dozens of small metal works. By the way, do you want Miss Culworth and her brother to hear all this?"

"Yes, if you don't mind, Superintendent. They're related to Noreen Wilks."

"Oh—well, they'll be glad to hear what I have to say." He twinkled round at Maggie and Alan. "You must have been down in the dumps listening to what Dr. Salt had to tell you. And I did warn him against trying any amateur detective work. He probably reads too many of these detective-story books. Eh, Dr. Salt?"

"I read very few." Dr. Salt looked at him steadily. "But what's happened at Comdon Bridge to make you feel so delighted with yourself?"

"Well," Hurst began, pulling out and opening a notebook. "It's where Noreen Wilks went on the morning of September

143

thirteenth. She stayed there a couple of weeks and then left for London. And it's just about what I told you she'd do, when we were talking on Tuesday morning. Another of these little fly-by-nights, I said to you. Remember?"

"Certainly. And I said you were wrong. I still think you're wrong."

"And I don't think—I *know* you're wrong, doctor. She *did* leave Birkden and she *isn't dead.* And we're not guessing. We have evidence." He looked at his notebook. "She stayed about ten days with a Mrs. Duffy at 86 Gladstone Street, Comdon Bridge. And then she went to London. Mrs. Duffy says so. Her daughter, Rose, says so. And her brother, Michael Corrigan, says so. And I've had all this, over the phone, from a Sergeant Driver, who's interviewed all three of 'em. So there you are, Dr. Salt."

Maggie noticed Alan giving her an I-told-you-so look, making her feel almost sorry that the wretched Noreen Wilks, though now apparently her stepsister, was still alive. But though Dr. Salt ought to have been feeling crushed—and the superintendent's manner was meant to be crushing—quite clearly he wasn't.

"I'm sorry, Superintendent, but I don't believe it."

"Calling me a liar?"

"No, of course not. Neither you nor the Comdon Bridge sergeant. It's those three in Gladstone Street I don't believe. How did they come to volunteer this information? The Comdon Bridge police can't have been advertising Noreen's disappearance. They can't have been calling at every house asking about her. So what happened?"

"That's a fair enough doubt, coming from a member of the public, doctor. But, you see, as soon as we've put out an inquiry of this sort—especially if it concerns a young girl—it soon gets around. You don't need any advertising or house-to-house calls. The men on their beats say something, perhaps ask a question or two, and then all the Nosey Parkers and gossips know about it. I've known it happen dozens of times. So don't think there's anything suspicious about this lot coming up with their information."

"Well, I'll believe them after I've talked to them—and not before."

"My word, but you're obstinate, Dr. Salt. If you think she's dead, nobody can tell you she's alive."

"Something in that," Alan murmured.

Dr. Salt ignored him. "Now look, Superintendent. I've not set myself up as an investigator, and I'm not enjoying this Noreen Wilks business. I want to end it and go away." He waited for a moment but still looked at Hurst, large and complacent, half smiling. "Do me a favor, Superintendent. No—two favors. For your own sake as well as mine. I want to talk to those people now—as soon as I can—so will you please ring up Comdon Bridge, see if this Sergeant Driver is still on duty, and ask him to take me to call on those three? Next, I don't know what you're doing tonight—"

"One doubtful case of receiving and a breaking and entering. Why?"

"Because when I come back from Comdon Bridge, I'd like to ring you and ask you to come round here for a talk. But of course I'll only do that if I'm sure those people have been lying. Because that will mean I've something very serious to say to you. But if they've been telling the truth—and Noreen Wilks really *was* there—I'll let you know at once, over the phone, that I've been wrong all the time. If I haven't been, then you come here as soon as you can and listen to me. Two favors, please."

Hurst hesitated a moment, then nodded and lumbered across to the telephone. "Comdon Bridge? Superintendent Hurst here, Birkden Police. Is Sergeant Driver there?" There was a wait. "Sergeant Driver? There's a Dr. Salt here. That Noreen Wilks was his patient, so he wants to ask your three witnesses a few questions about her. I'd be obliged if you'd take him to see them. Good! He'll be with you as soon as he can. Take him what? About forty minutes? Right you are, then." He left the telephone to move towards the door, but he turned before he opened it. "I think you're wasting your time, Dr. Salt. But I'll be hearing from you later. Night, all!"

Alan was on his feet by the time the superintendent had left. "Jill insisted on giving me dinner tonight," he began.

"Oh, cooking for you already, is she?" said Maggie. "That usually comes a bit later, but of course you two are exceptionally fast workers."

"Shut up, Mag." He looked at Dr. Salt. "If my father's asleep, there's no point in my disturbing him. He's all right, isn't he? You're not worried about him?"

"Not now—no. He can probably go home tomorrow. But he'll have to take care of himself. Off you go, Alan."

"Well, I may be looking in later."

"Won't you be too busy?" Maggie inquired with mock sweetness.

"Drop it, for God's sake! I'm off, then." But he hesitated, ignoring Maggie now. "Doesn't it look as if all this fuss about Noreen Wilks—"

"No, it doesn't," Dr. Salt cut in sharply. "Not yet. I'll tell you later, if and when you come back." After Alan had mumbled something on his way out, Dr. Salt went closer to Maggie, who wondered what he was going to do. But he merely put a hand on her shoulder. "Maggie, I want you to come with me. I need a witness. I'm afraid it means no dinner for a long time."

"I don't care about that," Maggie told him rather breathlessly. "But what about my father?"

"We'll make sure he's asleep. And he'll be all right. After all, he's a grown man. Too old to need a baby-sitter. Too young to want a night nurse."

"Very witty, Dr. Salt. But suppose that man Russ and his horrible chums came back?"

"Even if they did, they're not interested in your father. And this time I'll lock the door. And anyhow, they won't come back.

You go and take a peep at your father while I telephone our friend Buzzy."

Maggie found that Dr. Salt had already drawn the curtains in the room where her father was sleeping, and had switched on a heavily shaded standard lamp, well away from the bed. He must have done this, she realized, when the room was still in broad daylight, so that her father ran less risk of being disturbed. She crept to the bedside and stayed there several minutes, staring down at her father, who was sleeping peacefully. After telling herself that already he was looking much better, though in fact she could not see him very clearly, she began to wonder about him and that little secret life he had had, but more in compassion than in curiosity, and in the end she began to feel sad about him, about herself, about everybody. Was the best part of us—without doing anything wrong—forever sentenced to solitary confinement? She longed to talk about this to Dr. Salt, but could see little chance of doing so; he hated talking when he was driving and anyhow, he would be working away at this Noreen Wilks puzzle. But even if he were making a fool of himself about Noreen Wilks, being too clever and elaborate while the police were simply being sensible and realistic, he had found her father, and her father had immediately trusted him.

When she rejoined Dr. Salt, he had just finished telephoning. "Buzzy says that his boys have just seen off Russ. This sounds more sinister than it is. They haven't done anything to him—except to describe what they would do if he refused to go. We shan't see Russ again. Buzzy says he was being paid, to frighten me out of Birkden, by Aricson. Buzzy also sends his respects to you. I believe he thinks you're living here."

"And did you tell him I wasn't?"

"There wasn't time. I let it ride. Let's go, Maggie."

"No talk, I suppose?" said Maggie when they were in the car.

"Not much, if you don't mind, Maggie," he told her. "I want to get to Comdon Bridge as soon as I can, and there may still be a lot of heavy traffic on the road. Why—something on your mind?"

"Just a kind of large, vague sadness hanging over me."

"Your father's secret—his loneliness—your loneliness—all our lonelinesses—the human condition—um? Fair enough, but don't bother with it, not now. Ask yourself if I'm such a chump as Superintendent Hurst and your brother are telling themselves I am. But don't give me the answer. No more talk, I'm afraid."

Maggie tried to think about this Noreen Wilks puzzle, but soon gave it up. Cars were flashing and screaming at them. Lorries, looking gigantic in the dusk, lumbered past them or remained maddeningly in their way. Maggie had that feeling she often had when she was being driven, especially at this time of day, along a main road—as if everybody were fleeing in a panic, trying to escape from the threat of some appalling catastrophe, as if our whole civilization were really quite mad. And she had a great longing, which rather alarmed her, just to touch this man sitting beside her who, whatever anybody might say, was sane and real and so ready to be helpful, so quick to understand.

At the police station, she waited in the car while Dr. Salt went to find the sergeant. They were talking as they approached the car. "All I ask," Dr. Salt was saying, "is that you let me do it my way. However I look and behave, whatever I say, just let it pass, without any interruptions—um? Oh, Miss Culworth—Sergeant Driver. You can direct me from the back seat, sergeant. And don't sit on that old bag of mine."

"Not going to take their temperatures or listen to their hearts, are you, Dr. Salt?" the sergeant inquired humorously as he got in.

"I hope not. But I never go very far without my bag. I never know when it might be wanted."

"Quite right, doctor. And once we're there, I'll let you play it your way. I think we'll find 'em in, because they've just bought themselves a new telly."

"They have, have they? Well, well, well!" Dr. Salt started the car.

"Go straight on till you come to the lights," said the sergeant, who was a heavy, middle-aged man with a lot of chin and hardly any nose, which perhaps explained why he seemed to have some difficulty in breathing. "Then make a left turn and carry on till I tell you to make another turn—straight into Gladstone Street."

Comdon Bridge was the kind of smallish industrial town— and there were lots of them in the Midlands—that Maggie could never imagine herself enduring. It was like the nastier part of a city, from which there was no escape to any better part. The shopping street they were in now offered a panorama of illuminated rubbish. Gladstone Street looked exactly like Birkden's Olton Street, where Mrs. Pearson lived—and once, of course, Noreen Wilks.

"This is it, doctor—number 86. End house." As they got out of the car, Sergeant Driver continued: "They're in, all right. You can hear the telly. Now I'll go first, then explain who you are—and then leave it to you. Right?"

They were not enthusiastically welcomed. "Oh, not again, sarge, not again!" a man shouted above the noise of the sheriff's posse firing at the rustler. "We're trying to enjoy ourselves—just for once, just for once."

The three of them had been looking at their new television set, which was on top of a chest of drawers, all seated at a small table on which were several bottles of beer and stout and the smelly remains of a chips-and-fish supper. All three of them

149

looked hot and greasy, but while Mrs. Duffy and her daughter, Rose, were not merely plump but fat, Mr. Corrigan was thin and had an angry, inflamed face. Sergeant Driver, once he had had the television switched off, said to them, "We shan't keep you long. But this is Dr. Salt and his—er—secretary, Miss Culworth, and as Noreen Wilks was a patient of Dr. Salt's, he just wants to ask you a few questions." All three, sitting round the table again and leaving their visitors standing, nodded solemnly and looked important.

Even before he spoke, Maggie realized that Dr. Salt was going into his hopeful simpleton act again, offering them the apologetic smile that she hadn't seen since their visit to the Fabrics Club. "I'm very sorry to bother you—some of these Western serials are very good, aren't they? take you right out of yourself, don't they?—but, strictly for medical reasons, I must ask you a question or two about Noreen Wilks. That's not unreasonable, is it?"

"No, it isn't," said Mrs. Duffy, who looked rather like an enormous parrot. "Quite all right, doctor."

"Quite all right," said Mr. Corrigan, who still looked angry but contrived to sound polite but important, as if he might be a doctor himself. "And not unreasonable—no, no, not at all."

"Thank you, Mrs. Duffy, Mr. Corrigan. You see, Noreen had been a patient of mine for several years. She even insisted upon giving me a photograph of herself, and signing it too, like a film star, but not quite so grand, of course. 'Yours gratefully, Noreen.' Unusual, but very nice of her, I thought." And to Maggie's surprise, he handed over a postcard-size photograph.

"Nice—very nice," said Mr. Corrigan, after looking at it and then passing it to Mrs. Duffy. "And the spit image, I'd say—the spit image."

"No," said Mrs. Duffy, who now shared it with Rose. "It's a nice photo, but doesn't do her justice. Does it, Rose?"

"You need color for Noreen," said Rose, shaking her head so that her fat cheeks wobbled. "I'd know it was her, of course, but

150

she ought to be in color. Don't you think so, Uncle Mike?"

Uncle Mike wasn't sure. Color or no color, it remained a spit image.

"I agree with you, Mr. Corrigan," said Dr. Salt, smiling and holding out his hand for the photograph. "By the way, Mrs. Duffy, what made Noreen come here?"

"I can explain that right off. She wanted to get out of Birkden. And she knew me because me and her mother worked side by side for years at United Fabrics. I lived in Birkden then, of course. And if there's anything else you'd like to ask, doctor, don't hesitate. I know Noreen thought the world of you."

"There's just this," said Dr. Salt apologetically. "She was having some medicine from me that I told her she must take, without fail, night and morning. It wasn't pleasant to take, and you might have noticed it because it was a very unusual dark-green color—horrible-looking stuff, I'm afraid. But I'd like to think she was taking it regularly."

"Like clockwork," said Mrs. Duffy. "She kept it down here specially so we'd notice if she missed a dose. You remember that nasty green stuff, Rose, don't you?"

"Of course I do. The faces she pulled!" cried Rose. "And when I asked her why she bothered with it, she said she'd promised her doctor."

"That's right, quite right," said Mr. Corrigan. "She said that even if she was running off, she was going to carry out Dr. Salt's instructions."

"Oh, it was Dr. Salt this, Dr. Salt that, till I felt like telling her to shut up sometimes." This was Mrs. Duffy again, all nods and smiles. "But the time she was here, before she went to London, she must have got through a whole bottle of that nasty green medicine—poor girl. But I suppose it was doing her some good. She always said it was."

"If she said it to me once," Rose put in, "she said it a dozen times."

Dr. Salt turned to Sergeant Driver, and Maggie knew at once

that the simpleton act was over. "I see no point in going on with this, sergeant. There never was any such medicine. And the photograph they recognized at once was of a niece of mine who lives in Melbourne. Noreen Wilks never came here. They've never set eyes on her."

"They're all lying?"

"Of course they are."

"How d'you mean we're lying?" cried Corrigan belligerently, jumping up.

"You keep still and keep quiet," said Sergeant Driver. He turned to Dr. Salt. "But if they are, what's the idea?"

"Money." And Dr. Salt pointed to the television set. "A down payment on that came out of it."

"That's a dirty lie," Mrs. Duffy screamed. "Coming here and soft-soaping us—"

"And I'm not keeping quiet," Mr. Corrigan told the world, "when I'm called a liar."

"Corrigan, just listen to me," said Dr. Salt in his sharpest tone. And he moved a little, and then Maggie felt his hand on her arm, as if to give her some kind of warning. But he didn't look at her, only at Corrigan. "You're in a hell of a pickle, Corrigan. I'm now looking after the man you coshed on Monday night, outside the old Worsley place." Maggie felt the pressure on her arm again, and now she understood it. "He happens to have a thin skull and a bad heart. He might live—and he might die. It's touch and go, Corrigan."

"I didn't hit him so hard. How did I know he'd go out like that?"

"You bloody daft idiot!" Mrs. Duffy screeched at him. "Now you've done it."

"What is all this?" Sergeant Driver inquired severely.

"Honest to God, sarge—" began Corrigan.

"Let's go," Dr. Salt cut in sharply. "I can't waste any more time listening to these people. I must get back to Birkden. I'll drop you at the station, and explain everything on the way. Come on, man, let's go."

"Yes, go on, bugger off," cried Mrs. Duffy, the stout-hearted member of the trio. "Call yourself a doctor—coming and deceiving innocent people like that!" She may have enlarged on this topic, but they didn't stay to listen.

"I dislike talking while I'm driving, sergeant," said Dr. Salt when they were in the car. "So I'll be as brief as I can. I'm not interested in those people, only in Noreen Wilks. If you want to charge them, you won't get any help from me. They were bribed to tell that story. It hadn't to stand up as evidence in court. It was just a delaying tactic. Corrigan was the link with the Birkden end. I'll admit that was a lucky shot of mine, though it wasn't just a wild guess." He concentrated now on his driving; they were out of Gladstone Street and in the traffic again. Then he had to wait for a light.

"Corrigan had been employed as a caretaker-cum-watchman by United Fabrics. On Monday night he knocked a man out. He was probably afraid to stay, and anyhow was taken off the job. Somebody—and I think I know who it was—paid him to concoct that story about Noreen Wilks with his sister and niece. Noreen Wilks is dead, probably murdered."

"That's nothing to do with us, Dr. Salt," said Driver hastily. "You'll have to take that up with Superintendent Hurst of the Birkden Police."

"I know that," Dr. Salt told him, and then said no more until they were back at the police station. "All I ask you to do, sergeant—and I think you owe it to me—is to phone Superintendent Hurst, tell him what happened and remind him that he promised to come and listen to me if that story was proved to be false."

"Well, I can do that," said the sergeant rather dubiously. "But what kind of report I'm going to make out—"

"Don't make any report out. Forget it. Comdon Bridge is now

out of the picture. It's all bonny Birkden. Leave it to Hurst—
and to me."

"Well, doctor, I suppose you know what you're doing."

"Sometimes I do, sometimes I don't. But thank you very
much, Sergeant Driver. Sorry to bustle you like this, but I'm in
a hurry."

And he was in a hurry all the way back to his flat. Which
meant that he never spoke a word and Maggie was left to her
own thoughts, which she found very confusing indeed, almost
as if she were going at a mile a minute round and round a maze.

ELEVEN

1

As soon as they were back in the flat, Dr. Salt took Maggie to see her father. "I doubt if he's even moved since we last saw him," Dr. Salt told her as they left the room. "And he'll wake up in the morning twice the man he was this afternoon, you'll see. Now let's eat and drink."

She had a gin and tonic and he had a small neat whisky, and they stayed in the kitchen. "I'm famished, I warn you," said Maggie. "What have you got we can cook quickly?"

"I suggest spaghetti. And I've a little tin of stewing steak I can combine with it somehow. You do the spaghetti while I attend to the meat department."

"Please," she suggested.

"No, not 'please,' Maggie." He was good-humored but firm. "You've just said you're very hungry. It's going to be your dinner as well as mine. We're doing it together. So one of us doesn't have to say please to the other."

"Perhaps not. But does one of us have to sound so bossy—just giving curt orders?" She wasn't angry, but her tone was sharp. However, she wasn't looking at him but at the spaghetti.

"You're quite right. It's living alone so long—being a doctor too, giving curt orders because you're so often pressed for time. Now where's the tin opener?"

"I noticed it somewhere. Oh, there—look. You don't like living out of tins, do you?"

"Of course I don't. But there again, it's living alone and being a doctor. I couldn't go shopping because I was always busy with patients. And as soon as I had a little free time, the shops were all closed. It's one reason—and there are plenty of others—I'll be glad to get out of this country. Most of its arrangements are dead against people who do any real work. Everything, from the tax system downwards, is in favor of betting men and lay-abouts. It's turning into a dreamy country with a bad climate. Lazy long-haired young men, not lolling in the sunshine but snarling in the rain."

"I know." She waited until she had filled the pan with water. "But is it any better anywhere else?"

"I'm going to see. There are disadvantages and drawbacks everywhere, and it's a question of adding and then subtracting them from the advantages."

"I don't think my mind works like that."

"Neither does mine, in the last resort. I've an onion some-where. We need one for this stewing steak—no flavor. That's another thing now about life here. Not enough flavor. No onion. I'm talking about people like us, not about people who still live in delightful old country houses with a few devoted old retain-ers."

"I wouldn't know how to behave to devoted old retainers, even if I had any."

"Neither would I, Maggie. What about that man you were in love with in London?"

"Who told you about him?" She turned to stare at him.

"Nobody. I was just guessing. But we don't have to talk about him."

"We're not going to. Have you any cooking salt? Oh, yes, I

see. I'll tell you about him one day." Then she checked herself abruptly, and they hardly spoke again until they were ready to sit down.

"There's a touch of cheese and some fruit," he said cheerfully. "So it'll be something like a meal. I ought to have some wine for you, but I've been too busy to buy any. More gin?"

"No, just water, thank you. I think you've been rather clever with that boring meat. And I'm going to have a great fattening helping of this pasta."

A few minutes later, he began, "Now—about Noreen Wilks—"

"Oh, dear! You never stop, do you, Salt? We were being so cozy. I wanted to forget about her, just for a little while, even if she is—or was—my stepsister."

"That's the point, Maggie. I doubt if she was."

Her fork never reached her mouth as she stared at him. "You mean it was some other man—not my father?"

"Yes. I can't prove it. But I've remembered something Mrs. Wilks once said. And now that I've seen your father, I doubt if Noreen was his child. She wasn't like her mother—quite a different type physically—and so I assumed that her father's strain was strong in her, as often happens with daughters. You are obviously your father's daughter, for example. But Noreen didn't resemble your father—or you—at all. She suggested quite a different strain, entirely different from you Culworths. And from what I knew of Mrs. Wilks, I can easily believe she had a night or two with some dashing young pilot. It was never easy for her to say no, and it must have been particularly hard then, when so many of them flew away and never came back. No, Maggie, I don't think Noreen was your half-sister."

"Are you going to tell my father?"

"I don't know. What do you think?"

"Dr. Salt, don't tell me you're actually asking for my advice?"

"Why shouldn't I? I've never pretended to know everything, have I?"

"Not everything, perhaps—but almost."

"Nonsense! I'm not that kind of man at all."

"Aren't you?" She laughed at him.

"Certainly not. It just happened that you walked into the middle of something that I knew a little about and you knew nothing. It might easily have been all the other way round."

"I can't imagine it—unless it was something like making clothes. And even then you'd probably turn up with some strong opinions and a few sharp orders. No, listen—I'll be serious now. I think my father ought to be told, but perhaps not just yet. What worries me is what we're going to tell my mother—tomorrow morning too."

"Leave that to me. You must bring her here yourself, then you can listen carefully to what I'll tell her."

"Which won't be the truth."

"Do you want it to be the truth?"

"No, I don't," she said. "But I thought you might."

"A doctor learns to be very careful with the truth. Not everybody is ready for it."

"But do you enjoy lying?"

He gave her a grin. "Not much, though I'm pretty good at it."

"On the whole, you're rather pleased with yourself, aren't you?" It was not an attack; she said it lightly.

Nevertheless, he gave it a moment's serious consideration. "Not specially, I think. But I'm tired of that gentlemanly English modesty which often covers conceit a mile thick. I prefer men who seem to be more pleased with themselves than they really are."

"What about women?"

"Women too. I like women, but I don't like English ladies—not that I've seen very much of 'em. Do you feel like helping me to clear and then wash up, Maggie?"

They had just finished when Alan and Jill arrived. "I thought you wouldn't mind Jill coming along," said Alan. "I wanted to know about my father."

"I imagine he's still asleep," Dr. Salt told him. "And I certainly don't want you to disturb him."

"I'd no intention of disturbing him," said Alan stiffly.

"Well, what about Noreen Wilks?" Jill inquired, not without a touch of malice. "I suppose she's in London now, trying to get into a strip-tease act in Soho."

"No, she isn't," said Maggie sharply. "That story was all nonsense. Dr. Salt soon proved that."

"I'll bet he did. No, don't fly at me, dear—I mean it." Now she looked around. "But what's been happening here—an earthquake?"

"Alan, give me a hand," said Dr. Salt. "We can at least clear all the chairs and the center of the room. You girls needn't do anything, except give yourselves and us a drink. I'm expecting Superintendent Hurst here any time, so we'll need another chair or two."

"I'll help," said Maggie. "I know about these things now. Jill, the drink's in the kitchen—through there."

"What does everybody want? I might as well do some barmaiding," Jill told them. "I'll be out of United Fabrics any moment now, and looking for a job."

Twenty minutes later, when they had all had enough of room clearing, they were sitting round the electric fire in something like comfort.

"Hadn't Alan and I better go when this policeman comes?" Jill asked.

"If Hurst doesn't strongly object," said Dr. Salt, "then I'd like you to stay. You're all involved more or less in this Noreen Wilks thing, and I want you to hear what I have to say to Hurst. He won't like what I have to say, and if there weren't three other people here he might be tempted to shrug it all away." He looked at Jill, then at Alan, then at Maggie. "I want you to understand—even if Hurst won't—that I'm not simply airing little theories for my own amusement. Noreen Wilks is dead, has been ever since the night of September twelfth, and I think I know where we can go to prove it."

"Not us?" Jill cried in genuine alarm.

"Of course not. Hurst and I—and anybody he wants to go with us. And not tomorrow—*tonight.*"

"But how can you know—" Maggie began.

"No, Maggie, let's wait. I don't want to go over it twice."

The two girls exchanged a glance. "I'm not sure I want to hear it even once," said Jill, stretching a hand out to Alan. "Just to hear you talk like that gives me the creeps. Oh—what's that?"

"The bell—and Superintendent Hurst, I hope," said Dr. Salt, getting up. "Excuse me, ladies."

"Women, you mean," said Maggie, with a nervous laugh. "He told me earlier that he likes women, but doesn't like ladies."

2

"Now I'll play fair with you, doctor," said Hurst as soon as he had been settled into the largest armchair. He had not objected to the others' being there. After all, Maggie and Alan had been there when he had told the Comdon Bridge story—and had tried to make Dr. Salt look silly—and it appeared that he had already met Jill at some United Fabrics function. "Yes, I'll play fair, though I know some police officers who wouldn't. I'll admit we were taken in by those three at Comdon Bridge, lying their heads off. You were right about them, but that doesn't prove you're right when you say Noreen Wilks is dead."

"Possibly not. But let's take one thing at a time, Superintendent."

"Go on. Anything you know that I don't, I'll be glad to hear about, doctor."

"Fair enough. I'll tell you all I know, but don't ask me how and when and why or we'll be here all night. Now we'll start with the Comdon Bridge story. Corrigan was employed by

United Fabrics as a caretaker-cum-watchman for the old Worsley place. On Monday night, probably half drunk, he knocked a man out, a man who had to be rushed into a nursing home—"

"Hold on a minute, Dr. Salt. All this is new to me."

"Just take my word for it. Otherwise, as I said before, we'll be here all night. Corrigan, who was frightened anyhow, was told to clear out, and he went to stay with his sister, Mrs. Duffy, in Comdon Bridge. A day or two later, he and his sister and his niece were bribed to come up with this nonsense story about Noreen Wilks staying with them."

"I'll grant you the nonsense story, doctor. But who bribed them—and why?"

"Who? I'd say Aricson of United Fabrics, acting on behalf of Sir Arnold Donnington."

"Now, now, wait a minute—"

"I'm not waiting a second, Superintendent. If you interrupt me every time the sacred name of Sir Arnold is mentioned, we'll never get anywhere. Now you asked me why they were bribed. Well, just remember how you behaved when you told me their story. Noreen Wilks was alive and I was making a fool of myself. There was nothing for you to investigate and I might as well clear out of Birkden and forget about Noreen. That story was never meant to stand up as evidence in a court. It was cooked up to stop me going round asking questions. If the rough stuff wouldn't work, then this might. It was worth trying. But it didn't work, just because Noreen had been my patient—"

"And she'd have to have medical attention, as you told me right at the start. And I believed you, of course, but I also knew these little fly-by-nights can easily forget what they've promised their doctors."

"I know that, of course—I ought to, by this time—but even so, I knew that I'd thoroughly frightened Noreen. I also knew she'd never gone back to her lodgings for clothes and other things. She could be silly, but she wasn't a complete idiot, and I couldn't see her going away with nothing but the party dress she was wearing." He glanced at Maggie and Jill, and they offered him an immediate murmur of agreement.

"All right," said Hurst. "You didn't believe that Comdon Bridge tale and then made us look a bit silly. But now what?"

"On Tuesday morning, when you and I were talking in your office, Sir Arnold Donnington marched in and asked you to tell your man on the beat up there to keep an eye on the Worsley house. Remember?"

"Of course I do. And you're saying that's because this man Corrigan had been taken off the job—eh?"

"Yes, but that's by the way." Dr. Salt stopped to relight his pipe. "While I was listening to Sir Arnold, I asked myself two questions. First, why was he worrying about the old Worsley place, which was going to be a sort of extension or annex of the club, when he's not supposed to be interested in the club at all? Jill, you know about that."

"I know he was against our having the club at first, and that even when he finally agreed, he never took any interest in it." She looked at the superintendent. "And that's the truth."

"I'm sure it is, if you say so, Miss Frinton. But after all, his firm had bought the place—"

"Next question," Dr. Salt cut in sharply. "I asked myself why this important man, talking about an unimportant matter, was obviously in a state of great tension."

"Was he?" Hurst sounded very skeptical. "He seemed all right to me. A bit high and mighty as usual, that's all."

"He has high blood pressure, I imagine," said Dr. Salt coolly, as if Hurst had not spoken. "He was doing his damnedest to appear casual, and his tone wasn't bad, but his eyes and his hands were all wrong. So I asked myself why he was feeling so excited. And I came up with two answers. First, he was making himself talk about the old Worsley place. Secondly, he was talking about it in front of *me.*"

"Now, now, doctor. Sir Arnold hadn't to bother about you."

"Yes, he had. You're forgetting that you'd just introduced me to him as a doctor who was making inquiries about *a patient called Noreen Wilks*. And he was about to talk to you about the Worsley house. Could he risk it? He decided that he could, after first letting off some steam about industrialists and working women who behave so badly. You remember? No—let me go on. That outburst helped to relieve some of the pressure, so then he felt able to talk to you about the Worsley place, after telling you he hadn't been near it for months. Then, feeling he'd carried it off very bravely, suddenly bursting with a kind of impudent self-confidence, as he was about to go he said to me, 'Dr. Salt, I hope you find your patient—Dora Jilkes,' and I had to tell him he meant Noreen Wilks."

"I remember that, but aren't you making a lot out of nothing?"

"I don't think so, Superintendent. Don't forget, you were seeing him as a familiar and important figure. I wasn't. I was watching and listening to a man who thought he was covering himself up nicely when in fact he was giving himself away. When he insisted upon telling you he hadn't been near the Worsley place for months, I felt sure he'd not only been near it but inside it quite recently. And when he insisted upon calling my missing patient Dora Jilkes, he was really telling me he'd never heard of the girl before, and I knew he was lying."

"And I'll bet he was," cried Jill. "Because somebody must have told him that Derek was going around with her."

"Right, Jill," said Dr. Salt. "But I'm coming to that in a minute. Now, Superintendent, I may be making a lot out of nothing —and in terms of your kind of evidence, probably I am—but I'm trying to explain how I came to certain conclusions. And I left your office on Tuesday convinced that Sir Arnold Donnington was deeply concerned about Noreen Wilks and the old Worsley place, and that quite possibly they were linked together in his mind. And everything I've learned since, with a lot of hocus-pocus you know nothing about, has told me I was right. Now let's leave Sir Arnold to consider his son, Derek. And don't let's have any nonsense about accidents. He shot himself. You know it, I know it, everybody knows it. And he killed himself early in the morning of September thirteenth, at the end of that night of the twelfth when Noreen Wilks vanished." He stopped, looked around and then added, "I think we all need a drink. Superintendent, you've had a long day and needn't consider yourself on duty now, listening to me making a lot out of nothing. What about a little whisky? Girls, wait neat-handedly upon the weary men!"

"My God, he's a bossy type, isn't he?" said Jill as she and Maggie made for the kitchen.

"I've already told him so," said Maggie.

Alan had included himself among the weary men to be waited upon, and now, perhaps feeling he had been silent too long, he spoke to the superintendent. "I just want to say this. I've kept thinking—and it's happened several times—that Dr. Salt must be wrong. But so far he's always been right. I hate to admit it, because I like to think I'm as clever as he is, but his mind works faster than mine—"

"Only in a very different field, Alan," said Dr. Salt. "But thank you for the testimonial."

"I'll admit he's made me look a bit silly tonight," said Hurst. "I mean over that Comdon Bridge story. But sooner or later, if he's carrying on with this Noreen Wilks business, he'll have to come into *my* field, where he doesn't belong—police work and real evidence—and then we'll see who's right and who's wrong. With all due respect, doctor."

"Yes, but don't forget, Superintendent, I'm not trying to put somebody in the dock. That's your business. I'm only trying to find out, for my own satisfaction before I leave Birkden, what really happened to Noreen Wilks. That's all."

"Here you are, you lazy stinkers," cried Jill, returning.

"And don't waste too much time boozing," said Maggie. "I'm half frightened, but I'm dying to know the truth about poor Noreen Wilks."

After they had settled down again, Dr. Salt pointed his pipe stem at the superintendent. "Noreen and young Derek Donnington weren't just messing about with each other. They were in love. I've now read some of his letters and notes to her—"

"You would, wouldn't you!" Jill sounded disgusted.

"Well, why shouldn't he, if they're both dead?" This was Maggie, in a flash.

"I'd be obliged if you young ladies would leave this to Dr. Salt and me." The superintendent was not heavily disapproving—after all, he had just been given some whisky—but clearly he meant what he said. "I might want to see those letters—you got them from her landlady, I take it—but go on, doctor. They were in love."

"They were in love and were busy making love, as you can imagine."

"I couldn't at one time, but there's nothing in that line I can't imagine now. Straight to bed, these days."

"Now they had to go somewhere to make love," said Dr. Salt.

Hurst interrupted him again. "Nothing in that. Young Donnington had a car. And they were meeting when nights were still warm. They could have gone anywhere."

"But they didn't. That's clear from what he wrote. They had 'a place,' the same one each time. Now Derek was hard up—I know that because his sister, Erica, called to see me, and I extracted a little information out of her—and he couldn't afford to rent a room."

"He might have borrowed a pal's flat," said Hurst. "It's been done before—often."

"But it's not always easy," Dr. Salt objected. "And especially if it has to be used late at night—say, after a party at the Fabrics Club. But there was one place they could use anytime, quite close to the club—the empty Worsley house that Sir Arnold was so concerned about. Now Noreen Wilks was never seen again after she left that club party with him on the night of September twelfth. All we know for certain is that Derek, who was in

165

love with her, went home and killed himself early next morning. Why? Nobody knows. And if Noreen Wilks is dead, as I believe, it's not unreasonable to assume that she met her death that night in the old Worsley place. It's highly unlikely she died a natural death. She may have lost her life as the result of an accident of some kind. It's just possible. But I can't help believing she was killed—yes, *murdered*."

"You've no real evidence," said the superintendent very sharply. "It's just a tall story to me, doctor."

"But all the facts surrounding it would seem a tall story if I didn't know they were facts. Ever since I started asking questions about Noreen Wilks, I've been elaborately lied to, threatened, told to shut up and go away. Now, I went to see Aricson —you know him, Sir Arnold's dog's-body at United Fabrics?— and he practically admitted he was trying to shut me up. Not because he knew anything about Noreen Wilks—he told me that, and I believed him—but because Sir Arnold was afraid of a scandal in which his son would be involved."

"Well, I can understand that," said Hurst. "Can't you?"

"No, I can't. Like Aricson, who's no fool, you're accepting the scandal excuse because you're refusing to take a long, close look at it. You're both saying in effect, as I told Aricson, that there can't be anything wrong, but it mustn't get out. If Noreen simply cleared out that night, then there's no scandal. If she didn't, then there's something terribly wrong that has to be uncovered."

"No, no, Dr. Salt, that doesn't follow. For instance, suppose Sir Arnold discovered that night that the girl was pregnant and made arrangements at once for her to go away."

"I was her doctor, Superintendent, and in her confidence, and I'd seen her that very morning. Pregnancy's out. But what stays *in* is Donnington's peculiar state of tension on Tuesday morning. And also all the attempts, made on his behalf chiefly by Aricson, to confuse or block my inquiry."

"An inquiry entirely in a private capacity," said Hurst

heavily. "Remember that, doctor. I doubt if you could bring a single charge—"

"I don't want to bring charges," Dr. Salt shouted, suddenly out of temper. "I'm a doctor, not a policeman. Now I'll say it again—and I hope for the last time. Noreen Wilks was my patient, in my care, and I want to know exactly what happened to her. And now I'll make a lot more out of nothing for you, Superintendent. I say that Noreen died in that house and that Sir Arnold Donnington knows all about it."

"Doctor, you're going too fast."

"If I slow down, I'll be run out of Birkden before I can prove anything. I think she was murdered."

"You'd have to show me a body before I believed that."

"Well, I'm going to have a look," said Dr. Salt, now on his feet. "I'm not asking you to come with me—"

"If I didn't, our man up there wouldn't let you go near the house. Besides, this is police work, no business of yours."

"So?"

"I'm coming with you." The superintendent finished his whisky and pushed himself out of his armchair. "Good night, ladies. Yes, Mr. Culworth?"

Alan gave a quick glance at Dr. Salt's retreating back. "Do you believe he's right, Superintendent?"

"I do not. I think it's all moonshine. But there's never any harm in taking a look. And if he can't convince me, perhaps I can convince him. But I'd be obliged—and this applies to you too, ladies—if you'd keep this caper to yourselves—eh?"

3

"Now, Pickles," said Superintendent Hurst to the young constable. "Dr. Salt and I are just going to take a look round inside, and you can come with us."

"Yes, sir. But the doors are locked, front and back, and I haven't any keys. But perhaps you have, sir."

"No, I haven't. But there are usually ways and means of getting into a house this size that's been empty a long time. Wood gets warped or rotten and catches don't work. Go round and try some windows, Pickles, then give us a shout if you can get one open."

After a few minutes they climbed in by way of a small side window. The electricity had been cut off but all three of them were carrying large torches, and if there had been anything worth seeing on the ground floor they would have seen it. The house was not really old; it had probably been built—and very solidly built too—in the 1890s; and it had more than its share of colored leaded lights, Dutch tiles, cozy corners in light oak. A stag's head, which nobody had thought worth taking away, mournfully presided over one room. There was a sad reek of damp and decay. If the Worsleys, whoever they were, had been happy in this house of theirs, they had left no trace of it to lighten the moldering air.

Superintendent Hurst was very thorough, far too thorough for Dr. Salt, who was impatient to explore the upper parts of the house. "We'll find nothing down here," he grumbled.

"Maybe not," said the superintendent, "but I like a bit of method. And if a thing's worth doing, it's worth doing well— that's what I say."

"Well, I don't," Dr. Salt told him. "A lot of things are only worth doing if they don't take too much time and trouble. If those two youngsters used this place, then it's a hundred to one they went as high up as they could go. So I'm going to try the top floor."

"You please yourself, doctor. But it's not the way I like to work."

The top floor consisted of several small bedrooms and a couple of large storage rooms still half filled with moldy trunks, broken suitcases, piles of old magazines; and there seemed to be a scampering of rats in far corners. An immense melancholy descended upon Dr. Salt as he stared about him. He wished he were somewhere else, preferably about eight hundred miles farther south, sitting at a small table in the sunlight. For the first time since he had started asking questions about Noreen Wilks, he half wished he had left Birkden without giving her another thought. Hadn't he been overworking for years? Didn't he need —if ever a man did—a change, a rest? Why the hell should he be poking about in this place—and with everybody thinking him a damn nuisance?

As soon as he turned the handle and found the door was locked, he was ready to swear—in a still lower depth of misery —that the dead girl's body would be somewhere in there. Feeling no excitement whatever, only this huge blank wretchedness, he went down to the floor below, where Hurst and Constable Pickles were systematically examining master bedrooms and guest bedrooms and finding nothing but peeling wallpaper and bits of felt on the floor.

"No sign of anything here, you know, Dr. Salt. I think we're wasting our time."

"You may be, but I'm not. There's one locked door on the top floor, and it's not a heavy door. Two of us could charge our way in."

"Well, I don't know about that. There's a question of damage."

"Oh, for God's sake—come on, man. If they were here at all, that's where they were. If they weren't, then I'll admit I've been wasting your time—and I'll promise not to waste any more of it."

"That's a fair offer. Don't you think so, Pickles?"

"I do, sir. Though, of course, I don't rightly know what you're looking for, Superintendent—sir."

"You will in a minute," Dr. Salt promised him grimly. And led the way upstairs.

Challenged by the door, Hurst suddenly lost his reluctance. "I've done this job before. No need to start bruising our shoulders. There's a knack in this. Dr. Salt, you stand there and keep

your light on it. Pickles, you just hold me up on this side. Now
—watch!" He hopped towards the door, with his right leg stiffly
extended, and then used his leg, ending in a heavy size twelve
shoe, as a battering ram. At the third attempt, something
snapped, and the door flew open.

"Now I'll take charge here," said the superintendent as all
three torches swept the room. "A bed of sorts. Couple of old
blankets. Not for sleeping, this bed. Chair of sorts. Bit of a
mirror on it. Face powder been spilled about. Smells funny—
but then some of it does nowadays. Well, I think you were right
up to a point, Dr. Salt. I'll buy this. This is where they came to
do their lovemaking. Now what about these three trunks up
against the wall? Going to tell me there's a body in one of 'em,
are you, doctor? Well, Constable Pickles and I will see about
that. Leave it to us. I'd be obliged if you didn't touch anything.
This is police work now. Take that top trunk down, Pickles, and
then open the other two. You can shine your torch, doctor, and
that's all the help we need from you."

There was nothing in the three trunks but newspapers and
odd bits of rubbish. Hurst turned triumphantly. "You see, you
were right only up to a point, Dr. Salt. If you're looking for
another trunk murder, you won't find it here. Might as well put
'em back, Pickles."

"Just a minute." Dr. Salt moved forward. "Could I have a look
at those two strips of wallpaper?"

"The same as that already on the wall, sir," said Pickles, holding them up.

"I know," said Dr. Salt, moving again. "Just step aside, please,
constable." He bent down to look at that part of the wall which
had been covered by the trunks. "Now I'd like a little more light
here, please. Could you shine your torches where I've got mine?
Thanks." Then he straightened himself and looked at the superintendent. "I think you'd better take a closer look here. It's the
same wallpaper, of course, but it seems to me a bit newer."

"It might be—yes," said Hurst, after he had taken a look.

Now Dr. Salt shone his torch downwards. "And the floor here is interesting, don't you think? Doesn't it look as if somebody cleaned it thoroughly before pulling that trunk over it?"

"It's a possibility," said Hurst rather reluctantly.

Dr. Salt began moving his torchlight again. "Now let's have another close look at the wall." He began knocking against it until he heard a hollow sound. "I think there's only very thin board here—might be only cardboard. Certainly no solid wall. And this is where it's been newly papered. Either of you got a good strong knife?"

Pickles said he had, and he handed it over.

"Now steady on, Dr. Salt," cried the superintendent hastily. "You can't start damaging property."

"*You* can't. I can. Look the other way." Dr. Salt cut into the wall and pulled out a section of it, about two feet long and a foot wide, which was simply cardboard covered with wallpaper. He shone his torch into the hole, saw something there, and then stepped back, with an "Ugh!" of disgust.

"Yes, Dr. Salt, can't mistake that smell," said Hurst quietly. "That's a corpse, all right—what's left of it. And this is where you do nothing but look, doctor. Come on, Pickles. Let's get this over with. Give me that knife, doctor. And you keep back. Police work now."

Dr. Salt held his own torch and the superintendent's, giving them as much light as possible while they hastily enlarged the hole and then brought out the body. As soon as it was out, Pickles, handkerchief to mouth, hurried away, and a moment later he could be heard being sick just outside the door.

"All right, lad," the superintendent shouted. "Get to the nearest phone, sharp as you can. Tell Sergeant Broadbent or whoever's on the desk that we've found a body here. He'll know what to do. D'you hear me?"

"Yes, sir." It came in a kind of gasp, but then they heard him clattering down the stairs. "Now then, doctor, I can't stop you having a look—and anyhow, I'll ask you to identify her—but

171

don't lay a finger on that body. I'm sorry, but that's how it has to be. Is it Noreen Wilks?"

"No," said Dr. Salt harshly. "It's a lump of putrefying meat. But when it wasn't, it belonged to Noreen Wilks. Your man will give you all the details, of course, but I can tell you this—it was a nasty kind of murder. Lot of hate in it. Madness, perhaps." He moved away, and now lit his pipe.

The superintendent followed him, and also lit a pipe. "It was young Derek Donnington, of course," he began, almost in a whisper. "He brought her here as usual. And I'll admit you were clever working that out. He brought her here, but then they had a quarrel. He did her in, put the body where we found it, then went home and shot himself."

Dr. Salt stared at him. "Queer program that, isn't it? Why spend two or three hours hiding the body—even doing a repapering job in the middle of the night—if you're going home to shoot yourself?"

"He was going to brazen it out, then changed his mind. They often do."

Dr. Salt still stared at him. "I've several other questions, harder to answer than that one."

"And if you've any sense, Dr. Salt, you'll keep them to yourself. You wanted to know what had happened to your patient. Now you've found out. And I'll admit it was a brilliant bit of work. A lot of guessing in it, of a sort we're not encouraged to indulge in, but all very clever guessing." He moved slowly towards the door. "But now forget it, doctor. Just go away and forget it."

"Tell me why, Superintendent." Dr. Salt had followed him to the door, and now spoke quietly at his elbow. "You'll agree I'm entitled to an explanation, after finding her for you."

"Certainly you are, Dr. Salt. And I'll give it to you, in confidence—the strictest confidence." They were now out on the landing, and Hurst behaved as if the big, empty, dark house was all curious ears. "It's like this," he whispered. "Whatever you

172

may read in the papers, this case is closed—here and now. There's absolutely no doubt in my mind that young Donnington killed her and then killed himself. But I can't say so because we arranged for a verdict of 'Accidental Death.' And this one will be 'Person or Persons Unknown.' Can't do it any other way. We're stuck with it. Oh, we may have to pretend to make some inquiries, perhaps bring a vagrant or two in for questioning. But as I know who the murderer was, really the case is closed."

"Will you let me see your police surgeon's report?"

"No, I won't, Dr. Salt." The superintendent raised his voice now. "I'm sorry to be disobliging. But the case is closed. And don't try an appeal to the chief constable because he knows already you've been going round asking questions, and he's dead against you. And you want to leave Birkden, so now you can. Let's see," he added heartily, "you came here in your own car, didn't you? So now you can go home and leave me to it. Good night, Dr. Salt."

"Good night, Superintendent." He walked down several stairs before turning and shining his torch up at the superintendent, who had not moved.

"But I can't leave Birkden just yet," he called up quietly.

"Now why—why?"

"Because I've a case too, Superintendent. And *my case isn't closed.* Good night."

4

As he let himself into his flat, he heard angry voices that stopped as soon as he opened the door into his sitting room. All three were still there; the girls' eyes still sparkled with anger; and Alan looked hot and uncomfortable, a man who had just been dragged into some scene of ruthless feminine fury.

"You'd better quarrel with me now," he told them rather sourly. "But not until I've had a drink." He went into the kitchen and found there was some whisky left, not much but some. He drank about half of what he had poured out before taking himself and the glass into the sitting room. "Has anybody had a look at my patient?"

"Yes, I did," said Maggie, "only about quarter of an hour ago. Still asleep." She hesitated a moment. "What happened in that house?"

"Behind the wallpaper in a locked attic room," he said slowly, "we found what was left of Noreen Wilks." While they exclaimed, he took a sip of his whisky.

"And it wasn't some accident?" said Alan. "She'd been murdered?"

"Yes. All very nasty. I'll let you off the details. Just take my word for it. But this is how we came to find the body." And he described what had happened in the locked room, how he had noticed a slight difference in the wallpaper. "Hurst might have spotted it if he'd been looking really hard. But he didn't believe her dead body was somewhere in that house—he thought it was all a tall story, you remember?—whereas I felt at once, as soon as we were inside the house, that we'd find her there. I'm not a psychic type—"

"Are you sure?" asked Maggie. "Because I think you are."

"Whether I am or not, I felt in my very bones she was there. I moved in that house in a black cloud of horrible conviction. Damn it—I'm in it yet."

"Yes, you are," said Maggie.

He gave her a sharp glance, said nothing for a moment or two, then continued: "I'm a doctor, not a detective. You can say I'd given a lot of time and trouble to the job of trying to provide that girl with a reasonably healthy body. She was a special case, remember? So I didn't enjoy seeing what was left of her taken out of a cavity in the wall, like an oversize chewed-up rag doll. She'd gone there to make love as usual—"

"Oh, don't, Salt, don't!" And Maggie began crying.

"I'm sorry. Forget it."

"Do you think she'd been there," said Jill hesitantly, "ever since that night—September twelfth?"

"Of course. I'd felt that all along."

"Then Derek Donnington must have done it," said Jill, with no hesitation now. "And that's why he shot himself."

Alan cleared his throat. "That's fairly obvious, isn't it?"

Dr. Salt looked at him. "It is to Superintendent Hurst, who warned me that the case was closed, so far as he was concerned, and told me in effect to go away now and mind my own business."

"Why should he say that?" This was Alan again.

"Because I told him that *my* case wasn't closed. In other words, I don't believe for a moment that young Donnington killed her. And—as I've said too many times already—I'm not leaving Birkden until I know exactly what happened to Noreen Wilks."

Jill jumped up in a sudden rage. "Oh, for Christ's sake, stop it—just stop it!"

"Steady, Jill!" And Alan got up and made a move towards her.

"Steady be damned! I'm telling him he's got to stop it—*now.*"

"And I hate to agree." Maggie looked at Dr. Salt. 'We've been quarreling—as you guessed. But I know what she means—and I think she's right. Just stop it."

"Stop what?" He was genuinely bewildered.

"Let me tell him," cried Jill. "Just pack up and get out, go wherever you want to go, leave Birkden alone, and stop playing at being God."

"I see." He nodded, then turned to Maggie. "Is that what you meant too, Maggie?"

"Yes, it is—more or less. Though she doesn't really like you and I do. And I know it isn't just enjoying being cleverer than anybody else—"

"Yes, it is," Jill put in quickly.

"Oh, do shut up and let me say something. After all, I know him ten times better than you do—"

"Oh, that's it, is it? My dear, as soon as a woman starts saying that—"

"Shut up, shut up, shut up! Alan, why don't you take her away?"

"I'll be glad to. I've had enough of this screaming match."

"No doubt," said Dr. Salt, getting up. "Now listen to me, all three of you." He spoke very quietly, but there was something in his manner and tone that made it unlikely that he would be interrupted. "I know very well that young Donnington didn't kill Noreen. It's a very convenient explanation, but quite unreasonable. And if he didn't kill her, then somebody else did. And I don't want to spend the rest of my life wondering who did it —and why. The truth, you might say, will set me free. The other thing is, I'm rather obstinate, so when people start trying to bounce me out of something I feel I ought to do, I'm more determined than ever to do it. From tonight there'll be more and harder bouncing. Better keep out of the way. You can always tell yourselves you're against people playing God. And now, Alan, if you're not ready to go back to Hemton yet, I'll run Maggie home."

When Jill and Alan had gone and he and Maggie were in his car, but not moving yet, he said, "Don't talk. You're angry with Alan, with Jill, with me, with yourself—partly because you've had an exhausting day and now it's late. Same applies to me. I seem to have had a hell of a long day. So no talking. Do far more harm than good."

He said no more until he began slowing up within sight of Maggie's front door. "If the shop can spare you, I suggest you come with your mother tomorrow morning. Then you'll hear what I'll say to her. I'll have already told your father what I'm going to say. I'll have to tell him about Noreen too, of course."

"What about my father? When can he come home?"

"Tomorrow, probably. But he'll have to take it easy. However, I'll explain what I think he ought to do—not playing God, just doctor." He leaned across, reached out to open the door for her and said, "Good night, Maggie. And don't talk to anybody about anything tonight. You've had as much as you can take."

And so had he, he thought as he drove off, suddenly feeling deathly tired. A hell of a long day. And he'd had hundreds and hundreds of them. When and where could he go to sit in the sunlight? And whose long and strong fingers had made sure that Noreen Wilks would never see the sun again?

TWELVE

Maggie awoke on Friday morning to find herself under what might be called either a weighty cloud or a cloudy weight. She then discovered that it consisted of some apprehension about taking her mother to Dr. Salt's to see her father, of a lingering horror concerned with the murder of Noreen Wilks, and of a kind of angry disgust with Dr. Salt for being so stubborn and so blindly and obtusely masculine. (It annoyed her, too, to have to agree with Jill.) She put on a suit that she kept only for mornings like this, when she disliked everything in sight: a two-year-old mistake in mustard tweed that was always trying to put ten years and fourteen pounds on her. "What—that one again!" cried her mother, as soon as Maggie was downstairs. "It's all wrong for you, dear."

"It's what I'm feeling like," Maggie muttered.

Alan said he would just have time to drop them at Dr. Salt's and that was all. After that he never spoke another word, but ate a lot of buttered toast and marmalade and probably thought about subatomic particles, moths or Jill Frinton. But their mother chattered away, rapidly and rather nervously, as if she were not having breakfast with her own two children but were entertaining somewhat difficult company. This may have been because she had dressed herself this morning with great care. And then Maggie saw how pathetic this was, disliked herself for being so sulky and silent before, tried to be brighter and more sympathetic but was defeated by this dislike of herself. What hard work it was being a female! Probably in all their lives Alan and Salt had never worried a moment about this sort of thing. Meanwhile, her mother was explaining that they wouldn't have to clear and wash up as she had a woman coming in for the morning. "I want everything looking nice if Dr. Salt says your father can come home. By the way, I forgot to ask. Will this be on National Health or will he be sending us a bill?"

Maggie found herself giggling. The last thing she could imagine was Dr. Salt presenting them with a bill.

"I don't see anything funny about it."

"No, Mother, it's a sensible question. And I'd say no bill," Alan told her gravely.

"Thank you, Alan dear. Y'know, I can't really make out whether Maggie likes him or not. What about you, Alan? You know about clever people. Would you say he's a clever doctor?"

"I think he might be," Alan began slowly. And Maggie could not help waiting intently, ready in a flash, if need be, to confirm or deny what he might say next. "I know he's extremely sharp and observant, and his mind works quickly."

"Isn't that nice? Maggie never told me that."

"Well, now Alan's told you," said Maggie. "So that's better still, isn't it? Dr. Salt's very clever—odd but rather sweet—and terribly obstinate. Alan, you'll have to wait a few minutes. I've decided I can't wear this stinker of a suit."

It was just after ten when Alan dropped them at Dr. Salt's. To Maggie's relief they didn't discover Dr. Salt in a sport shirt and baggy old pants, still sorting out books and records. He looked like a respectable doctor, and his manner might have been borrowed straight from Harley Street.

"Naturally you're anxious to see your husband, Mrs. Culworth," he began. "And I shan't keep you from him more than a minute or two. But there are one or two things I must explain."

"Yes, yes, of course, Dr. Salt—I understand."

"Your husband came to Birkden on Monday to make some inquiries about a girl, Noreen Wilks, who was missing. She was the daughter of an old friend of his—somebody he'd known in the Air Force. This girl was a patient of mine—that's how I come into the picture—and I was making inquiries too. Last night, the police and I discovered her body in an empty house. She'd been murdered. Of course, your husband knew nothing about this. On Monday he met with an accident and was sent to a nursing home, suffering from some concussion and a heart condition he'd known about for several years. He couldn't get in touch with you because he was being kept under sedation. Yesterday I brought him here. He's made a splendid recovery, Mrs. Culworth, and you'll be able to take him home this morning and it'll probably do him more good than harm if you let him pay a short visit to the shop this afternoon to see if all's well, sign a few checks, look at some bills—spend an hour there, let us say. So far, so good, but—" And here he broke off to hold up a warning finger, at which Mrs. Culworth stared as if she were already half hypnotized.

"*But* I must ask you to remember this. After the shock and then sedation, his mind is naturally confused about events earlier this week. You must ignore them, Mrs. Culworth. Don't begin questioning him, reproaching him or in any way raising the emotional temperature. He'll have to take care of himself from now on—you'll have to watch that—and indeed I've suggested to him already that if he can afford to do it, he ought to give up the shop, though that doesn't mean he ought to do nothing; he needs some occupation. Now Maggie'll go in with you, just to say hello to her father, and then she'll leave you.

Take everything easily and slowly—chat about this and that—help him to dress and pack up—keep him smiling. You know?"

"I should think I *do* know," said Mrs. Culworth, though not indignantly. "I understand perfectly—and thank you very much, Dr. Salt. Come along, Maggie dear."

Maggie kissed her father, said he looked wonderful—though he didn't—and then, sensing her mother's impatience, hastily left them together and rejoined Dr. Salt. "And I must say, though I'm rather cross with you this morning," she told him, "that speech to my mother was a masterpiece. You might have been dealing with her all your life."

"Not quite, but I've spent some years talking to anxious and suspicious wives. By the way, you'll be glad to know I've got two men calling this afternoon—one to buy the books I don't want, the other for the records. They'll both swindle me, of course, but most of this clutter will be off my hands. All the rest of the stuff will go into store on Monday, when I hope I'll have gone."

"Gone where? You don't even know that, do you?" She spoke sharply, trying to reject a sudden little sad and empty feeling.

"Yes, I do. Paris first—to pick up a car from a friend of mine there—and then the Dordogne. But why are you feeling annoyed with me this morning, Maggie?"

"After last night, of course. I mean not letting well alone, wanting to go on and on about Noreen Wilks when it could be all over."

"All over but not done with. And I don't want to spend the rest of my life with the mystery of Noreen Wilks. What I do want—unlike these other people—is to lay that poor ghost, clear away and tidy up, then leave Birkden with an easy mind, a clear conscience. How can I—"

But he never finished the question because somebody was at the door.

"I'm Sims—*Birkden Telegraph*," Maggie heard the man say. "Like to have a word with you, if I could, Dr. Salt." He could, and was admitted and introduced to Maggie. He was a middle-aged man with a fat, sagging face and a sad voice, and he smoked his cigarette with a hissing noise, as if he were a very polite Japanese. "You're leaving Birkden, I understand, Dr. Salt?"

"I am, yes." Dr. Salt, who was still standing, picked up a book from the nearest pile and looked at it as if he had never seen it before.

"Any particular reason?"

"I'm tired of it. Need a change."

"No wife and family to bother about?"

"No. All alone."

"Sometimes I wish I hadn't."

"And sometimes I wish I had." Dr. Salt replaced the book. "Now your next question is, what am I going to do? And the answer is, I don't know. Haven't made up my mind where to go next. Need a holiday first."

"You've been in practice here seven years, haven't you?" Sims now sounded bored as well as sad. "What do you think of Birkden?"

"Not much. However, I've been in worse places—mostly on the Persian Gulf."

"What's the matter with Birkden?"

"Nothing—if you read the *Telegraph*. So just say that Dr. Salt had found it a fascinating town, with a charm all its own, filled with varied life, color, an eager friendliness and that civilized gaiety discovered in so many English industrial towns."

"Well, don't think we won't print that, though we have a few readers—just a few—who'll write in to say you must be barmy."

"Just please yourself, Mr. Sims." But then the telephone was ringing. As Dr. Salt went across to answer it, Maggie was astonished to see Sims give her an enormous wink.

"Yes, this is Dr. Salt. Who? Colonel Ringwood? Right, put him on."

"Our chief constable," Sims told Maggie in a loud whisper, and then gave her another wink.

"Yes, Colonel Ringwood? . . . No, I can't come and see you. . . . Possibly it *is* urgent, but if it is, then you can come here. . . . Well, it's equally inconvenient for me to leave this flat—and I don't even *want* to see you." Dr. Salt put down the receiver and looked at Sims. "Bad-tempered chap, isn't he?"

"He isn't used to people talking to him like that. Is *he* coming *here?*"

"I don't know and I don't care. But he seems to imagine I'm still in the army."

"Were you in the army once, then?"

"As an MO—yes. Burma campaign."

Sims nodded several times. "I'm getting the idea you're a lot tougher than you look."

"Oh, he is," said Maggie. And then wished she hadn't.

Dr. Salt lit his pipe and said nothing.

Sims waited, cleared his throat, then said, "Well, now—what about Noreen Wilks?"

"Ah, I've been waiting for that. The real reason why you came to see me, isn't it, Mr. Sims?"

"You don't know what goes on round here, Dr. Salt."

"I'm beginning to learn."

"I can print all that guff about Birkden—taking the sarcasm out of it, of course," said Sims. "But there isn't going to be any Noreen Wilks story in the *Birkden Telegraph*. You see, it's owned by the Birkden and District Newspaper Company. And the chairman of that company—"

"Don't tell me. Let me guess. Sir Arnold Donnington."

"Right first time, Dr. Salt."

"He's a kind of Louis the Fourteenth round here, isn't he?

183

Let's see—finance, industry, property, the law, the press. Every time I turn a corner he's there."

Sims grinned. "And sometimes he's just behind you telling you not to turn corners. But now you can understand why anything you tell me about Noreen Wilks will be off the record."

"In Birkden. But what about London—or Birmingham?"

"We're under contract not to do anything for the nationals or the agencies. The last chap who tried it was sacked at once. And I've got four children and a mortgage. So I'm just curious, that's all. Now the rumor's going round that late last night it was you who led the police to the body, but that then you told Hurst that his account of the murder didn't satisfy you at all. Now, off the record, is that right?"

"Quite right, Mr. Sims."

"Are you going to do anything about it?"

"Well," said Dr. Salt in a mild, half-ruminating manner. "Having established, after some opposition, that the girl wasn't merely missing but had been murdered, I'd certainly like to know who killed her. Before I leave the town, y'know."

"And when do you think that'll be?"

"Sunday—or Monday."

"You'll have to work fast, won't you?"

"Work fast? I don't intend to work at all."

"Just sit around and think—is that the idea?"

"More or less," said Dr. Salt. "Not much thinking, though. You're looking skeptical, Mr. Sims."

"I think you'll have your work cut out just keeping out of trouble, Dr. Salt."

"And I'm sure that's true," Maggie told them both, earnestly. But somebody else had arrived.

Colonel Ringwood had a beaky nose and fierce mustache, but the remainder of his face suffered from a droopy, old-hound effect. He was obviously out of temper, and his bark was almost that of a young hound. "Morning! Dr. Salt, eh?" He marched in and then stopped to glare at Sims. "We've met before, haven't we?"

"Yes, Chief Constable. I'm Sims of the *Telegraph*."

"Good God!" He turned angrily to Dr. Salt. "You've brought the confounded press in already."

"Don't be silly," said Dr. Salt mildly.

"I came to interview Dr. Salt on his leaving Birkden—what his plans are, how he's liked Birkden—that kind of thing. Any objection?"

"If that's all it is—no. Why should there be?"

"That's what I was wondering," said Sims, who was now sauntering towards the door. "Well, thanks, Dr. Salt—and have a good holiday. Bye-bye!"

"What's this about a holiday?" said Colonel Ringwood very sharply, as soon as Sims had gone.

"I'm about to take one."

"When are you going?" It was another bark.

"As soon as I can." Then he suddenly started barking too. "What do you have for breakfast?"

"What?"

"You heard me," barked Dr. Salt. "What do you have for breakfast? And why?"

Maggie began giggling.

"What the devil has it got to do with you, man?" Colonel Ringwood was furious. "And why are you taking that tone with me?"

Instead of replying, Dr. Salt gave him a long, slow smile, compelling him to understand the point of the burlesque.

"I see. Bit brusque with you, was I? Sorry!"

"Not at all, Colonel. Oh, this is Miss Culworth, who's acting as—er—my confidential assistant."

"How d'you do? Though I don't pretend to understand this confidential assistant business."

"Neither do I," said Maggie sweetly.

"Having a worrying sort of morning, partly thanks to you, Dr. Salt."

"But if young girls disappear," said Dr. Salt, mild as milk, "somebody ought to try to find them, don't you think?"

"Well, she's been found. And now you ought to feel satisfied and go and enjoy your holiday. What you won't do, if you've any sense, is to hang about here playing detective and interfering with legitimate police work."

"And what would that work be, in the case of Noreen Wilks?"

"None to speak of. We consider the case closed."

"Well, then, if you're not doing any work, I could hardly interfere with it, could I?"

"There's nothing to be gained by mere quibbling, Dr. Salt. You know where we stand. Superintendent Hurst told you last night. This girl was undoubtedly killed by her lover, Derek Donnington, who had the motive, the opportunity, the means. And as young Donnington's dead, that's an end to the whole wretched business. This is Hurst's view. It's my view. And it ought to be yours."

Dr. Salt smiled at him. "I'm sorry, but it isn't. In fact, it's quite ridiculous. You and Hurst are trying to paper over this case just as somebody papered over that hole in the wall where we found the body last night. You're not solving the riddle. You're just giving it up."

"But if young Donnington didn't kill the girl, then who did?"

"I don't know. But I'm sure he didn't."

"Have you any evidence that would stand up in a court of law?"

"None whatever," Dr. Salt replied cheerfully. "But then I never have had. Nevertheless, now you have the body."

"You're being frank with me, Dr. Salt, so now I'll be equally frank with you. You've probably got some fine-spun theory, a typical intellectual amateur approach, that any experienced police officer would reject at once. And for the sake of that theory, you're probably prepared to let loose a lot of dangerous

186

stuff that might do a great deal of harm to this town. I live in Birkden. You're about to leave it. Well, I'm here to make sure you don't do it any harm."

"But I don't want to do it any harm. I'm sorry for it."

"I don't know why you should be." Colonel Ringwood looked and sounded outraged.

"Let's not bother about that, then."

"Very well, then listen to me. To begin with, Sir Arnold Donnington is a friend of mine, I'm proud to say. He needn't live here—he could live anywhere—but he stays on to do what he can for Birkden."

"And I think it's time he stopped. Let Birkden do what it can for Birkden."

"Will you kindly listen to me? Sir Arnold felt the death of his son very deeply. If that wound is reopened, it's going to hurt him like hell. Then—United Anglo-Belgian Fabrics are our biggest employers. Any scandal involving them won't help Birkden. And if we all find ourselves splashed across the pages of the sensational Sunday press, a lot of innocent people will suffer."

"That really *is* true," said Maggie, giving Dr. Salt an appealing look.

"Thank you, Miss Er," the colonel continued. "And all because Dr. Salt, who's leaving the town anyhow, has a fancy theory about a murder case that's already solved itself."

"But it hasn't, y'know," Dr. Salt told him.

"Why the devil can't you attend to your own affairs and leave us to attend to ours? What would *you* feel if I marched into your surgery one morning and told you what was wrong with your patients?"

"Some mornings I'd hate it. Some mornings I'd love it."

"Well, I don't want you meddling with police work. And I warn you, Dr. Salt, that I'll tell my men not only to offer you no assistance whatever—"

"Oh, that reminds me," Dr. Salt cut in coolly. "What was your police surgeon's report on the body?"

"Hurst told you that you couldn't see that report. Damned impudence asking me now! I'm telling you, as plainly as I can, that not only will you get no help from the Birkden force, but that if there's the slightest infringement of the law on your part, you'll take the consequences."

"Better keep away from my car, hadn't I?"

"You'll do your preposterous amateur detecting entirely at your own risk."

"You mean that if I should be beaten up—"

"It's not a question of beating up. This isn't Chicago."

"No, but it's doing its best," said Dr. Salt. "Where have you been, Colonel Ringwood? I don't work in casualty wards, and even I've attended at least eight men who were badly beaten up—one of them shot in the leg, three of them probably maimed for life. Ever since we never had it so good, this has been a rough town."

"If you believe that," Colonel Ringwood told him, "then the sooner you leave Birkden, the better." He was now on his feet. "And I've said all I want to say, so—"

"But wouldn't you like to know why I'm sure young Donnington couldn't have killed her?"

"No," the colonel bellowed. "Lot of damned nonsense!" And he banged out without offering a word or even a look to Miss Er, who pulled a face but then unpulled it to give Dr. Salt a stern look. It missed him, however, because he was busy relighting his pipe. So finally she had to say something.

"Don't think I'm on that one's side," she began. "I'd be against him whatever it was. All the same, Salt, you're not being very sensible. I thought so last night. I think so now. The only difference is that I'm no longer feeling cross about it. But I have to tell you that I think you're behaving like an idiot." It came tumbling out before she really knew what she was saying. Then she felt terrified as he stared at her for a moment, all bristling eyebrows. But his lined and weathered face cracked into a grin.

"I'm sure you do, Maggie. There's a point past which each sex finds the other idiotic or childish. This is still true however much a man and a woman may find they have in common."

"Do you think *we* have much in common?"

"I don't know yet—and anyhow, that's not what we're talking about."

"Oh, all right," said Maggie impatiently. "But if you want to know why I think you're behaving like an idiot, I'll tell you. And please don't interrupt. You say you want to leave here as soon as possible—to have a holiday and then start again, probably somewhere thousands of miles away. Well, I understand that. I feel like that myself sometimes. But if that's what you want, then why entangle yourself—running risks too—in something that nobody—but *nobody*—asks you to bother about at all? You're alive, and Noreen Wilks is dead and Derek Donnington's dead, and the police are quite happy believing he killed her and then himself. I didn't like Colonel Thing, the chief constable, but there was a lot of sense in what he said. Leave it alone. Don't interfere. Young Donnington and Noreen are dead and can't run into any more trouble. You're alive, and you can. And why should you? I don't say you like playing God—that's a bit much —but I do say it's mostly a kind of conceited obstinacy in you—and it frightens me and I don't like it."

He waited a moment. "Finished?" He wasn't aggressive, just calm and quiet, which in a way made him all the more maddening.

"Yes," she said defiantly. "Though I could go on and on. But I won't."

"It's a sound feminine point of view," he told her rather slowly. "Really, the let-sleeping-dogs-lie approach—um?"

"If you like—" But the telephone was ringing.

"Who?" he asked it. "Mr. Aricson? Certainly. Put him on. . . . Yes, this is Salt, Mr. Aricson. What can I do for you? . . . All right, then, what can you do for me? . . . I see. I'd like to repeat that, if I may. A check for seven hundred and fifty pounds, for services rendered, will be available today, whenever I want to pick it up, but only today. Right? . . . In other words, you're ready to pay me seven-fifty to clear out and mind my own business—um? Very tempting, I must say, but I'll have to turn it down. . . . No, no, I've hardly any scruples at all. But I want to leave everything clear and tidy. . . . Oh, no, it won't be. . . . We can leave Colonel Ringwood out. He's just downright stupid—I agree. Hurst is experienced and honest. He's not consciously trying to deceive me or anybody else. But he *is* busy deceiving *himself*. It's our great British vice—haven't you noticed? . . . All right, try to swallow this. A young man is in love with a young girl. He takes her to a party. Later, they leave it, as they've done before, to go to an empty house to make love. But on this particular night the boy suddenly turns into a maniac. He strangles the girl and mutilates her body. Then he not only hides the body but very carefully and neatly papers over the gap in the wall. He then goes home and shoots himself. Even if I'd no other evidence—*and I have*—I could never accept that story. I'd feel ashamed of myself for the rest of my life even if I pretended to accept it. Thank you for ringing me, Mr. Aricson, but you can tear up that check. Good-bye!"

Coming away from the telephone, he looked steadily at her. "If you listened to that, Maggie, then you heard most of my answer to you. I don't say conceit and obstinacy play no part here—"

"Of course they do. And all that money too," she added rather crossly. "What a waste! Just to prove some theory you have! I know I'm sounding like Colonel Thing, who's supposed to be so stupid, but as I said before, I thought he talked sense."

"There's something you're all overlooking," he cut in harshly. And the change of tone gave her a shock. "If I believe young Donnington didn't kill Noreen, then I must also believe that somebody else did. So what do I do then? Leave Birkden with a homicidal maniac still at large in it? Go far away knowing that the *Birkden Telegraph* won't catch up with me, to tell me about the next victim?"

"Oh, all right, I can understand that—*if* what you believe is true." She still sounded cross, crosser than she really felt. "And I'm not sure it is, because if that Donnington boy was more than half mad, he might easily do all kinds of contradictory things. And what was all that about evidence? How can you get any evidence, just sitting here?"

"I know—you feel I ought to be running round taking finger-prints and collecting tobacco ash. But that's not my method, Watson. My method is to do nothing in particular, just drop a remark or two and watch the pressure build up. The other people do all the work, giving themselves away."

"Oh, I realize you're very clever, Salt. But you do a lot of dangerous bluffing too. You announce you're leaving in a day or two—and tell everybody they're all wrong, and there's a murderer around—but can you honestly tell me you really have a clue?"

"My dear Miss Culworth"—and she knew at once that this was half mockery and that behind it he was serious—"believe it or not, I need only one other piece of information, and then I think my case will be complete, and the mystery solved."

But that was all he told her. There was a lot of noise outside, then some simultaneous ringing and knocking, and they were joined by Mr. Buzzy Duffield.

3

"Before the talking starts—and don't think I haven't plenty to say because I have—*bzzz*—step out an' have a look at it. Talk about class! I'm more than halfway to Buck House with a car like this. *Bzzz.*" As they followed him out, he waved a hand at a long black car standing at the curb. "Got it from a punter instead of the money he owed me at the betting shop. Talk about a bargain! He's more than two thousand nicker down on this lot. *Bzzz.* That's Whitey pretending to be shuvver. The cap's good —he insisted on it—but the rest of him's dead off key. And so far I have to open the bloody door all the time. *Bzzz.* How about taking a ride in her? Drive slow, lift your hand now an' again —give the peasants a treat."

"No, thanks, Buzzy," said Dr. Salt. "I haven't time. But I can use that car. Whitey can take the Culworth family home to Hemton while you're talking to me. Mr. Culworth hasn't been up and about for days and could do with a smooth ride. Maggie, go and see if they're ready."

"Please," said Maggie.

"This time you win. *Please.*"

Maggie found her parents all ready in the sitting room, wondering what was happening. Five minutes later she was sitting in the car with them, on her way home. She was not very happy about it, even though she knew she would have to be in the shop sometime in the afternoon, to clear things up with her father. But she couldn't help wishing that Salt had insisted upon her staying with him, at least for another hour or two. He hadn't exactly hurried her away with her parents, but he'd assumed she was going with them just a bit too quickly and easily— almost, though not quite, as if he wanted her out of his way. And what was he up to? And what did Buzzy want with him? And did he feel she was being stupid, an ally no longer, when all she really wanted was to keep him out of trouble? She went back over their argument. She was still going over it when Whitey brought them to their front door.

About the middle of the afternoon, when she and her father had dealt with checks and bills in the little back office at the shop, her father drew his chair nearer to hers, looked hard at her and said, "There's something I have to discuss with you, Maggie. And I think this is the best time to do it."

"Not if you're feeling tired, Daddy."

"No, I'm all right. Y'know, I've great confidence in Dr. Salt's judgment. I feel he understands me as a man and not just as so much blood pressure, temperature, heartbeats and the rest. And he told me that if I could get a good offer for this shop, I ought to give it up. On the other hand, even if I could afford it, I oughtn't to go away and do nothing."

"And I'm sure he's right. He isn't always right, but he is about you, Daddy."

"Do you mean he isn't right about *you?*"

"No, I don't," said Maggie hastily. "It's something else, quite different. I don't suppose he ever gives me a thought."

"Oh, yes, he does. However," he continued, to Maggie's sharp disappointment, "we're talking about me and the shop now. Now I didn't tell you this, but as a matter of fact I can get a very good price indeed for the shop and the business. And I could come to an arrangement with my old friend Sayers in Birmingham to help him—on a part-time basis—with the rare-books side."

"Well, that would be just right for you, wouldn't it?"

"It would. Give me something to do—and not too much."

"Then that's settled. So what are you looking and sounding so doubtful about, Daddy?"

"About you, Maggie, my dear," he replied promptly, surprising her. "I was talking it all over with your mother this morning, and we agreed it would be just right for me. But what about you?"

"What about me?"

"No shop, don't you see? I'm not worried about the other three. Bertha Chapman can go back to teaching, and I believe would be glad to go. No difficulty there. Sheila's out of her element here and could find a better job tomorrow. I don't know about young Reg—I have a notion he's really cut out for the book trade, that boy—but I'm certain I could find him something. You're the only one I'm worried about, Maggie. I have an idea you wouldn't want to go back to London, doing secretarial work. And I don't think there'd be much of an opening for you here in Hemton. Of course, you could easily find a job in Birkden—"

"No fear! I wouldn't be found dead in Birkden." She spoke

with a vehemence that surprised herself. "I *loathe* the place, always have done, and now I know it better I see I was quite right."

"Not just because of what happened to me, I hope, my dear."

"There's that too," she said hastily. "But also for all kinds of reasons. But it's absurd to bother about me, Daddy. You go ahead with your plans and don't think about me. Really I'm glad you're giving up the shop. Lately I've been feeling restless, needing a change—to do something different, though I don't know what."

"Dr. Salt half hinted at that."

"Oh—what exactly did he say?" she demanded sharply.

"Well, various things—you know."

"No, I don't know," she told him even more sharply, maddened by his vagueness. "How could I? Can't you remember even one of them?"

"Let me think. Yes, he said—what was it?—potentially you were a very fine woman but that your real life hadn't begun yet."

"Oh, he did, did he? A fat lot *he* knows about my real life—or anybody else's."

"No, Maggie, you can't say that. He's a man with a lot of insight as well as a lot of experience. I thought you'd have noticed that."

"All I've noticed," she replied, sweeping this reproach away to the rubbish heap where it belonged, "is that I'm beginning to feel rather restless." Then, thinking that she had been behaving badly, she smiled at him and changed her tone. "So you haven't to worry about me, Daddy. You do just what you want to do. It's time you did, bless you!"

He left early, at her insistence, but she stayed later than usual, clearing up and exchanging gossip with Bertha. Then, back at home, she really did begin to feel restless. What was Salt doing? Why had Buzzy wanted to see him? What was *happening* while she was just mooning around, miles away, here in Hemton?

Finally, after going to look at the telephone several times and then hardening her will against using it, she rang up Salt. No reply. There was something peculiarly desolating about hearing the phone ring and ring in the flat she now knew so well, and within a few minutes of putting down the receiver she was hurrying to the bus.

It was nearly half past seven when she rang Salt's bell and somehow knew at once that it wouldn't be answered. Feeling small, stupid, unwanted, she turned into the main road to find a telephone box. Her heart thumping away—and anyhow, the air in there was horribly foul—she rang up Buzzy's club and, after some delay, was able to speak to Buzzy himself. "I wanted to thank you first, Mr. Duffield, for letting us use that wonderful car of yours—you remember, to take my father home."

"Don't mensh—it was a privilege and a pleasure, Miss Culworth. *Bzzz*. You're a friend of Dr. Salt's, so am I."

"Well, that's what I wanted to ask you," she cut in desperately, afraid he might ring off. "I can't find Dr. Salt. Do you happen to know where he is?"

"I do. But keep it quiet. Strictly between us, this is. *Bzzz*. After a little talk we had this morning—and as a favor to me— he's moved into the Beverly-Astoria. You know it? Brand-new place on the Coventry road. They're still blowing the sawdust off it. *Bzzz*. That's where you ought to find him. If you don't, then come here to the club and ask for me. And not a word to anybody—you never know who'll start talking. You can't move for big mouths. *Bzzz*."

The Beverly-Astoria was the newest hotel she had ever walked into; it really did look as if it had just been unpacked out of a crate twelve stories high; and it also looked very grand, altogether too grand for Birkden. She decided to look around before asking for Dr. Salt. It was rather dimly lit and confusing, crowded with notices and glass cases, and seemed to smell of hot tin and varnish, rather like a magic lantern that Alan had once had. She contrived a peep into the dining room just before being accosted by a man with a pale face and a waxed mustache, like a croupier in a film, who was holding a number of menus about a yard square. She decided against going down below to Ye Olde Englishe Grill and instead ventured rather uncertainly into the cocktail bar, which was very dim indeed, almost blacked out, and had very soft and sickly canned music coming out of the wall. For a few moments she stood there, unable to see anybody or anything, but then—and it was the strangest experience—she heard his voice, heard a woman laugh and heard him laugh with her, from somewhere in a corner at the opposite end of the room. She took a few tentative steps in that direction—nobody was bothering about her—and then, her sight adjusting itself to the gloom, she saw him and his companion, not a young woman, no girl, but one of those ripe, smart, handsome and sophisticated women who represent The Enemy everywhere, and especially in cocktail bars where men drink double very dry martinis like water. And she was honest enough to recognize and name the knife that was turning in her.

It was jealousy.

THIRTEEN

1

"Now then, Buzzy," said Dr. Salt as soon as the Culworths had gone. "If you're ready to talk, I'm ready to listen—up to a point. No, sit in that chair—it's the only one that'll hold you." He waited until Buzzy had made himself comfortable and was lighting a cigar. "Now—what is it?"

"A bit of info first, doc. There's a lot of talk going round, but none of it's coming from you. Just exactly where do you stand on this Wilks kid's murder?"

Dr. Salt explained briefly and clearly where he stood.

"That's all I want to know. *Bzzz.* Anybody been round from the police this morning?"

"Yes, Buzzy. Colonel Ringwood himself. He lost his temper and almost told me I was outlawed."

"I buy that, doc. And it's just what I thought. *Bzzz.* And if it wasn't Friday I'd have two of my boys looking after you here. But Friday, like Saturday, can be a bloody great dogfight down at the club. They come in from other planets. *Bzzz.* I need more hard boys than I've got, both Friday and Saturday. So what about you, doc?"

"I'm not worried, Buzzy."

"Never said you were. But I am. So I want you to do *me* a favor by letting me do *you* a favor, if you see what I mean?"

"Not yet, Buzzy."

"I want you to take a load off my mind. *Bzzz.* I'm not going to spend tonight watching all those baboons and their scrawny little birds at my club an' wondering what the hell's happening to you here. I want my mind on my business. *Bzzz.* So you do me a favor. You stay away from here tonight and tomorrow—see?"

"But I'm not leaving Birkden, Buzzy."

"I know you're not. This is where I do you a favor. I've booked you into this posh new hotel—the Beverly-Astoria. Only opened this week. And you're in a suite—not just a bedroom, mark you, a *suite*—on the tenth floor."

"I'm not. I can't afford it. Neither can you."

"Me? I could afford to take the whole bloody floor if I wanted to. *Bzzz.* But don't get the idea I'm throwing good money away on this caper. They aren't full yet—they need people to dress it up—and I have an in with a couple of the directors, who've been betting with me for years. *Bzzz.* Your number's 1012. You ask for the key and walk straight in. All brand new. Deluxe. Four star. And it's time you poshed it up a bit, isn't it, doc? Gracious living an' all that. Look at this lot. Either you need a woman here or three furniture removers. *Bzzz.* Joking apart, doc, I'd feel a damn sight easier in my mind if I knew you weren't waiting for trouble here but were up there in the Beverly-Astoria—among the top people, we hope. Just as a favor, doc, eh? *Bzzz.*"

"All right, Buzzy. It's very kind of you to have taken so much trouble. Though I doubt if it's my kind of hotel."

"It's the last word. It's jet-age hospitality—"

"I'll bet it is. That's what I'm saying."

"It's what the young executive demands. It's for trend setters. Haven't you seen any of the ads?"

"No, Buzzy."

"Then you're not with it."

"I know I'm not."

"Me neither. Silly twerps!" After a pause, Buzzy gave him a long, hard look. "If the boy didn't do her, then who did?"

"I'm not sure yet, Buzzy. Don't press me."

"Okay, doc. *Bzzz.* But you told 'em she was dead, didn't you? Then took 'em to that house—eh? Just explain that part of it, doc. As a favor. What with punters all day and rockers and rollers all night—no brains anywhere—my mind's going an' I'll be a bloody imbecile shortly. *Bzzz.* So if you've anything clever to tell me, let's have it, for God's sake!"

"It wasn't that clever, Buzzy. But this is what happened." And by the time he had explained all that had happened, Whitey was hooting outside.

"Listen to that," said Buzzy, getting up. "Must have a shuvver's cap, then makes that bleedin' din. No class, no idea! *Bzzz.* Okay, then, doc. You'll move into the Beverly-Astoria this afternoon—eh? Tenth floor—1012. And of course, if you an' Miss Culworth would like to come an' see me at the club, you'll be heartily welcome. But tomorrow—good old Saturday—is the best night. *Bzzz.*"

"At its gayest, is it, Buzzy?"

"Gay? That's gone out. But I can show you the biggest mad monkey house of the week. It's an education. *Bzzz.*" He lowered his voice now as they moved out of the room together. "Another thing is, if you're down there nobody'll be trying to kick your teeth in. I'm serious, doc. You'll have to watch it now. If they can't frighten you out, they'll try to frame you. *Bzzz.* So watch it closely. And if I don't see you tonight, I might see you tomorrow—eh?"

"You easily might, Buzzy. And thank you for everything."

Outside his work—and especially at times like this, when he was really waiting for something important to happen—Dr. Salt was anything but a methodical man. He kept lighting his pipe and then letting it go out again. He looked at several suitcases in his bedroom, then wandered back into the sitting room, carrying the smallest of them. Realizing that he ought to have left it in the bedroom, to be packed there, he dropped it on the floor. Then he looked at some books—on a pile of those he intended to keep—and chose two of them and put them into the suitcase. Not long after that he drifted towards the telephone, picked up the receiver and then put it down again, looked in the directory for Alicia's Boutique and dialed its number.

"Mrs. Marton, please. Dr. Salt here. . . . Oh, Alice—how are you? . . . Good, good . . . Are you still thinking about starting a branch boutique swindle in Hemton? . . . Well, I might have just the right girl for you. . . . No, not over the phone, I think. There are things I have to explain. Why don't you join me for a drink in the cocktail bar—it must have a cocktail bar—of the whatsit—Beverly-Astoria, that place that's just been opened? About seven—um? . . . Good, very good . . . What am I up to? Oh, just playing God. Bye."

Absent-mindedly he returned to the bedroom, wondered why he was there, then collected pajamas, a dressing gown and slippers, took them into the sitting room and dropped them into the suitcase. After looking at his watch, he went into the kitchen, examined what was left on its shelves and in the refrigerator, took down and opened a tin, French and good, of onion soup and spooned it out into a saucepan to heat it. He cut a slice of bread for toast, and found all that was left of his Parmesan cheese. Two oranges—and he hadn't anything else—would have to complete the meal, such as it would be. Then he drank a little neat whisky and stirred the soup. For the first time he felt rather glad he had accepted Buzzy's invitation to enjoy the jet-age hospitality of the Beverly-Astoria.

"Oh, then you're not here for either the books *or* the records." Dr. Salt was addressing his first caller of the afternoon.

"Not me. My card." He was a tall, thin man who wore a nasty green tie and a suit the color of faded chocolate. He suggested a Dante half ruined by too many late nights, too much whisky and not enough money, and was not an appealing figure. Above some address in Birmingham, his card read: *Herbert X. Coleman—Confidential Investigations.*

"What's the *X.* for?" Dr. Salt was genuinely interested.

"Just a front—part of the build-up. You're Herbert Coleman —who cares, who remembers? But Herbert *X.* Coleman—wow! Even the wife calls me Herbert X. now."

"Good for her! But I don't want any confidential investigations, Mr. Coleman."

"Do you mind, Dr. Salt?" He was offended. "I don't go asking for clients on doorsteps. I'm not looking for business. Just wanted to have a little chat—in comfort and not where everybody might see us and hear us, don't you think?"

"I'm not sure I do. But come in."

"Mind if I sit here?" said Mr. Coleman, now near the suitcase. "Packing, eh? Clearing out?"

"I'm moving into the Beverly-Astoria for a night or two."

"Any particular reason, Dr. Salt?"

"Yes, it isn't costing me anything. And I'm curious. Jet-age hospitality."

"I don't follow you."

"You don't have to. Or do you, Mr. Coleman? Perhaps you already have a client here in Birkden."

Instead of replying, Coleman stared hard at him. Dr. Salt was a good starer himself. So they both stared.

" 'Bout this Noreen Wilks murder," said Coleman. "I have a

little idea of my own that ought to interest you. Now you say the boy didn't do it."

"How do *you* know?"

"It's going around. Now my idea is this. *You did it.*"

"*I* did?"

"Why not?"

"Well, to begin with, if I'd done it I wouldn't have insisted that the girl wasn't missing but dead and then have found the body for the police—would I?"

"Why not? It's happened before. Say you're really a psychopath. You've done a girl in—a patient too. You're going away and nobody knows about it. That won't do. So you insist that the girl didn't leave town but is lying dead somewhere, and as there isn't much time, you lead the police straight to the body. Then when they say the boy must have done it, you won't have that—it's your job, not his."

"And what do I do next? Give myself up? Confess?"

"Probably not. Depends how far gone you are."

"And how far gone am I?"

"How should I know?"

"Oh, come on. Why stop now?" Dr. Salt paused, realizing that the most withering irony had no effect on Herbert X. Coleman. "You can do better than that."

"I can try. I'd say there won't be any giving yourself up and confessing. The murder's out, that's enough. You'll prove the boy didn't do it, and that'll satisfy you. Then you'll go, quite happy, after celebrating at the Beverly-Astoria. What's wrong with that?"

"Nothing—except it's all balls."

"Could be. But one or two people round here might buy it. Then—when do you leave? You might be weeks—helping them with their inquiries, as they say."

"I see," said Dr. Salt, looking hard at him. "I began to think you were a complete crackpot. But you're not, are you?" There was somebody at the door. "That must be for either books or records. So now I'm busy, Mr. Coleman."

"Thanks for your time, Dr. Salt. I'll be seeing you."

"I hope not. Good afternoon."

3

Dr. Salt followed the youth who had taken his suitcase—a youth with a thick Birmingham accent but wearing a uniform originally designed for Hungarian bandsmen about 1908—and they arrived at the lifts. One was down and wide open. A middle-aged couple, looking indignant, were waiting inside. The youth pressed the number ten, which lit itself up. "All automatic—see?" he announced proudly to all three of them.

"I daresay," said the indignant man. "But when does it start?"

"Doors have to shut first."

"I know that—but when?"

"You can always close 'em yourself," said the youth. "You press this." He pressed it. Nothing happened.

"Now then—what?" And she sounded more indignant than her husband.

The youth pressed the same button and then tried lighting up numbers eleven and twelve, in the hope of making something happen. Nothing did until a short, fat woman, carrying two hatboxes, tried to enter. At once the doors came to life in a sinister fashion and smartly caught her between them. She gave a shriek; Dr. Salt tugged at one door, the youth at the other; the woman pushed her way in, ramming the hatboxes against the indignant couple; and the lift started.

"What floor?" the youth asked, ready for more pressing and lighting up.

"Second—and I wish I'd never bothered with this thing."

"It's what the young executive demands," said Dr. Salt.

"I don't know what you're talking about."

"Neither do I. But here you are. Now—watch those doors."

The doors parted an inch or two and then trembled, as if they were begging the short, fat woman to come and play. "Well, make your mind up," she told them. They did, and she charged out, but only just in time, nearly leaving a hatbox behind. The indignant couple wanted the sixth floor but the lift preferred the seventh, so they hurried out to walk down. Then the doors sulked again. The youth did more pressing. Fortunately another 1908 Hungarian bandsman arrived, and in trying to nip him the doors had to close. The lift went up and apparently reached ten, but the doors were not cooperating. Tired of them by this time, Dr. Salt gave the nearest one a kick. This opened them at once.

On their way to 1012, the youth noticed the old black bag Dr. Salt had insisted on carrying himself. "You a doctor?" he asked.

"I am. But I'm not here professionally."

"Maybe not," said the youth darkly. "But if you ask me, there's a woman on the next floor going to need one soon. This is it—1012."

The sitting room looked so new it might have been in a shop window. And not a particularly large window. It was a very small room, and there was space for a television set and a radio only because the two armchairs and the sofa seemed to have been designed for midgets. It was like a sitting room in science fiction—say, about A.D. 2250, in a block of flats two miles high, with the world population perhaps at 32 billion. Dr. Salt detested it at once. The bedroom and bathroom were better, and he gave the youth, who was fussing around and behaving as if the solitary suitcase were really three cabin trunks, half a crown instead of the shilling he had mentally promised him.

Left to himself, he went prowling around, like an animal moved into a new cage. His windows offered him what he had already been told was a "breathtaking view" of Birkden, but he found he could breathe quite easily as he stared out and down, nothing in sight being worth looking at. Hanging in the bedroom was a bad watercolor of Fountains Abbey, and in the sitting room was a guitar-bottle-newspaper mess painted by somebody who had once seen a postcard of an early Braque. He switched on the television set, which, after making a noisy protest, showed him a number of dazzling lines moving up and down the screen. So he turned it off, unpacked his suitcase, took his shaving kit into the bathroom. There was no toilet paper.

He looked in both the bedroom and the sitting room for a bell to summon the chambermaid. But progress and the demands of young executives and trend setters had left such bells far behind. Their place had been taken by the telephone, which proved to have a most elaborate dialing system, turning him into a switchboard operator; and an equally elaborate directory of services that seemed to include everything except any mention of chambermaids and toilet paper. He dialed the *Op.*, but found himself talking to *Valet Serv.*, tried again and got through to *Sten. & Copying Serv.*, finally reached *Op.* and told her he had no toilet paper. She said she would put him through to the housekeeper, and after some delay, during which he heard an angry man shouting, "Charlie said Tuesday? Charlie's always saying Tuesday," he was able to speak to some remote gentlewoman, who promised faintly to provide him with toilet paper. It arrived fifty minutes later.

Meanwhile, for want of something better to do, he took a bath. The bathtub was long, wide and rather low, unsuitable for reading, so he abandoned Tomlinson's *Tidemarks*, one of the two books he had brought, did some sketchy soaping and sponging, and then, for no reason at all, thought about a man called Hibberson he hadn't seen for ten years. Then it was time to get out. And this, he saw at once, could be tricky. He was a heavy man—even heavier than he looked—and the tub was slippery. There was nothing for his right hand to grip or rest on, and a one-handed job, with his left hand slipping along the edge, was impossible. However, about eighteen inches above the tub on the wall was a fitting that had a recessed soap dish and a handle above it for people like him to use. So he gave a push with his left hand and stretched to grab the handle with his right, and he had pulled himself half out of the bath when the whole fitting came out of the wall, a shower of plaster with it. He felt he might have broken his neck, and as it was, he had given his knee a nasty knock. After hurling the wretched fitting across the room, he managed somehow to get himself out of the tub, and then, wrapping a towel round his middle, he went padding out, wet and furious, to the telephone to call the manager. What he got was *Trav. & Trans. Bureau.*

When the management finally arrived, it was represented by a young man with a long, falling-away face who was wearing a black coat too large for him. "I am the assistant manager, sir. Mr. Mallini is out at the moment. What can I do for you, sir?"

"Come and look at this," said Dr. Salt, who was dry now and in a dressing gown, bought in Kowloon ten years before and well past its best. He pointed at the hole in the bathroom wall. He pointed at the fitting and at the plaster both inside and outside the tub.

The young man, who looked frightened, made a tuttering noise. "How did this happen, sir?"

"It came out of the wall as soon as I tried to make use of it. Gave my knee a hell of a knock. Look!"

The young man tut-tutted again. "If you'd like me to call a doctor, sir—" he began.

"I *am* a doctor. Who built this hotel? A women's magazine? Jet-age hospitality!"

"Pardon?"

"Never mind."

"I'm very sorry indeed, sir, this has happened. If there's anything we can do—"

He was wriggling inside the black coat, which had been designed for it, and he looked so like a terrified sheep that Dr. Salt hadn't the heart to be bad-tempered any longer. "No—forget it. And off you go. It's time I got dressed."

When he went down to the main floor it was still too early for his appointment with Alice Marton in the cocktail bar, but he felt that he needed a drink. On his way to it he noticed a tall, thin man talking at the reception desk. It was Herbert X. Coleman, apparently still engaged in confidential investigations.

4

He saw her approaching the bar and went forward to meet her. "Hello, Alice. You're looking healthy, prosperous and fine."

"Thank you, dear. I'd return the compliment, but I can't see how you're looking. Very dim, isn't it?"

"It's probably what the young executive wants. There's a table free in the corner. Are you still drinking gin and Campari?"

After he had ordered their drinks, she said, "Let's talk business first, Salt dear. Who's this girl you're wishing on me? Not some sweet little thing you've been amusing yourself with, I hope. I never trust a man's judgment—not even yours—if sex is mixed up in it."

"Nothing like that, Alice. I've never spent two minutes alone with this girl. And as far as I can gather, she's just fallen violently in love with a young man I know, Alan Culworth, who teaches physics at the university. And that's the point. She's lost—or will shortly lose—her present job, and I'll be partly responsible for that. They'll want to marry soon, and I don't suppose he has much of a salary yet, and running your Hemton boutique would be just right for her."

"Well, I'm looking for somebody, as you know. But don't forget, darling, I'm not a soft-hearted doctor—and you know very well you're just a lot of warm mush inside—but a tough business woman. So stop telling me how nice and convenient it would be for her and her boyfriend. What has she got to offer me and the job?"

"Rather a lot, I'd say. But you've probably run into her. Perhaps at the Fabrics Club, if you ever go there. Her name's Jill Frinton."

"Now wait a minute. A tallish, dark girl, rather smart, isn't she? But somebody told me she was the girl friend of one of the Fabrics directors."

"She was but isn't now. My dear Alice, do I have to explain all over again—"

"No. Shut up! I want to think."

Left to sip his whisky and water in silence, Dr. Salt began to listen to a voice that he felt he had heard before. It was coming from the opposite corner of the room, the one nearer the entrance, but it was high, nervous, rather loud, so not hard to hear above other, more subdued voices and the idiot music that was being pumped into the room. He half rose to stare across, saw a young man and a girl sitting at that table, and then concentrated on the girl. And as he sank down again he awarded himself a little nod.

"When you've finished bobbing about, Salt darling," said Alice, "I'll tell you what's in my mind. Unless, of course, you've lost interest and would rather join your friends over there."

"They aren't my friends, I haven't lost interest, and drop the sarcasm. It doesn't suit you and you have to work too hard at it. Now what about Jill Frinton?"

"You really have something there, Salt, my love. She certainly looks dead right, and she's had the social experience. It doesn't follow that she'll know how to run a shop of this sort, and for all I know she may not have the right temperament. But I'm going to talk to her—and as soon as possible. Do I arrange it through you?"

"I think not, Alice. She denounced me hotly last night—said I was trying to play God."

"Oh, that's what you meant on the phone."

"Yes. Everybody's denouncing me and threatening me, Alice, because I'm determined to find out who killed a patient of mine."

"Something Wilks. It's in tonight's paper—how you helped to find the body. Isn't it *exciting?*"

"No," he told her flatly. "It's miserable, nasty, horrible. Let's get back to Jill Frinton. I suggest you ring her up and ask her to visit the shop in the morning. But leave me out of it. She doesn't like me."

"Then that's one bad mark, my pet. I ought to tell her I love you. I do in a way too."

"I love you in the same way, Alice, my dear. Only it's not the right way for either of us, as we both know very well. We enjoy each other's company, but don't *need* each other. What you need is a slender man with a beard, a delicate chest and wood engravings nobody wants to buy."

"I'd kill him in a week. I don't know what you need, but I know what you'll get sooner or later. A nurse—with a very straight back and a will of iron. But how do you come to be mixed up in this Jill Frinton thing?"

"This Noreen Wilks business, which I don't want to discuss, involved her boyfriend's family. Culworths—keep a bookshop in Hemton."

"I noticed it the other day when I was up there. Once you keep a shop, you notice all the other shops. But tell me, Salt, my pet, why did you ask me to come here? Not your sort of place, unless you're not the man you were."

"I'm staying here."

"Why, for God's sake?"

Then he explained about Buzzy and jet-age hospitality and young executives and trend setters and all that had happened to him so far under this roof, probably due to collapse at any

209

moment. And she laughed and laughed, and he began to laugh with her. Then he saw Maggie.

He hurried across, to catch her before she turned away. "Maggie, come and join us. Unless, of course, you're looking for somebody else."

"Well, I was just wondering—" she began vaguely.

"Come on, come on. I've been discussing something with an old friend—something that'll interest you, but I'll explain later. In point of fact, I was going to telephone you. Now then—this is Maggie Culworth, Alice. Maggie, this is Mrs. Alice Marton, of Alicia's Boutique fame. "Alice, order something for Maggie. I'll have to leave you women for a few minutes."

He moved briskly towards the entrance, but then swerved and went up to the table in the corner. "Miss Donnington, isn't it? Thought I recognized your voice. I'm Dr. Salt, you remember?" He looked at the beefy young man whose cheeks were dark and his eyes glittering and insolent with drink. "Let me see," he said in his special innocent-chump voice, "have we met? I seem to know your face."

"My name's Walsham. And I don't think we've met. Can't imagine why we should have."

"He's really telling you to go away. Aren't you, darling?" And Erica Donnington, who had obviously had her share of drink too, gave a shriek of laughter.

Dr. Salt showed no sign of embarrassment. He grinned, nodded and hurried away. A few moments later he was at the reception desk. "I have an idea that a young man I know called Walsham is staying here. Could you give me his room number, please? I'm staying here myself, you know—1012."

"Yes, of course," said the receptionist. "Mr. Walsham is in 806. If I see him, shall I tell him you inquired?"

"No, don't do that. I'd rather like to give him a surprise."

He strolled away, like a man killing time and not looking for anybody or anything. But between half-closed lids his eyes were bright and sharp indeed, and very soon they saw, protruding from one of the large armchairs facing the hotel entrance, a pair of trousers of a faded-chocolate shade. They could only belong to Herbert X. Coleman, who was sitting there waiting for somebody to arrive. As if wondering whether to walk forward into Herbert X. Coleman's area of vision and perhaps accost him or to remain out of sight, Dr. Salt hesitated a moment or two. Then he moved slowly and thoughtfully towards the cocktail bar, but just before he reached it he went down some steps beneath the illuminated sign of *Gentlemen*, hoping that one of the urinals would not crumble as soon as he started making use of it.

FOURTEEN

1

After Alice had ordered a Dubonnet for Maggie, she said to her, "I'm opening a branch boutique in Hemton and I'm looking for somebody to manage it. Dr. Salt has suggested Jill Frinton. Is it your brother—at the university—who's her boyfriend?"

"Yes—Alan," Maggie replied rather shyly. But she no longer felt jealous of this large, plump woman. "They seem to be crazy about each other. And I know Alan, who's very serious, will want to marry her. And I was dreading it because he hasn't much money."

"And you just couldn't see her trying to make do on it, could you, dear? Well, if she was right for my job, I'd pay her at least as much as he gets. With commission, probably more. You know her. What do you think of the idea?"

"Well, I'm sure she's very clever about clothes and accessories and all that. She's that type. And I can see her being charming and tough at the same time, if you know what I mean, Mrs. Marton?"

"Alice, dear. And I know exactly what you mean. Between nine-thirty and five-thirty I'm *very* charming and tough as hell.

You just have to be. Anyhow, I'll have a talk with her—tomorrow morning, I hope. And if I do take her on, she'll owe it to our friend and poppet, Salt. And he says she doesn't like him."

"She would if he wanted her to, Alice." Maggie spoke with more conviction than she intended to convey.

Alice gave her a flashing look. "But you can't have known him very long, my dear."

"Only a few days. But it seems a long time because a lot of things happened—all part of this horrible murder business."

"He didn't want to tell me, so you needn't, Maggie. I've known Salt ever since he came here, though I saw a lot more of her than I did of him. He was always working so hard. I lost my husband—a car smash—just before he lost his wife. We're fond of each other, but only as friends. Couldn't be anything else. But he's a lovely man—very clever and yet kind and sweet, and very brave."

"I know he is," cried Maggie. Then she checked her enthusiasm. "But isn't he very obstinate and self-opinionated as well?"

"Of course he is, my dear. And why not? He's a real man—just as my Bill was. Maddening and marvelous. And getting damn scarce, let me tell you. I don't really know young men now, though I like the look of some of 'em, as if they didn't give a damn. But, say, between thirty-five and fifty-five, real men, like my Bill and Salt, seem to me harder and harder to find. Too many of 'em seem to be frightened of something—of us women or not pleasing the chairman of the board or not having enough money. You know."

"Yes, I *do* know." Maggie was emphatic.

Alice gave her a look. *"Aha!"*

"Yes—*aha!"* Maggie finished her drink. Then she hesitated. "What was she like?"

"In appearance, not unlike you, but a size or two larger all round—and of course much older. She was one of those rare women—and I'm not one but I admire them—who are serious but not solemn, boring. She could be very lively, quite gay, but she wasn't frivolous. She was a serious person, just as Salt, for all his talk and antics, is a serious person."

"Yes, I know what you mean, Alice. She must have been wonderful. What are you laughing at?"

"I don't know. Yes, I do. But here he comes. And I must fly. I've a dinner date." She got up to greet him. "I'm sorry to be running away, Salt darling, but I'm late already. When are you actually going?"

"Monday morning, probably. We must meet sometime on Sunday, Alice."

"Will you still be staying here?"

"Don't be silly, woman. I leave this gorgeous dump in the morning. I'll ring you."

"You'd better, Salt." She gave him a hasty comradely kiss. "And thanks for the drink. And the tip about the girl. *And* the nice talk with nice Maggie, who's pretending not to adore you. Bye."

"I heard all that," said Maggie, because Alice had moved a few steps away from the table. "I like her, but I'm *not* pretending not to adore you, because I don't adore you, Salt."

"Of course you don't, Maggie. But Alice says anything that comes into her head. Not that she's a fool—far from it. And she had a rough time but came through—bands playing, colors flying."

"Has she a lover?"

"Probably, but if so, I don't know who he is. I'm very fond of Alice, but I haven't seen much of her lately. I've had to work all hours, and she not only runs the shop but has to keep dashing off to London and Paris, buying her expensive nonsense. Perhaps it's a Frenchman—one of those with deep voices who stick out their lower lips."

"I'll bet he has a lovely time. Why are you doing this for Jill, when she was yelling at you only last night?"

"It's part of a tidying-up process. I'm not conscious of wanting to move people around like chessmen, as Jill—and you too, perhaps—seem to believe. But if she gets the job—and I believe she will—then you won't be worrying away thinking she's going to ruin Alan. So I might leave everybody feeling happier," he concluded lightly, not looking at her.

"But that doesn't mean you aren't really a bit of an old busy-body." She spoke lightly too.

Now he looked at her. "I'm not, Maggie. It's a wrong view of me. It just happens we've become friends at an odd time. You might as well imagine that I'm always sitting in a dusty room among piles of books and records. By the way, all those I wanted to sell have gone now. I was swindled, of course, but both chaps paid me in notes so that I feel as if I'm bulging with money. Let's spend some of it on dinner. Aren't you hungry? I am."

"I think I am too. But I'm not dressed for that dining room. I peeped in when I was looking for you—I rang up Buzzy and he told me where you were—and I wouldn't feel happy in there. We'd better go down to Ye Oldie Englishie Grillie Room. Unless, of course, we go out and eat somewhere else."

"No, Maggie, I'm against that," he said rather slowly and apologetically.

"Don't tell me you've fallen in love with this place."

"This place? Me? Didn't you hear Alice and me laughing when you first came in here? Well, I'd been telling her what had happened. I'll tell you later. But I must stay on now." Both his look and his tone changed. "I wanted to say something about that, Maggie. My own behavior may soon seem rather peculiar. I may want you to do one or two odd things."

"Nothing you learned from the Chinese, I hope, Salt."

"I'm serious, girl. Silly as I look and probably sound—and idiotic as this place is—I'm trying to do a bit of work here tonight."

"Work? On what?" Then she brought her voice down. "Not the Noreen Wilks thing?"

"I'm afraid so, Maggie." He leaned towards her, dropping his tone almost to a whisper. "And if you don't mind, we'll begin with a little odd behavior now. While I'm paying for the drinks, you go out—"

"To the ladies' loo first, if you've no objection."

"Perfect from every point of view. Then go down to the grill, and if I'm already there, then join me, of course—but if I'm not, simply ask for a table for two and wait for me. And get one out of the way, in a corner, if you can."

She stared at him for a moment. Even now she was never quite sure if he was really in earnest. "Now look—if you mean this, hadn't you better explain what the idea is? Have you some reason for our not being seen together?"

"Partly that. Partly too that there are some things I ought to do by myself. Now, Maggie, please, off you go." But he gave her a smile.

As she walked out slowly, she heard a scream of laughter coming from some girl in the corner on the left. Nearly all the tables were occupied now, and people seemed to be two deep at the long, curved bar. The two red-coated waiters were hurrying with loaded trays, and seeping through the mosaic of noise like warm, flooding syrup came the sound of the hotel's canned music. And it was hard to believe that she was here because Salt was here, because Salt was still thinking about a girl's body left in a cavity in a wall. No doubt he could join everything together, making one world out of it all, but she couldn't. It was all split up, and it split her up, making her feel bewildered and terribly inadequate. If she was so close to Salt that she saw everything through him, would that do the joining-up trick for her? But what would she be giving him then, what would she have to offer?

The ladies' didn't help. The woman looking after it was all right, quite friendly, but the place itself suggested it was waiting for girls more important and better dressed than Maggie Culworth of Hemton. Even when she had redone her face, putting in some rather reckless eye shadow work too, it still made her feel a rather shabby little thing. So when she reached

216

the grill room she was relieved to discover, after some staring around, that Salt was already there.

They had eaten avocados with a French dressing, saddle of mutton, cheese (for him) and fruit salad (for her), had drunk a bottle of a beautifully soft claret whose name she never bothered to learn, and were now talking idly over their coffee. Between the mutton and his cheese, Salt had asked her to excuse him and had then been absent for about five minutes. Throughout the meal nothing had been said about Noreen Wilks, young Donnington and old Donnington, Colonel Ringwood and Superintendent Hurst. And it seemed to her that just talking about other people and things was like escaping from a dark house into clear sunlight. Moreover, having been persuaded to drink some Cointreau with her coffee, she was feeling rather dreamy. She tried to imagine herself in the Dordogne.

"I've never been there, but Alan has and he showed me a lot of photographs."

"Been where?" But Salt wasn't really attending. He was busy with a cigar that was trying to unravel itself.

"Oh, sorry! The Dordogne. That's where you said you were going, didn't you?"

"Yes, yes—of course." He was now out of his cigar muddle. "I'll only be there a week or ten days. Then I drive to Barcelona, and then to Zurich. There's a man in Barcelona and another man in Zurich who are specializing in certain kidney diseases. Too late for me to do that—and anyhow, I like people, not microscopes—but I want to see what they're doing. And I have a few notes that might interest them."

"I must say, that's not my idea of a holiday. The Dordogne— yes. Marvelous! And Barcelona's rather exciting. I've been there. But then the kidneys take over."

"Given the right time and place, I could keep you enthralled by my story of the kidney—its disasters and triumphs, its hopes and fears. But not here, not now." He looked at his watch. "Just after ten. So—we go to work. You ready?"

"I suppose so," she said reluctantly. "But I won't pretend I'm in the right mood for it, especially if there's anything difficult to do."

"No, no. All as easy as pie."

"Pie can be terribly difficult."

"Not this one. I want you to go to the eighth floor. If there are any chambermaids or waiters around—and I think it's unlikely —just waste time until they've gone. Look at your nose, powder it—that sort of thing."

"You needn't tell me. I've done hours of it. Every girl has. So what do I do if the corridor's clear?"

"You ring, knock or bang on the door of 806. If it's not opened at once, don't give up. Try at least once again. If and when it is opened, then tell an urgent but rather confused story that will keep it open. You believe—let's say—that a small parcel intended for you in 906 may have been delivered to 806. You're awfully sorry to disturb him but would he mind making sure the parcel isn't there—you know?"

"He might want me to make sure with him. And a lot of things could happen after that, especially if he's a young man and has had a few drinks."

"If he asks you in, then he won't have anybody in there with him, and the whole exercise is washed out. Just mutter some excuse and buzz off."

"You mean I'm really trying to discover if this man has got a girl in there? While I'm telling my story and the door's open, I'm listening for any possible screams, giggles, scraps of girlish song or impatient cries from the bedroom—um?"

"That's very sharp of you, Maggie."

"No, it isn't. The female mind works like lightning along those lines, Salt. Then what do I do?"

"You don't come down again. You go up to the tenth floor—

stairs or lift—make sure nobody's watching you and then let yourself into my little suite, 1012. And here's the key." He handed it over. "Close the door, but don't let it lock itself. That's so that I can pretend to be unlocking it when I arrive. If somebody sees me, so much the better."

"Is this part of the room 806 plot or something different?"

"Quite different." He grinned. "But they both belong to a grander plot."

"Salt dear, do you really know what you're doing? Or is it the mixture of whisky, claret and brandy that's at work?"

"That's helping, no doubt. But I had all this in mind before the mixture began to work." The grin vanished. "I may be guessing a bit wildly, but I'm not just fooling around, Maggie. For one thing, I can't afford the time."

"A pity in a way." She sighed. "Now I come to think of it, I'm more in the mood for fooling around. But after all, it was your dinner that created the mood. And thank you, Dr. Salt. It was lovely. And now I'll go—a mousy type creeping around like a mouse." She got up.

"No, Maggie," he told her quite sharply as he got up too. "There's one thing wrong there."

"Oh, dear. What?"

"You're not a mousy type."

Her pleasure at hearing this lasted until the lift, which she had to herself, brought her to the eighth floor. No chambermaids or waiters or guests could be seen along the corridor that led her to 806. Outside the door she hesitated, rehearsing what she had to say, feeling silly. She pressed the button and heard the buzzer inside. Nothing happened. Resisting an impulse to leave it at that and hurry away, she pressed again, longer this time. "Oh, for God's sake!" she heard a man saying. "Now what is it?" Then he opened the door.

He was a big, youngish man who was pulling a dressing gown round him, and his hair was rumpled, his color high, his eyes rather bleary.

"I'm so sorry," she began.

"Wrong room," he told her.

"Well, that's the point. I'm in 906, you see, and I think that a parcel I'm expecting may have been delivered here by mistake."

"No parcel here."

"Are you sure?" He was already closing the door.

"Of course I am. 'Night."

And that was that. She decided against using a lift again, found the stairs and walked as fast as she could, in what she was certain must have looked a very suspicious manner, up to the tenth floor. But nobody was about. It was rather like wandering about a hotel in a dream. But then, on her way to 1012, she heard voices behind her. Two people must have just arrived by the lift. She stopped, took out her compact and looked at her reflected nose, to allow them to pass her. It was a nonsensical move, really; any girl in her right mind would either have fixed her nose downstairs or would wait now until she reached her room; but of course it worked and the couple ignored her. They had, in fact, disappeared by the time she moved on again slowly. She had a moment's panic when the door of 1012 didn't seem to respond to the key Salt had given her, but then a reverse turn took her in. In her relief she slammed the door behind her. After switching on some lights, she remembered what Salt had said about the door and she made haste to unfasten it so that he could push it open. By this time, after all that dinner and drink and anxiety, she felt hot and rather sickish inside, so she went to the bathroom and drank some cold water that wasn't cold and didn't taste like water. Then she returned to the idiotic little sitting room, kicked off her shoes and curled up on the sofa, and not only waited for Salt but thought about him.

"We'll have to talk very quietly, if you don't mind," said Salt, speaking very quietly himself.

"I don't mind. But I can't help wondering why. I mean, this is a sitting room—or it's trying to be."

"I'm not thinking about that. Something quite different. By the way, there's some whisky in my bag."

"No, thanks, not for me. What I need, after all that mysterious creeping around, is something for my tummy."

"Well, I've got something for your tummy too," he told her. And of course he had, being a doctor, and came back with something fizzy in a glass. She thanked him all the more warmly because he had attended to her before asking what had happened at 806.

"I feel I ought to have managed it better," she said. "But he was so determined to get rid of me. He was also rather tight, rather rude and quite ready to be still ruder. He wasn't prepared to be interested at all in female callers."

"Which suggests there was a girl in his room—um?"

"That's what I felt. Also, just as he opened the door I thought I heard a girl laugh. I never heard anything afterwards. I may have imagined the girl's laugh. I'm afraid this doesn't add up to very much. I certainly can't prove he had a girl in there. Sorry, Salt."

"Not to worry. I may try something else shortly. In the meantime, we'll just have to sit and wait and keep our voices down."

"I don't know what we're supposed to be doing," she said. "But if you want to suggest you're here by yourself, then why don't we turn on the television or the radio? My voice wouldn't be heard above it. Right?"

"Right. Let's try this radio." He fiddled with the set until there came out of it, booming and boring away, the voice of a man who was talking about railway trains. After a minute or two of this, he tried again and found some music. "It's the Mozart clarinet quintet," he announced with some satisfaction. "Let's stay with it—unless you have a very strong objection, Maggie. You're not a music *hater*, are you?"

"You ought to know I'm not. I like it, even though I don't know much about it."

"Listen to this, then. It's a masterwork—a credit to the human race."

It was five minutes later when the human race began discrediting itself. The door, which Salt had left unlatched, was flung open, and a young woman, wearing a dressing gown and apparently not much else, came charging in, looking as if she were about to embrace Dr. Salt with her dressing gown flung wide open. With only a few seconds' interval, she was followed by a tall, thin man who was holding a flash camera.

"Go ahead, Coleman," said Dr. Salt cheerfully. "Maggie, this is Herbert X. Coleman."

"Another sodding balls-up," cried the young woman bitterly as she stepped away from Dr. Salt and wrapped the dressing gown around her. "This is the last time, Bert."

"Perhaps you'd like *me* to take my clothes off," Maggie suggested sweetly.

"If you did, dearie, then something'd go wrong with his bloody flashlight. My God—I'll never learn."

"All right, all right," said Coleman. "So it didn't work out. Not that I did anything wrong, but he was too smart for me, that's all. It can happen."

"It's always happening," the young woman said contemptuously. "But not with me anymore." She looked at Maggie. "Sorry to have intruded, dearie. Nothing personal. Just business."

"Come on, Enid, and stop yapping. I must have telegraphed the punch somehow."

"You did, Coleman," said Dr. Salt sharply. "And we'll leave it at that. But try anything else and I'll make you wish you'd never left Birmingham. Now clear off—and don't frighten anybody in the corridor."

As the door closed behind them, Maggie switched off the radio. "I know it's lovely music, but you can listen to it some other time. He was trying to *frame* you, wasn't he? I've seen it in the movies."

"So has Herbert X. Coleman," said Dr. Salt, grinning. "He's the Birmingham model of a Hollywood private eye." No longer troubling to keep his voice down, he explained how Coleman had called on him early in the afternoon. "I guessed then he'd been brought here to run me into any kind of trouble. Then I spotted him down below, first waiting for somebody and then, later, talking to the girl. And that's why I didn't want us to be seen together and why I asked you to come up here first. They didn't know you were here, of course. Which reminds me." He went to the telephone.

"Now then, where are we?" He pulled a kind of miniature directory out of the base of the telephone. "This is all so modern and convenient they turn you into a switchboard operator to speak to anybody. This is it, I suppose. 'To call another room, first dial 17.' "

As soon as he had finished dialing and had waited a moment, the receiver produced some sort of screech that even Maggie could hear. "What did you say?" he asked the screecher. He listened and then, without speaking again, put down the receiver and gave Maggie a triumphant nod.

"That's all," he told her. "I can run you home now, Maggie. And thank you for being so patient and good."

"Do you mean you've finished now?"

"For tonight anyhow. I don't want you to go, but I think you ought just in case our friend Coleman thinks of something that might involve you. Ready?"

As they went down in the lift, she asked him if he had definitely decided to return to his flat in the morning.

"Certainly. I've a lot of little things to do. But I may accept

223

Buzzy's invitation to spend the evening at his club. Would you like to come and lend me a hand as soon as you're through at the shop? Saturday's a busy day, I imagine. I can't fetch you because I'll no longer have my car. I'm selling it tomorrow afternoon."

"Alan can run me down on his way to Jill." As they left the lift, she said, "What about dinner tommorrow night?"

"A very good question, Maggie. We'll eat at home, eh? No Saturday night table grabbing. We'll be up late, so we might risk chump chops and then Welsh rarebit. All right?"

"Lovely. Do you want me to bring anything?"

"No, my dear. I'll pop out fairly early in the morning. Now just hang on and I'll find the car."

As usual they said nothing while he was driving. However, when they stopped outside the house Maggie couldn't leave him without saying something. "I've been wondering and wondering all the way here. And I can't decide if I'm just stupid or you're being fantastic. You've spent tonight playing these games with Herbert X. Thing—Coleman—and those people in 806, and you're talking about selling your car tomorrow, buying chops and stuff, going to Buzzy's club—and yet at the same time you're defying the police and everybody and talking as if you'll prove young Donnington didn't kill Noreen Wilks."

"I am, yes. Quite right, Maggie."

"But if you mean it, then when—and how?"

"Better not stay here. Excuse me." He leaned across and opened the door for her.

"Oh, you're just being maddening now, Salt."

"I'm not trying to be. *When?* I'd say tomorrow night or Sunday night. *How?* Well, I think I know now who killed Noreen Wilks—and why. But let's leave it. See you early tomorrow evening, Maggie. Good night, my dear."

FIFTEEN

1

They had just finished washing up the dinner things when the telephone rang. Salt was back after a few moments. "That was Buzzy. I asked him earlier to ring me, if necessary. We'll go along to the club now."

"Not until I've changed," Maggie told him firmly. "Did you notice I arrived carrying a small suitcase?"

"I did, though of course I didn't know what was in it. Daren't even risk a guess. But you don't need to change to visit Buzzy."

"I need to change for my own sake. But I promise not to be long. And please remember, Salt, it's raining, it's Saturday night, and we must have a taxi—if it's possible to find one."

"Off you go, girl. I'll have an old chum of mine waiting to take us to Buzzy's long before you're ready."

And so he had, to her surprise. Often he seemed so vague that she tended to forget he was capable of all manner of clever little arrangements. Though she guessed what Buzzy's would be like, she couldn't help feeling in the taxi that she was going to a party. She slipped an arm through his and squeezed it, and tried some gay chatter. But though he nodded and smiled, he wasn't really responsive.

"What's the matter? The rain? The night? Buzzy's?"

"Probably they come into it, Maggie. I've never liked wet Saturday nights, and I don't think I'll enjoy Buzzy's. But it's chiefly something else. No thought in it. Just a feeling. One part intuitive apprehension to two parts melancholy. Sorry!"

"It's the Noreen Wilks thing, isn't it?"

"Yes. That and the poor bedeviled human race. And now I'm playing Buddha, not God. I'd better shut up."

Then they were climbing the stairs that led to Buzzy's peculiar office, long and narrow and with the window down one side, high above the dance floor. Buzzy himself, wearing a vast dinner jacket, was smoking a cigar and drinking whisky. He was delighted to see them.

"Miss Culworth—Dr. Salt—welcome to the big monkey house! *Bzzz.* Look at 'em down there. Did you ever see such a bloody spectacle? Two to three hundred of 'em twisting their guts out an' paying good money to do it—an' not one smiling face. *Bzzz.* That's progress, that is—affluence—technology—welfare—"

"She's still here, Buzzy?" said Dr. Salt.

"Of course. But not on the floor. My boys have her taped. *Bzzz.* What are you drinking? How about something fancy, Miss Culworth? Now you take your pick." He waved at the long table and its array of bottles. "I've got the lot there. *Bzzz.*"

Maggie said she would have some Cointreau, and as there really wasn't room for Buzzy to act as barman at that table, Dr. Salt attended to her before giving himself some whisky. She perched on a narrow sofa alongside the window, and stared down, fascinated, at the dancers.

"Colored lights now, Buzzy," she told him over her shoulder. "It's really quite pretty. Salt, come and look."

"They get the lot down there, same as we do up here," said Buzzy. "Only what they get's different. *Bzzz.* Lights all colors.

226

Sprung floor. Five-piece band on Fridays and Saturdays—costs the earth. All for long-haired young twerps an' their scrawny little birds. *Bzzz.*"

"And their money, Buzzy, don't forget," said Dr. Salt.

"No, doc, I don't make my real money here. That comes out of the betting shops, where they change their money for bits of paper. *Bzzz.*"

"Why bother about this place, then?"

"Bother? I love it, doc. Just sitting here gives me something to do with my evenings. *Bzzz.* Besides, it's prestige, doc. I'm Buzzy Duffield of Buzzy's Club. I'm one of Birkden's trend setters. That reminds me. How was the Beverly-Astoria?"

"Oh—I ought to have thanked you for last night, Buzzy. Now I do. But now I realize I'm old-fashioned. I like small, out-of-date hotels where you ring a bell and somebody answers it, and you haven't to operate a switchboard to ask for somebody and anything." Dr. Salt was ready to go on, but now he was interrupted.

"That's right, Super," said Buzzy, looking up. "Don't knock. No sissy stuff."

"This might be a raid," said Superintendent Hurst, who was standing in the doorway, shaking a wet mackintosh and looking rather grim. "Evening, Miss Culworth, Dr. Salt."

"Go on. *Bzzz.* We don't break the law here, Super. I know too much."

"No, you only think you do, Buzzy. People break the law all the time—especially in places like this—and if we wanted to catch them, we could. We nearly did tonight—yes, here. But I said no. I'd do it my way."

"Now what's this about? No, let me think. *Bzzz.* It hurts, but it's good for me. Otherwise, the stupid twerps I have to deal with, I'd be stupid forever. *Bzzz.* All right. I've thought. It's not me you're interested in. It's Doc Salt here. Right? An' you wouldn't know he was here if you hadn't put a tail on him. See how it is, doc? *Bzzz.* Try to help the police and they tail you. Disgusting!"

"Either keep quiet or clear out, Buzzy," Hurst began.

"Since when? This is *my* office, Super. Who you working for —Hitler or Stalin?"

"Not funny. Turn it off, Buzzy. I'm here to talk to Dr. Salt, for his own good, so if you're a friend of his, you'll let me get on with it. Now, Dr. Salt, what do you think you're doing?"

"People seem to have been asking me that for days," said Dr. Salt mildly. "Now let me see. This afternoon I sold my car—"

"All right," Hurst cut in roughly. "If you're going to take that line, then you'd better come along with me and make a statement."

"Certainly not. Unless, of course, you're thinking of putting me under arrest."

Salt had spoken quite gently, but Maggie knew him sufficiently well now to realize that he was nearly as angry as the superintendent seemed to be. She looked from one man to the other, feeling rather frightened. The hard beat of the band below was like a pulse, steady but throbbing with anger.

After a pause, Hurst said, "You think that's impossible, don't you?"

Salt offered him a shrug. "I've stopped thinking anything's impossible, Superintendent."

"You did me a good turn the night before last." Hurst hesitated. "So I didn't agree you ought to be brought in to make a statement."

Salt stared at him. "A statement about what?"

"Your concealing evidence in a murder case."

"I must be rather stupid tonight," Salt told him quite pleasantly. "I find this very confusing. I thought you people believed the case was closed. And I was unpopular because I said it wasn't. Now you talk about concealing evidence as if I wanted to close the case and you wanted to keep it open. I don't know where I am."

"Yes, you do. And you're meddling in police work, Dr. Salt."

"You're beginning to sound like Colonel Ringwood."

This brought a loud guffaw from Buzzy.

"Now let's stop this banter and backchat," said Hurst, raising his voice. "You've already announced you have evidence that Derek Donnington didn't kill the Wilks girl."

"Have I? What is it?"

"How the hell do *I* know?"

"Well, how the hell do you know I have any such evidence, Superintendent?"

"Let's stop being funny, shall we? This is serious. It could be very serious for you, Dr. Salt."

"Very well." And Maggie knew as soon as he had said this that Salt was now just as angry as the superintendent, but in a different way, cold and scornful.

"Now I'll talk seriously, Superintendent. If I hadn't planned to leave Birkden—on Monday, I hope—I'd ask in public, loud and clear, why the Birkden police think they're working for United Fabrics. No, no—don't interrupt now. I'm still serious, and I haven't finished. You got that information about my having evidence from Aricson. Has he been told not to meddle in police work? Has Sir Arnold Donnington been told? No, only Dr. Salt, who meddled and meddled until he found that girl's body, and who's meddling on until he discovers who killed her."

"You're bluffing."

Salt grinned at him. "I might be—yes. Then again, I might not be."

"What about that evidence? You told Aricson—"

"I told Aricson what I wanted him to believe. After all, he shouldn't be meddling in police work, should he?"

Hurst hesitated a moment. "Well, I'll go along with you there, Dr. Salt. But I'm warning you—you're going to have to be very, very careful. If they can get you on anything—from suppression of evidence to defamation of character—they will do so. And by this time tomorrow you'll have had it. But I'll give you a break tonight because I owe you something. And if you want to waste your time here, that's all right to me. I can't find you. Now,

Buzzy, one of my men said he'd seen Dr. Salt come in here tonight. Care to say anything about that, Buzzy?"

"Plain ridiculous, Super. *Bzzz.* Dr. Salt'd never come to a place like this. Besides, I'd heard he'd left Birkden. Still, if you're not satisfied, you could have a look down there."

"No, they make me feel dizzy. 'Night, Dizzy—I mean Buzzy!" And the superintendent went out without even a glance at Dr. Salt and Maggie. She drew a long breath. How oddly men behaved! Impossible to imagine women being so angry and then playing a sort of complicated silly game!

"He's not so bad, old Hurst," said Buzzy comfortably. "Live and let live. *Bzzz.* It's the colonel and some of these young busies, sweating for promotion, who are the bastards. Now drink up, you two, and have another."

Maggie shook her head at Salt. "Not just now, thanks, Buzzy," he said for both of them. Then, for himself, he added, "I have an idea I ought to keep my wits about me tonight."

2

For the next half hour or so nothing happened, except that the room seemed stuffier, the beat of the band began to be irritating, and Maggie started to feel she had had quite enough of this place. She was in fact feeling thoroughly bored when, as so often happens, the whole character of the evening suddenly changed.

There was no excitement at first. Somebody merely walked in. It was the Mr. Aricson that she and Dr. Salt had visited at his home.

Buzzy was not pleased to see him. "Now just a minute, just a minute. *Bzzz.* There's no reception going on, y'know. This is my office. *Private. Bzzz!*"

"If you want me to apologize, Mr. Duffield, then I apologize," Aricson said hastily. "Sir Arnold Donnington asked me to find his daughter, Erica, and take her home. I've been inquiring all over the place—and now I understand she's here."

"Oh, she's here, all right. Saturday night with the riffraff. *Bzzz.* And she was more than half stoned last time I caught sight of her. She's a bloody pest, your Miss Erica is. If I bar her, I'll run into trouble. If I let her carry on like this much longer, I'll run into trouble. I can't win with this bit. *Bzzz.* She's down there somewhere—maybe close to passing out. Black coffee and a lie-down in the ladies' cloaks—"

"Buzzy, I'm a fool," cried Salt, jumping up. "I must take a look at that girl. Come on, Maggie. You too, Aricson. Buzzy, lead the way downstairs."

The youngsters on the floor, moving energetically but as if in a trance, never noticed the four of them as they hurried towards the entrance. There was something half absurd, half sinister, Maggie felt, about this setting and this whole situation. They might have been hurrying around the edge of some complicated service that belonged to an utterly strange religion. Then Buzzy led the way to the ladies' and waved Maggie in. Three girls were staring at a fourth, laid out on a sofa and obviously unconscious. "Come on," said Maggie sharply. "We must get her out of here. There's a doctor waiting outside."

They carried her across to a small ticket office at the entrance. "What did I tell you?" said Buzzy. "Out like a light—see? *Bzzz.*"

"Quiet, Buzzy! This might be something different," Salt told him.

Maggie had time to see Salt begin examining the girl—raising her eyelids, feeling her pulse—but then he called over his shoulder. "Maggie, ring for the ambulance. Phone here, isn't there? Then after the ambulance get me the general hospital—doctor on duty. Say it's very urgent. Don't stand any nonsense from anybody."

"But look, doc," she heard Buzzy say. "She's only had a few too many, hasn't she?"

"No, it's different this time." Then Salt was at her elbow, and when she had called the ambulance and was through to the hospital, he took the receiver himself. "Come along, come along, come along.... Who's that? Dr. Harrison? This is Dr. Salt. I'm at Buzzy's Club and there's a girl here, Erica Donnington, who's been mixing barbiturates and alcohol. . . . Yes, coma, of course, but not deep yet. Pulse fifty-five. Respiration and heart not too bad. Corneal reflex present. . . . Yes, the ambulance is on its way. I'll bring her in. No, *we* can tell her father."

After putting down the receiver, he handed Maggie a key. "Go back to the flat and wait for me, Maggie. Aricson can drop you there. Where is he?"

"I'm here." He had been waiting just outside.

"Now, Aricson, this is what I want you to do. Drop Miss Culworth at my flat—it'll be on your way—then go out and collect Sir Arnold, tell him what's happened and where his daughter will be—the general hospital—ask for Dr. Harrison. Right?"

"Right. Ready, Miss Culworth?"

"Just a moment. That's not all. You can also tell him this: It's serious, but I think we've caught her in time. But—as soon as he knows she's out of danger, I shall expect to see him at my flat, whatever time it may be. Tell him I've too much evidence now to let this go any farther. *I have to see him tonight.* No, don't let's have any more blustering," he added severely. "I mean what I say. This is where we all stop playing games. Right, Maggie, my dear. Wait for me."

3

After she had spent about half an hour alone in Salt's flat and then heard somebody ringing at the door, Maggie felt frightened. This couldn't be Salt because the door wasn't locked and he could have walked straight in. And if it wasn't Salt, then who was it? But if they were dangerous characters, they could walk

232

straight in too, like those three horrible young men. She went and opened the door about three inches, at the same time asking who it was.

"Come on, you chump," said Alan. "It's only us."

Us already, these two, Maggie told herself as she let them in. Then she saw they had that sleepy triumphant look, that cats-full-of-cream air, of two people who not long ago had been enthusiastically making love.

"Where's Dr. Salt?" said Jill. "I've come specially to thank him."

"Oh, Jill!" cried Maggie, who was genuinely pleased. "Has Alice Marton offered you that job?"

"She has. You know about that, do you, Maggie?"

"Alice and Salt were talking about it last night, and she asked me what I thought." Maggie's tone was now perhaps rather lofty. "Salt and I were dining at the Beverly-Astoria, and we were talking to Alice in the cocktail bar."

Jill gave Maggie a look that said, What's going on between you and Salt, and Maggie gave Jill a look that replied, Nothing I can tell you and just mind your own business. Quite oblivious of this lightning exchange, Alan puffed at his pipe, regarded both girls benevolently, and then said, "If it comes off, it'll settle our problem very neatly. We're very grateful to Dr. Salt."

"You don't mind his playing God, then?" Maggie asked him, too sweetly.

Her brother remained unruffled. "Jill said that, not me. Anyhow, where is he, Mag?"

She explained what had happened at Buzzy's. "And I must say," she concluded, "this Erica Donnington looked terrible, but Salt said they may have caught her in time. And if he hadn't been there—and acted so quickly—she'd probably be dead now. Oh—and another thing. Salt told Aricson to tell Sir Arnold Donnington that as soon as he knew his daughter was out of danger, he—Sir Arnold—had to come here, whatever time it was. Salt didn't say so but I'm sure this is the Noreen Wilks thing. He's going to settle it tonight somehow. He says he's leaving on Monday morning."

"He won't want us here," said Jill hastily. She was looking frightened.

"You never know with Salt," said Maggie. "It's quite possible he might want you here. Anyhow, I'm expecting him any minute now."

"I brought some whisky." Alan got up. "It's not mine—it's Jill's."

"Strictly speaking, it isn't even mine," said Jill with a faint smile. "It was bought and paid for by United Anglo-Belgian Fabrics, and the last I shall see."

"Do you mind about that?" Maggie asked as Alan went to take the bottle out of his overcoat pocket. "I mean, no more free drinks, delightful flat, all the rest of it—um?"

"My dear, if I hadn't met Alan," she whispered, "and don't make any mistake, Maggie—I'd marry him tomorrow even if we'd only thirty bob between us—I say, if I hadn't met him and if I'd had another year or so of that Fabrics life, I know now I'd have been well on my way to becoming a hard-faced, hard-hearted bitch and tart."

"And you realize, don't you," said Maggie as Alan returned with the bottle, "that if it hadn't been for Salt, going round asking about Noreen Wilks, refusing to be put off, none of this would have happened? You owe it all to him, both of you." She looked at them almost defiantly.

"We'll drink his health," said Alan. "What about some glasses, Mag? You know your way around this joint."

"I ought to by this time." As she went into the kitchen, she heard them talking in low tones, perhaps about her. She returned with four glasses and a jug of water. "There isn't any soda. In fact, there isn't anything much, let's face it."

And then, before she could sit down, Maggie heard a taxi outside, knew that it must be Salt, and hurried to the door to meet him. He looked tired. Suddenly, and for the very first time, Maggie found herself disregarding his nonchalant air, his not-giving-a-damn attitude, his little eccentricities and jokes, and realizing, not without some self-reproach, that this man, who had been overworking for years and had promised himself a holiday, had been under an increasing strain the whole week. She could have flung her arms round him, wet overcoat and all, and pressed her warm cheek against his cold one.

"We were in time. She's going to be all right—at least physically. Who's here?"

"Alan and Jill. She wants to thank you because Alice has offered her that job."

"And I do," cried Jill, as they went in. "I really do. Most gratefully—most humbly—most apologetically. I mean, after screaming at you the night before last. Here." She was already standing, and now she swiftly kissed his cheek.

"We were just about to drink your health," said Alan, grinning.

"In your own whisky too," said Salt. "Well, now we'll drink to somebody or something else."

"Let me pour out the booze," cried Jill. "My God, I ought to be good at it by this time." But a little later, after they had all had their first sip or two, she looked doubtfully at Salt. "Maggie told us you insisted upon Sir Arnold Donnington coming here. Aren't Alan and I going to be in the way?"

"I told them I wasn't sure," Maggie added.

"He might object," said Salt slowly, "but I think for once an objection of his is going to be overruled. I'd like you to stay. You've both been mixed up, one way or another, in this sad, messy affair. If you didn't stay, then you'd never know how it came to be cleaned and tidied up." He looked around at all three of them. "I say that because I don't want a single word about it to be spoken outside this room. In other words, I want to bind you to secrecy here and now. This is really important —very serious. Maggie, you promise?"

"Yes, of course, Salt. Solemnly I do."

"You, Jill? You, Alan? Good! Donnington ought to be here quite soon. He knows his daughter's out of danger now. On the other hand, she isn't conscious yet and he might as well leave. Now let's talk about something else."

"All right," said Maggie. "When I went into the kitchen to get the glasses, I suddenly realized there isn't a thing for breakfast, Salt."

"Well, dear," said Jill softly and sweetly. "That can't be any concern of yours, can it?"

"Men want breakfasts, don't they? And I'll bet you've got a whacking great breakfast all planned for Alan. Sausages, I hope. That's what he likes on Sunday."

"You've missed the point, Maggie dear," Jill told her. "Alan and I are no better than the wicked. Whereas you—"

"Oh, do shut up!" Maggie jumped to her feet, went across to one of the remaining piles of books and did something quite unnecessary to three or four at the top. The back of her neck looked hot.

"As a matter of fact, Maggie," said Salt, "I remember now I left a bag of groceries in the spare bedroom. I must have been thinking about something else." Then he stopped because he had heard the car. "I think that'll be Sir Arnold Donnington."

Maggie turned, found she had suddenly gone cold, and shivered a little.

SIXTEEN

1

Sir Arnold Donnington was wearing a long, dark overcoat that he refused to take off. He also dismissed with a quick shake of the head the chair that was offered him. He just stood there, looking as if he would be gone in a minute—a stiff elderly man with a narrow head. Maggie remembered now having seen photographs of him in the local papers. He didn't look at her or at Alan and Jill, only at Salt, who was standing too.

"I'm not staying long," Sir Arnold announced. "I had an anxious time at the hospital, as you know, and I'm an elderly man. I wouldn't have come here at all if it were not for the fact that I felt I owed you something. Dr. Harrison said my daughter might have lost her life if you hadn't acted so promptly. So I felt I ought to spare you a few minutes. Though nothing was said about all your friends being here too."

"Not all. There are three or four elsewhere. But allow me to introduce Miss Culworth, Miss Frinton and Dr. Culworth. Miss Frinton is—or was—one of your employees. It was she who organized the parties attended by your son and Noreen Wilks. And Culworth is the name of the man who was knocked out by your caretaker on Monday night, and then rushed into a nursing home and kept under sedation. So you might say they're all in the picture."

"Well, Dr. Salt?" said Sir Arnold, just as if not a word had been spoken to him. "I can only give you a few minutes. What do you want?"

"I want you to drop that tone, Sir Arnold," said Salt, quite easily and cheerfully. "Come down a few pegs."

"I'm afraid that doesn't mean anything to me, Dr. Salt."

"I see. You're staying on that lofty height, are you? Well, you'll have to come down from it sooner or later. And staying up there you only increase the tension."

Maggie knew he was going to pounce now—she had learned a lot about Salt in a few days—and she felt a kind of choking sensation as her heart went faster.

"Look at your hands, man," said Salt very sharply.

Sir Arnold didn't look at them, but hastily thrust them into his overcoat pockets.

"Ah, but there's something else," Salt continued, easier now. "Something you can't control—which gives you away—like a visible pulse. I noticed it when I saw you in Superintendent Hurst's office the other morning. High tension. I knew then that Noreen Wilks was important to you. Ask Hurst."

"Rubbish! I never knew the girl. And if that's all you have to say—"

"You're running your own lie detector, you know, Sir Arnold. Every time you speak, your blood's going to contradict you. By the way, you'll have to do something about that blood pressure."

"I have quite a competent doctor," said Sir Arnold dryly. He was now in better control of himself. "He's never suggested a second opinion. And if he did, I'm quite sure it wouldn't be yours, Dr. Salt."

"So am I, though you needn't work so hard to be offensive. Hypertension, to use the new and fashionable term, has never

238

been one of my special studies," he continued cheerfully. "But now I'm wondering how far it might affect the eyesight of an elderly man. Now you're not a slapdash type. You're a careful man. And you had to be very careful that night—I mean the night of September twelfth, when Noreen Wilks was murdered. I think you were, but your eyesight was at fault."

Salt paused as if he thought the other man might like to make some comment. Maggie thought she heard Jill draw a deep breath, but it was difficult to tell because she was breathing hard herself.

"You see," Salt continued, "there were two bits of evidence up in that attic room that you overlooked. I have them—at least I *had* them. But now they're in a little packet I sent to a colleague of mine, together with an account of what I think happened that night. He's not in Birkden, by the way, so you can't get at him. And if he doesn't hear from me during the next twenty-four hours, I've asked him to open the packet, read what I've written inside and then get in touch with Scotland Yard."

Sir Arnold was obviously under some strain now. "I don't know what you're talking about," was all he could manage.

"I'm talking about the possible effect on eyesight of a state of hypertension. Take another example. I'm sure you tried to be very careful matching that wallpaper exactly. Yet I saw at once that it didn't match."

"That's a lie. It matched exactly." And then Sir Arnold realized what this outburst had cost him. For the first time he looked around—rather wildly, like a trapped creature—at Maggie and the other two.

"Now you've really torn it, haven't you?" said Jill.

"So there you are in that room, covering the cavity in the wall where the body was hidden." Salt didn't sound triumphant; rather sad, if anything. "And don't tell me now you were doing it for your son. I'd be too ashamed to listen."

"Don't imagine you're making any sense, Dr. Salt. And if you've anything worth hearing to tell me—"

"Oh, drop it, man!" Salt was impatient now. "Your son never killed that girl. He was in love with her. I've read his letters to her. And don't forget I've also seen the body. Your son loved it —and her. And he was your son—and he's dead. Do we have to pretend now he was a homicidal sexual maniac, to keep you safe? I tell you I'd be too ashamed to listen." And Salt pointed an accusing finger at him.

Sir Arnold shook himself, then glanced at Alan.

"If you're appealing to me," said Alan, "then don't. I believe you killed her. You might as well admit it."

"Very well." He looked at Salt. "I killed her." There was no more shaking. He was a stone man now. And Maggie, though she didn't want to, suddenly found herself feeling sorry for him.

"So you killed her, did you?" said Salt very softly. "Why?"

"I'll sit down, if you don't mind," said Sir Arnold, staring about him in a curiously vague way. Salt, who was still standing, offered him an armchair. Sir Arnold sank into it, closed his eyes for a moment or two, then looked up at them all and, making an obvious effort, took them all into his confidence.

"I'd heard rumors of this affair," he began. "I'd heard too that they were using the old Worsley place. So I went there that night—and found them. I was deeply shocked, then very angry. I ordered Derek to get dressed and clear out, and though he didn't want to go, I made him leave me with the girl. Then I appealed to her to let him go, even offered her money to go away. She not only refused but she taunted me, saying she was going to marry him. She was an evil little slut, flaunting her sex, lying there half dressed, jeering at me. Then something snapped. I can't tell you exactly what happened because I can't remember. But then I found myself staring at the body. What happened afterwards you seem to know, though I can't imagine what possible evidence you can have found."

"And your son?"

"By the time I'd done everything I could to hide the body and remove all traces of the girl, it was very late, nearly morning.

Derek had been drinking. I tried to make him believe at first that the girl had agreed to go away, but something in my manner made him suspicious, so finally I had to tell him what had happened. He rushed out of the room. Then, before I could do anything to stop him, before I knew even where he'd gone, he shot himself. And now you know the truth, all of you."

"And I believe you," said Jill.

"So do I," said Alan.

Maggie heard herself making some sort of agreeing noise. And then Salt astonished her.

"Certainly not. We're miles from the truth yet. But let's have a drink." He was lively, cheerful, bustling. "Sir Arnold, some whisky—"

"Thank you. I need a drink."

"Maggie, give me a hand. Oh, we must have another glass. I'll get it, for Sir Arnold. You pour out for the others." He rushed into the kitchen while Maggie, still bewildered, busied herself with the bottle and the jug of water. He was back again in a flash. "Here—I'll attend to Sir Arnold. He needs a stiff one. Neat, perhaps."

Jill spoke for Maggie. "You really are the most extraordinary man, Dr. Salt. You begin talking about drinks just when I think you'll call for the police."

"Police? Police?" Salt was contemptuous. "I've nothing to do with the police. Sir Arnold's the man who hobnobs with the police. I don't. I'm a doctor, not a detective."

"Yes—but—" And Sir Arnold, looking as bewildered as Maggie felt, left it at that.

Alan was frowning. "If the police don't come into it, then what's the point of all this?"

"I'll tell you." Salt, serious now, addressed them all. "There are two points, both equally important. The first is the discovery of the truth. In this case, what really happened to Noreen Wilks. The second point is, having discovered the truth, to decide what best can be done. It's the sort of thing a conscientious doctor has to do all day long. I've not been amusing myself playing God, as you suggested, Jill. I've simply been applying a familiar method outside my usual field. I say I've *been* doing it, but of course I'm still doing it. Hard at it this very minute."

"But, Salt, you're not *doing* anything," Maggie objected.

"I never have done anything very much, have I? My method doesn't involve me in scurrying around and putting cigarette ends in envelopes."

"What about those bits of evidence you said you sent to a colleague?" asked Sir Arnold. Salt made no reply. The two men stared at each other in silence for seveal moments. "If you were bluffing, Dr. Salt," Sir Arnold said finally, "then you'll never prove a thing, you know. And if you insist, I'll keep on saying I did it."

"But you did, didn't you?" said Alan.

"Of course he didn't," Salt told him.

Then Salt finished his whisky and water, put down his glass and went closer to Sir Arnold. "Why won't you remember I'm not a policeman, prosecutor, judge and jury—I'm a healer. And what I want to do now, Donnington, is to take you off the hook that's kept you in agony ever since September twelfth. Now there could be only one reason why you were willing to let the police think your son had killed that girl. Or why, when I challenged that story, you confessed to the murder yourself. You were protecting the only person left for you to protect—your daughter, Erica. She killed Noreen Wilks."

Maggie heard herself exclaiming with the other two. Sir Arnold said nothing and put his head into his hands.

"You don't have to talk about it, Donnington," Salt went on, quite calmly. "But you'll have to listen for a minute or two. It was you who hid the body, of course, after your son came home and told you what had happened. But it was Erica, insane with jealousy, who did the strangling and mutilating. She and her brother were very close. There may have been an incestuous

242

sexual relationship, and it was probably to cover this that she pretended to be a Lesbian. Yes, Jill?"

"I was only going to say she did seem to parade it too much."

"And it was all talk," Salt continued. "Late last night she was up in a man's room at the Beverly-Astoria—"

"Oh—806," cried Maggie, before she could stop herself.

"She must have followed her brother and Noreen that night, somehow got rid of him, perhaps told him you were looking for him, and then, starting a violent quarrel with Noreen—"

"She blacked out, Salt." Sir Arnold's voice was loud and yet curiously hoarse. "She never knew afterwards she'd done it. She thought she'd dreamt it. And then when Derek understood what had happened, he shot himself. What was I to do, man? What was I to do? I mean, beyond wishing I was dead too and done with it all."

"I think what you did was wrong," said Salt gently. "Even for Erica, as we've seen tonight. Besides, how can you be sure she won't black out again?"

"I know, I know, Salt. But what are you going to do now?"

"I'll get you off this hook. No police, no trials, no scandals. Now I know the truth, I'll take the risk of burying it. But you must swallow your pride, Donnington, and submit to two conditions."

"What are they?"

"First, Erica. She's just as sick as if she had typhoid. But if she can be cured—and I believe she can, though it'll take time— then here's a man who might do it." He scribbled a name and address in a notebook, tore out the page and handed it over. "Take her to him as soon as she's ready to leave hospital. He runs his own small mental home. Stay nearby. See her as often as you can. And that brings me to the second condition I propose." He broke off to stare at Sir Arnold, who was now sitting up.

"I seem to have been told all this week," Salt went on, his tone

243

much sharper now, "that if you were taken out of Birkden, it would fall to pieces. All right. Let it. Then perhaps out of the pieces another and better Birkden might be made. Stop trying to own everything and run everything. There's been far too much Sir Arnold Donnington here. Every time I've turned a corner, all this week, I've run into somebody or something you owned or controlled. This is bad for Birkden and bad for you. So this is my second condition. You stop being Birkden's Mr. Big."

"I can't accept that, of course," said Sir Arnold coldly, getting up. "You're taking too much on yourself now, Salt."

Maggie was alarmed by Salt's howl of fury. The next moment he had thrust Sir Arnold back into the chair.

"Now listen, Donnington. All this week you and Aricson between you have put every sort of obstacle in my way, not caring a damn what might happen to me. I've been willing to forget it. I've taken you off the hook. But power—power—you can't let it go, can you? And in thirty seconds flat, by God, you're telling me to know my place. All right, then, Donnington. *Stay on the hook and wriggle.* If you can't let Birkden go, then I'll spend my holiday bringing it down on top of you. Don't forget, four of us know what happened. If you still want to be Mr. Big, then you're going to be the Mr. Big who hid a body and said nothing about a murder. Maggie, get me the police."

Maggie began a slow vague move towards the telephone, almost certain that if Salt had been quite serious he would have rung the police himself.

"No, no—stop," she heard Sir Arnold croaking.

She stopped. Everybody and everything—time itself—stopped.

Sir Arnold had to restore at least a little of his lost dignity before he spoke again. He was that kind of man. "If I have to stay near my daughter," he began slowly, "then I can start easing out. So you'll get your way, Salt. I'm assuming, of course, that you'll all keep quiet."

"I can promise you that," Salt told him.

Sir Arnold levered himself out of the chair, looked around and produced a small gray smile, and cleared his throat. "Then I'll say good night."

"And I'll say good-bye," said Jill.

Salt went to let him out. Maggie looked at Alan and Jill, but they were looking at each other.

"I'm feeling hungry," said Alan.

"My God—not again, darling! Not after that dinner you ate," Jill continued. "It's going to be like keeping an elephant or something."

"Stuff him with cornflakes and cheap sausages," Maggie suggested.

"That reminds me," said Alan. "How are you getting home tonight, Mag?"

"Oh, don't be so dense," cried Jill. But then they heard Salt closing the door and Sir Arnold's car starting up. They kept silent until Salt joined them.

"Did I finish my whisky?" Salt asked. He looked tired again now, Maggie thought.

"Yes, but you can have mine. I don't want it," she told him. "Here. And, Alan, you must take the bottle back with you."

"Oh—must I?" Then he looked at Salt. "Several times this week—as you must know—I've thought you were merely fooling around. I've even argued with Jill, who wasn't always on your side but always thought you were devilishly clever. Now I know how wrong I was. By the way, what *was* that evidence you had against Donnington and his daughter?"

"I hadn't any—not a sausage. All bluff. That—and knowing something about people. Maggie, I believe I'm hungry."

"Oh, for God's sake—another of them!" Jill grabbed hold of Alan. "Come on, man. We'll see you both sometime tomorrow."

Left to themselves, with the whole place suddenly very quiet and somehow expectant, Maggie and Salt looked at each other. Then he made a slight movement with his arms and she ran into them, and they began kissing. "Are you really hungry?" she asked, after an interval.

"Fairly—yes. We'll scramble some eggs soon. No hurry."

"I think you've been wonderful—so clever, so patient, so kind. I wish you'd explain sometime exactly how you worked everything out."

"I'll do that, Maggie, my love. One night after a damn good dinner, probably costing the earth now, somewhere in the Dordogne."

"I can pay for myself—"

"Not with me you can't, girl. Besides, I've spent very little the last year or two. High time I began spending again. You don't mind, do you?"

She laughed. "No fear. But I warn you. If we're any good together, I'm marrying you."

"And I warn you. Once we *are* married, and the holiday's over, you're likely to find yourself on the Persian Gulf or in Penang or the Australian outback."

"I don't care. Though—" and now she hesitated, moving a hand across his cheek.

"Though what?"

"Well, it's just that I'd hate to think that you of all men were running away from anything—from England, let's say. Or am I being stupid?"

"Not a bit. Just remember I've had seven hard years of it. I need a change. And I get along with people in rather outlandish places. We English seem to have got stuck in a nasty place. It's possible to make a class system work with a certain amount of ease and dignity. But we've done with that. It's also possible to make a clean, fresh start. But we daren't risk that. So we're bogged down in a morass of meaningless snobberies, sulkiness, anxiety, resentment; and for the time being I've had enough of it, Maggie, my love."

"I see. Which doesn't mean I agree with you. How many eggs did you get?"

246

"Enough for now—and breakfast."

"For two?"

"For two."

"Taking some things for granted, weren't you, Dr. Salt?"

"No, I can always use some extra eggs, Miss Culworth. Whereas—"

"I can always use that overnight bag I happened to bring."

He laughed, and then she laughed. And they went together to remove the groceries from the spare bedroom to the kitchen, rather as if they had to practice at once doing things together.

FINE MYSTERY AND SUSPENSE TITLES FROM CARROLL & GRAF

- ☐ Allen, Henry/FOOL'S MERCY $3.95
- ☐ Blanc, Suzanne/THE GREEN STONE $3.50
- ☐ Brand, Christianna/FOG OF DOUBT $3.50
- ☐ Browne, Howard/THIN AIR $3.50
- ☐ Boucher, Anthony/THE CASE OF THE BAKER STREET IRREGULARS $3.95
- ☐ Boucher, Anthony (ed.)/FOUR AND TWENTY BLOODHOUNDS $3.95
- ☐ Buell, John/THE SHREWSDALE EXIT $3.50
- ☐ Carr, John Dickson/THE EMPEROR'S SNUFF-BOX $3.50
- ☐ Carr, John Dickson/LOST GALLOWS $3.50
- ☐ Coles, Manning/NIGHT TRAIN TO PARIS $3.50
- ☐ Coles, Manning/NO ENTRY $3.50
- ☐ Dewey, Thomas B./THE BRAVE, BAD GIRLS $3.50
- ☐ Dewey, Thomas B./DEADLINE $3.50
- ☐ Dewey, Thomas B./THE MEAN STREETS $3.50
- ☐ Dewey, Thomas B./A SAD SONG SINGING $3.50
- ☐ Dickson, Carter/THE CURSE OF THE BRONZE LAMP $3.50
- ☐ Douglass, Donald M./MANY BRAVE HEARTS $3.50
- ☐ Douglass, Donald M./REBECCA'S PRIDE $3.50
- ☐ Fennelly, Tony/THE GLORY HOLE MURDERS   Cloth $14.95
- ☐ Hughes, Dorothy/IN A LONELY PLACE $3.50
- ☐ Innes, Hammond/ATLANTIC FURY $3.50
- ☐ Innes, Hammond/THE LAND GOD GAVE TO CAIN $3.50
- ☐ Innes, Hammond/SOLOMON'S SEAL $3.50